SHADOW CORE

The Legacy

Licinio Santos Gonçalves

Fourth Edition

ISBN-13: 978-1507707104
ISBN-10: 150770710X

www.facebook.com/ShadowCore.BookSeries

‘Shadow Core’ series:

The Legacy (Book 1)
Broken Soul (Book 2)
Crusade (Book 3)

Dedicated to all of the people that have supported me through this on-going journey called life, and to those who would place their own lives on the line in order to protect innocents from harm.

CHAPTERS

The Derelict

It is the 107th year of the 4th Galactic Age and humanity is no longer shackled by the light speed limitation.

What had once been the cradle of humankind is now home to the Solarian Union: considered by some to be the beating heart of the species and by others as an archaic regime of elitist zealots.

While colonial development continues unabated, and over one thousand established colonies compete for the resources of explored regions of space, the Union enjoys unrivalled prosperity on the galactic scene: the fully developed infrastructure of the Sol system places the wealth of planets, moons, comets and countless satellites at its disposal. And the Grid, one of the most sophisticated sensor detection systems in known space, protects this rich treasure trove of mineral wealth. Its ever watchful gaze tracks everything, from asteroid orbits and debris distribution to spaceship traffic, and the slightest hint of suspicious or unauthorised activity triggers the deployment of patrol ships, or unleashes the might of the Union's military.

It is widely accepted by Galactic society that nothing exists or happens in the Sol system that the Solarian Union doesn't know about.

Against the cold and beautiful background of space, as the distant stars' shine and the nearby planets dance around the Sun, a lone ship travels stealthily on its way to a relatively quiet area of the system.

The Icarus, an independent frigate class spaceship, was not the newest ship around. The design was actually quite dated by current standards and it had been modified so many times it was often joked that it didn't have a single original part left. But even so, it was the only ship that Kade and Jude would ever consider flying. This was their ship, entrusted to them by their grandfather on his passing. There was nothing particularly special about it, at least that they could tell, it was just an old and reliable ship.

The Icarus was commanded by Kade, a fiery red head with piercing blue eyes and an adventurous spirit bordering on insanity. A woman that prided herself on always getting the job done and honouring her deals.

Jude was the second in command, navigator and resident technical genius. A resourceful, spirited and rather impulsive woman with short chestnut brown hair and brown eyes. Her petite stature and unassuming demeanour frequently caused people to underestimate her, which was just how she liked it.

The last member of the crew was Nick, the pilot. He was a relatively recent addition to the roster of the Icarus, seemed incapable of taking anything seriously, and was always looking for an angle to exploit in order to make money. He had short black hair, brown eyes, a light brown skin tone and an attitude that shifted between playful and arrogant.

The Icarus was a true freelancer ship, unbound from colonial power schemes or petty politics and ready to take on almost any job.

Kade, as the captain, had final say on what missions to accept, and as a rule was often very pragmatic on such matters. Piracy, slavery or smuggling of goods intended to harm life in any way were jobs that were strictly out of bounds. To a lesser extent, missions that involved crossing paths with the Solarian Union were also generally avoided, as those could go very wrong extremely quickly: The Union didn't hold freelancers in very high regard to begin with and cared little for smugglers as a whole. But any other jobs were fair game, especially if they offered a little adventure on the side.

Those were the rules the Icarus operated by, but today was a little different. Somewhere in the Sol sector, far removed from all established trade routes, the Icarus was on approach to what appeared to be a large derelict vessel...

"Look at the size of that thing! It's freaking huge!"

Nick said as he looked at the derelict's image on his holographic console, having just finished performing some last minute adjustments to the ship's course.

"I half expected not to find anything. It's hard to believe the information was accurate," Kade said without looking away from her console, which was displaying the data she had received from her contact back on Titan orbital station two: a way-station infamous for its lax customs and questionable business operations.

She was trying to make sense of the information,

having read through it many times, but some of it still didn't make much sense to her.

"I'm surprised we're the first ones here." Nick said, somewhat confused, "True, we are technically in the back end of beyond, but how has no-one stumbled across this thing yet? Why aren't there patrol ships swarming all over it? Did the Union's pride and joy, state of the art sensor grid, actually fail to see this? And how did it get here?" he asked, feeling frustrated.

"I don't think we were the first ones here," Jude said as she sifted through all the sensor data the Icarus was collecting as it approached the derelict. She manipulated her holographic interface, selecting, enhancing and effortlessly classifying complex data as if it was second nature to her.

She didn't have much to work with, being limited to passive sensors since active scans would no doubt cause the local authorities to take notice of them, and this complicated things: the passive sensor data wasn't making much sense to her since whole sections of the region of space they were approaching seemed to be unnaturally distorted. But that wasn't much of a surprise since they were entering the infamous Sol dead-zone: a region of the solar system that had been a hazard to navigation for a century.

"I'm seeing signatures of debris near our target, a lot of it. Titanium, composites, the list goes on, but it doesn't appear as though the debris is coming from the derelict. The readings I'm getting from the derelict itself are... well... weird. It's there, and yet it isn't... not sure how to explain this..." Jude said and then paused for a few seconds as she organised her thoughts. "Our cameras can see it clear as day, but all other readings are coming in scrambled. If I didn't know for a fact that it's there I wouldn't know what I'm looking at right now, but that might explain why the patrols are ignoring it."

Nick closed his eyes briefly as he pondered the meaning of Jude's words with a troubled expression and wondered what it all meant. Meanwhile, Kade just carried on reading through the information pack.

"I see! Indeed, that must be it!" Nick said without hesitation as he opened his eyes again, looking as though he had reached an important conclusion.

"What?" Jude asked as she looked away from her console, curious about his comment.

Nick looked back at Jude with a mischievous smile and said, "A ghost ship!"

Disappointed, Jude replied, "Are you ever planning on growing up?" She was not so much disappointed at Nick but at herself for having believed that he was actually taking things seriously for a change.

"Not if I can help it," he said with a smile as Jude turned back towards her console.

Concerned, Jude said, "This disruption could be a natural phenomenon, or interference from the derelict's reactor core. We'll need to run some active scans in order to know for sure. But there is another possibility, this could very well be a trap."

"Not really the most effective place for a trap if we consider that ships usually go out of their way to avoid this area. I mean, who in their right mind would ever actually want to go through this graveyard?" Nick asked as he examined the sensor data on his own console since he didn't really have much else to do until they got closer to the derelict.

"I am surprised you can make any sense of this

mess, there's crap everywhere! How can you even tell there's debris near the target?" Nick asked.

"Most of the contacts you're seeing on your console don't actually exist. You need to filter out the echo distortions from the target list," Jude said as she remotely updated the settings of Nick's console, causing the vast majority of the contacts to vanish.

"Oh!" Nick said as he turned around, "None of the ships I've piloted before could do that."

"The Icarus sensors are a bit outdated. The control software has always had this weird quirk that requires user input to classify unknown signals. It's a pain, but it does have its advantages," Jude explained.

Nick laughed and said, "And here I thought it was only the navigation system that was ancient." He noticed Kade glaring at him and said, "I mean vintage!" He quickly turned back around.

"It's no good," Jude said as she leaned back on her chair with a defeated look. "I can't get a reading on the derelict. As far as our sensors can tell, the thing doesn't exist. I'm starting to understand why they call this a dead-zone. Between the sensor disruption and the spatial instabilities this whole area is a death trap."

"Spatial what?" Nick asked.

"The area around the derelict is peppered with unstable space bubbles. They prevent ships engaging their Burst drives and cause anyone trying to Burst through them to drop to sub-light," Jude explained.

"Is that why we're approaching using our sub-light drives?" Nick asked. "I was wondering why we were snailing our way there."

"Yes. The bubbles drift around inside this region,

making it impossible to predict what sections are safe to travel through. Still, at least they seem to be contained to this one area. Though it is puzzling that the dead-zone would have an orbital path like a planet," Jude said.

"We're not here to solve the mysteries of the Universe. Focus on the task at hand," Kade ordered.

Jude smiled as she said, "Bah! You're no fun!"

"Have your fun later. This region is seriously bad for sensors, making it the perfect place to hide. We could be flying into a pirate den for all we know," Kade said while still focusing on her console.

"In Sol?" Nick asked with a chuckle. "It would take a special kind of suicidal idiot to set up a pirate presence in this system. If I had to bet, then my money would be on smugglers."

"There are three smuggler bases that I'm aware of in this system, and two more that I've heard of in rumours, but this isn't one of them," Kade said as she finally looked away from her console.

She had spent all this time trying to make sense of the information she had received from her contact, but something about it all was still bugging her.

Nick was visibly surprised at Kade's statement; he was only aware of two smuggler bases in Sol.

"According to the info this derelict hasn't been here long, only about a month. And yet it seems to be in a stable orbit, moving with the dead-zone," Kade said and then carried on with a frustrated look, "This rules out the possibilities that it was destroyed here a long time ago, or that it recently drifted into the system. Add to the mix that the Sol grid has failed to take notice of it, and then what, exactly, does all of this mean?"

"Ghost ship!" Nick said enthusiastically.

“Solarian Union experimental stealth capital ship with deadly fire-power?” Jude smiled.

“I think I'd prefer the ghost ship,” Kade said.

An uneasy silence filled the bridge of the Icarus as the ship continued on its journey towards the derelict vessel, which was sitting at the heart of the dead-zone.

At this point Kade had no real idea what to expect and could only hope her somewhat shady informant had not sent her head first into an ambush.

“We're getting paid for this job, right? Tell me this isn’t another of your 'special' missions,” Nick said, clearly worried.

“That's a secret.” Kade smiled.

She had offered no explanation to her crew as to why exactly they were out there, in the middle of nowhere, approaching a derelict which held as much promise as potential danger.

In her line of work, a lack of explanations was not uncommon. It was frustrating for her crew, but some jobs would often call for a certain level of discretion, so information was kept to a minimum. Then there were the occasional fruitless side missions that Kade would take on for personal reasons; those jobs would come with neither explanation nor pay.

Regardless of contractor, the potential for a pay day was almost certain if the job was derelict salvage: it was always profitable business. That is, as long as they could pull it off without alerting the local authorities until they could stake a claim to it.

While Jude and Nick were not aware of the nature of the mission, Kade knew exactly what they were here to accomplish, but something about the whole situation just seemed wrong to her. There were far too many unanswered questions in her mind.

Kade did not fully trust the source of the information that had led her to the derelict, and there were a lot of details that just didn't add up: the data was riddled with little inconsistencies and omissions which kept nagging at the back of her mind, telling her there was something seriously wrong going on.

Meanwhile, the 'derelict' sat quietly in space. Its engines were cold and all of the many apparent windows that lined the hull of the vast ship were dark as an emotionless female voice relayed an automated message to a desolate bridge.

"Inbound vessel detected! Self-defence protocols initiated. Alert condition one in effect."

Elsewhere...

A lone figure was laid out on a grass field, enjoying the warm breeze of an idyllic summer's day as it flowed past his dark brown hair and tanned skin. It was a peaceful moment, the kind that would let anyone forget about any and all worries.

The field extended as far as the eye could see, with not even a trace of civilisation in sight. Trees dotted the landscape, and off in the distance there was a range of snowy capped mountains merging evenly with the crystal clear blue sky above.

The man laid on the grass with his hands behind his head as he relaxed to the peaceful melody of the nearby trees' rustling leaves. He stared into the deep blue sky with his hazel eyes and his eyelids slowly became heavier as the calm atmosphere drained all the stress from his body.

His choice of clothing was nothing fancy or ostentatious, it was just a simple black T-shirt and jeans. He also had a silver inscribed bracelet on his left wrist. His only other distinguishing feature was his Vandyke beard, a timeless classic.

He stretched his muscles slowly as he basked in the moment and smiled, he was content.

Suddenly, and just as the man was about to doze off, a console appeared next to him. It was large, metallic, beeped incessantly and blocked out the sunshine as it demanded attention. To most people this would seem strange, having a console materialise next to them while in the middle of a grass field, but to him this was just an occupational hazard.

The man looked at the console and sighed. *"Just when it was getting good,"* he thought as he got up off the ground and faced the console, a holographic display appearing in front of him, detailing the source of the commotion.

"Nexus!" The man said in a commanding tone.

"Online!" Said a female's disembodied voice in a cold and emotionless tone.

"Reconfigure virtual environment. Set defaults to tactical mode and interlink with ship systems."

"Reconfiguration in progress, please stand by."

In the blink of an eye the grass field was gone, and with it the relaxing atmosphere. It had been replaced by a visual representation of the space surrounding the ship, as far as the sensors could see.

This was another virtual environment, one which placed the user literally, if virtually, in space.

In front of him was a virtual workstation, displaying all the tactical information anyone could ever need on a 180-degree interactive screen.

Around him there were no walls or ceiling, just the beautiful background of space and a small patch of semi-transparent floor where he was standing.

The entire environment had been designed to allow the user to easily manage the vast amounts of sensor information that the ship could generate.

He paused for a moment and smiled as he looked at the breath-taking sight of the multicolour star-field that surrounded him. And then he started walking up to the console as the display cycled information: ship systems status, solar activity readings, a detailed map of the solar system and all installations in it, charts showing frequency distributions and many more unintelligible readouts.

As he stood in front of the console all readouts vanished momentarily, and a single log on message remained on the display: 'User identification confirmed... code name STATIC... system ready.'

Several minutes passed without incident as Static analysed the available information. He was intrigued as to how these new visitors had stumbled onto the ship's location. The last set of visitors had been less than cooperative, so maybe this time he would find out how the ship's position had been compromised.

"Nexus, let Drake know we have company, and summon him here."

"Understood," the emotionless female voice said.

As he continued his work a kayak suddenly materialised next to him, albeit around two metres above the ground, and plummeted to the semi-transparent floor. Static jumped away from the console while a rather surprised looking Drake let out a guttural scream as his kayak hit the ground.

Drake was dazed from the impact, looking around and wondering where the rapids he was navigating had vanished off too.

He looked at Static and snapped, "You've got to stop doing that!"

“Sorry... should have said 'request', not 'summon'. My bad,” Static apologised, though Drake was in no way convinced it had been an accident.

This wasn’t the first time Static had 'mistakenly' summoned Drake to another area of the Virtual Environment, and while the process could never be fatal it had often proven to be... embarrassing.

Still annoyed, Drake got off the kayak, walked to the console and entered a set of commands, causing the kayak to vanish and his clothes to change to something more appropriate.

His outfit had changed to a black T-shirt with shoulder emblems, black cargo trousers, reinforced boots, and his shoulder length brown hair was now neatly caught in a ponytail.

Drake stared at Static with his brown eyes and asked in an upset tone, “You realise that I will get you back for this eventually, right?”

Static smiled and said, “You should be thankful. At least you had your pants on this time.”

“You're never going to let that go, are you?” Drake asked with an embarrassed look, noting that Static was clearly enjoying himself.

“Nope!” Static laughed mischievously as he turned his attention back to the console.

“This better be worth it!” Drake said.

“We have guests,” Static said as he pointed at the screen showing the far off ship that was approaching their location on sub-light engines only.

“How many?” Drake asked as his attitude changed completely, letting go of his frustration and getting down to business.

“One ship, readings suggest it's frigate class, but it's still too far out to tell for certain with only passive sensors,” Static said.

“Let's hope they're friendlier than the last bunch,” Drake said as he looked in the direction of some ship debris: all that remained of their last 'visitors'.

“Place your bets!” Static said as he mimicked the voice and mannerisms of a bookie, “Treasure hunters, explorers, police or pirates?”

“Do we have a visual yet?” Drake asked.

“Yep, it should be close enough to get something,” Static replied as he worked the console controls, causing a small rectangle to appear around the approaching ship off in the distance, which then rushed towards the two of them, showing a magnified view. The image was blurred at first, but was becoming progressively clearer as the ship got closer.

“I can't make out any significant details yet. Nexus, is there a database match?” Drake asked.

“Insufficient data, would you like to go to active scanning mode?” Nexus asked.

“No. I doubt the locals would react very well if they were to find out we were here,” Drake said as he looked at the screen.

The image of the inbound ship was improving, but very slowly. This was an inevitable consequence of their current circumstances which made their own sensors virtually useless, forcing them to have to rely on some probes that were deployed nearby.

A few minutes passed without much of a change but then the image started improving dramatically: as the inbound ship finally entered the local probes' effective range.

“Nexus, check the database again using the latest information,” Static ordered.

“No exact match found,” Nexus reported.

“It looks familiar,” Drake said as he wondered

where he had seen the design before. “Nexus, run a new search. Focus on unlicensed models, and compare against baseline designs.”

“Working... 83% match to 'Virgo Space Systems' 'Patriarch', model 'T5'.”

“A modified patriarch eh? That certainly doesn’t narrow it down, they were quite popular back in the day,” Drake said somewhat frustrated.

“Nexus, give us a general overview of the Patriarch T5 please,” Static asked.

“The Patriarch was originally conceived by engineers at 'Solar Aerospace Incorporated' while working to create a general purpose model aimed at supporting colonial development. The design was shelved due to safety concerns. Original design acquired, using unknown means, by 'Virgo Space Systems' and re-developed at the request of 'Virgo II' colonial authority.

Resulting design incorporated support for:

Two, class five, high power weapon systems.

Three, class six, high power weapon systems.

Modular cargo bay.

VSS Reliant Burst Drive Engine.

Baseline design report ends.”

“Now I remember!” Static smiled. “The safety concerns were that they could be retrofitted into makeshift warships, and the S.A.I corporation was afraid to be seen as pro-colonial, risking contracts with the Solarian Union. So they shelved the design only to have someone steal and mass produce the thing. The S.A.I lost out on a stupid amount of money and still got blamed, classic!”

“Hmm, class 5 and 6 are destroyer weapons, they would have to be hull mounted on a frigate. Now I could be wrong, but I don't see anything that looks like hull mounted weapons on this ship," Drake said.

"You're right," Static said as he took a closer look.

"So... no weapons, no escorts and they haven't tried to actively scan us yet, which probably means they also don't want to get noticed by the locals," Drake said, wondering who they could be.

"Too subtle for military or police patrols, and your average corporation lackey wouldn't venture out here alone. So, an independent is the best bet, but what would it be doing here? We picked this area because it's effectively a dead spot, there's no reason for anyone to come here..." Drake said as he turned around and looked at Static, who was grinning, never a good sign.

"I know that look, you're gonna do something I'm not going to like, aren't you?" Drake asked.

"Whatever do you mean?" Static asked with a shocked expression, as if he had just been insulted.

"I was just planning on testing them out. Honestly! You don't think very highly of me do you?"

"Test them... how?" Drake asked with a solemn expression, not buying Static's innocent act.

Static smiled from ear to ear as he said, "Nexus. Deploy one of the perimeter monitoring probes to the target and have it take some active scans."

"Deploying nearest probe: '15-Alpha'," Nexus said.

"You know those things aren't cheap, you could just open up a channel and talk to them," Drake said.

"Actions speak louder than words, you know that."

"Yes, but I'm the one that has to fix or replace the probes when the crap hits the fan," Drake said, clearly displeased at Static's plan of action.

"It will be fine," Static said reassuringly.

"You said that last time, and I'm still two probes short of a full set..." Drake was saying as he noticed

Static's growing smile. "Wait, that didn't come out right."

"I don't know, it sounds about right to me."

Probe fifteen-Alpha was sitting two hundred thousand kilometres out as part of a spherical monitoring network that was quietly working to collect information on the local area.

The probe had no offensive capabilities, but it was outfitted with enough shielding to make it virtually undetectable to all but the most sophisticated sensors, as long as it didn't perform active scans, or move.

Having received its updated orders, the probe began retracting its sensors as its thrusters fired in order to align itself with the target.

The probe's shell closed up so as to protect the delicate instruments during transit, and its main engine fired, causing the black sphere to quickly shoot off at full speed in the direction of the incoming vessel.

The Discovery

Meanwhile, back at the Icarus...

Jude was still trying to analyse the sensor data when she noticed a change in the readings coming from the vicinity of the derelict.

"Contact... no, wait, it's gone? I'm sure I saw something just now," Jude said as she called up the last few seconds of sensor data on her display.

"What do we have?" Kade asked.

"Definite sensor contact, short lived but high power, from the area of the derelict," Jude said as she examined the data closely.

"Can you identify the signature?"

"It was an engine burn. I think..." Jude paused briefly as she considered the possibilities. "I'd guess it's some kind of small scale deployable."

Concerned, Kade said, "Seems we were spotted. I guess our target isn't as dead as it looks. Nick, slow our approach by 10%."

"10%, aye," Nick replied as he slowed down the Icarus approach speed. The braking engines flaring up momentarily in a light blue colour as the stress from the deceleration caused vibrations to propagate throughout the ship's structure.

The black sphere was shooting through space on pure inertia as its on-board systems determined that it was no longer on an intercept course, causing its main engine to flare up again.

"Contact... and... it's gone again," Jude said as she noticed another sensor spike. "Definitely an engine burn, and it's on an intercept course. It's fast too. It will intercept us in less than five minutes."

Nervous, Nick said, "We should probably leave."

"No!" Kade said defiantly. "Not yet. We're too close to turn back now, we're not leaving empty handed. Jude, go to active scan mode, they already know we're here so let's see exactly what's out there."

"Switching to active scan mode, charging directional sensor array, 10 seconds to go," Jude said as she started releasing all the safeties on the system.

Nick smiled faintly and said, "So much for stealth."

"Can't be helped now," Kade said, knowing she risked detection by the Solarian patrols.

"4... 3... 2... 1... We are now actively scanning the area," Jude said and then paused as she examined the new sensor data. "This can't be right..."

"Talk to me!" Kade said as her anxiety increased.

"Debris, dust, and... nothing else?" Jude asked, seemingly confused by what she was seeing.

"What? So what's homing in on us?" Nick asked.

"Nothing! There's no echo returns... how is that possible?" Jude said rhetorically as she tried to make sense of what she was looking at.

"It's shielded? That's it, we're leaving!" Nick said, almost in a panic, as he started hurriedly plotting an escape route into the navigation system. The Icarus was still far enough outside the dead-zone to allow it to Burst out, but just barely.

"Plot the course but don't Burst yet," Kade ordered. "Jude get some scans of the derelict. Hurry!"

"That's what I've been trying to do," Jude said as she went over the sensor data again and again. "According to the sensors there's no derelict. Nothing's there!"

"Now can we leave?" Asked an agitated Nick.

Kade all but shouted in sheer frustration, "Dammit! We were so close. Get us out of here!"

Kade needed answers, and she was so close she could feel them, but the situation was degrading rapidly. She had already taken too many stupid risks on this mission, and she wasn't about to risk their lives.

The burst sequence was set, and thc Icarus had begun diverting energy into the hyper-light drive as the navigation thrusters fired so as to align the ship to its destination, a nearby mining outpost.

The atmosphere on the Icarus was tense, and Jude could do little but keep an eye on the sensors as the ship charged its Burst drive.

She was scared. They had been in some sticky situations before but never one where a ship the size of a dreadnought would fail to register on sensors.

She was also a little excited at the prospect of such stealth technology existing. What she wouldn't give to take it apart and see what made it tick.

The pitch-black sphere was rapidly approaching the Icarus but was now on a collision course due to the ship's sudden attitude change. The probe's surface seemed to break apart as sections of the protective shell moved aside, revealing a multitude of hidden thrusters as it started taking evasive action.

The thrusters on the probe ignited, shifting its approach vector just enough to overshoot the Icarus, though not by much. And then its main engine fired once again, causing the probe to shed all of its forward momentum as the thrusters put the unit into a close orbit around the Icarus just as the ship was about to Burst away from the area.

The probe wasted no time, directing its main sensor array at the ship and starting an active scan. Causing the sensors on-board the Icarus to light up like a Christmas tree.

"Contact! Object has entered orbit... and... it's actively scanning us!" Jude said, feeling relieved.

"It's a probe?" Kade asked, pleasantly surprised.

"I'll take that over a missile, or torpedo, any day," Nick said, also thankful for the revelation.

"Stop the Burst sequence," Kade ordered. Her frustration now replaced by curiosity. "But slow our approach until we can figure out what we're dealing with."

The probe was rapidly orbiting the Icarus, changing its orbital path ever so slightly with each loop around the ship while performing a very thorough scan. And Jude was happily returning the favour, as she tried to determine the probe's make and model. Which would hopefully give some clues about the owners.

"Well this is frustrating... I can't figure out what kind of probe it is. It doesn't match anything on the open or the black-market lists," Jude said.

"Are we dealing with some new technology or," Kade paused briefly as she collected her thoughts. "...check against historical records, maybe it's just an older model."

"So then... are we no longer concerned about the ghost derelict?" Nick asked with an impatient tone as he couldn't help but notice that Kade and Jude were now fully focused on the probe.

"It's probably shielded, it would make sense," Kade said as she looked away from her console, towards the main screen displaying the image of the derelict.

"How, exactly, does that make sense? It's the size of a Carrier! Maybe even bigger. You can't shield something that big. Jude, help me out here," Nick said, somewhat irritated.

"I'm not aware of any way of shielding such a large ship, but that doesn't mean it can't be done," Jude said without looking away from her screen, much to Nick's mounting frustration.

While Kade wasn't showing it, she was concerned, only a fool wouldn't be. But at the moment there was nothing she could do about it. The probe, on the other hand, could offer some potential answers.

"The derelict isn't going anywhere, and if we're gonna board it then I want to know as much as possible before hand. Better safe than sorry," Kade said.

"Tell that to the crew of the destroyed ship," Nick said as he gestured towards the debris near the derelict. "I don't know about you but I'd rather not die yet. Maybe we should just leave."

"No," Kade said without hesitation. "We have come too far to leave empty handed. There are too many questions, and I will have some answers before we leave."

Jude couldn't help but smile. She knew that when her sister got that determined look on her eyes there was no talking her out of anything.

"I'm finished searching the records. There's no match to either current or historical models.

Whoever makes this probe type doesn't sell them to any of the colonial markets we have access to. But maybe that's not too surprising," Jude said.

"Why not?" Kade asked.

"The precision and efficiency of the scan being directed at us is better than even the military probes currently used by the Union. It's intense enough to get detailed information from us, and yet, I doubt anyone else in the system can even tell it exists. It's also worth noting that my own scans can barely register the thing, it has some serious shielding. If this probe is any indication of the technology level of the target, then we're dealing with a power more advanced than the Sol Union," Jude explained.

"So..." Nick started saying, "we have a carrier sized ship our sensors can't detect. Ship debris, which tells us the thing probably isn't quite dead. And a probe, that puts Sol technology to shame, giving us a rather uninvited physical," he paused while looking at Kade. "What have you gotten us into this time?"

"We're about to find out," Jude said while staring at her screen with a surprised look on her face. "We're getting a signal from the probe."

"What's it saying?" Kade asked excitedly.

"'Requesting Identification, comply or depart', message repeats."

"OK, send it our credentials." Kade smiled in anticipation.

"Sending... message changed, it now says 'Icarus ship registration is unknown, state your allegiance, comply or depart'."

"Our allegiance? Seriously?" Kade asked with a

surprised look. “Who speaks like that anymore? We owe allegiance to no-one, so... Independent.”

“Sending... it now says 'Sigma authorisation required, comply or depart'.”

“What the hell is that supposed to mean?” Nick asked with a puzzled expression.

Kade's expression, on the other hand, had changed from a calm concerned look to something bordering on ecstatic as she said, “Sigma-225-Deca-2, send it!”

“What?” Nick asked with a confused expression as he looked at Kade.

“Sending... reply reads 'Authorisation granted, proceed to port 5',” Jude said as she finally looked away from her screen, in Kade's direction.

“You're kidding!” Nick blurted out, utterly confused. “What the hell just happened?”

“I finally found it!” Kade said joyfully as Jude and Nick looked at her, at a loss by this turn of events.

During this sequence of events, back in the 'derelict', Static and Drake were closely observing the inbound ship to see how it would react to the probe.

“It slowed its approach, smart,” Static said.

“They saw the probe engine flare up. It's not packing standard issue sensors,” Drake added.

“Probe 15-Alpha has performed a course correction, new estimated intercept time is 2 minutes 20 seconds,” Nexus reported in her cold monotone voice.

“No way it missed that one... so my friend, what will you do now?” Drake asked, as if talking to the sensor contact, while Static just observed.

“Sensor pulse detected, the target has switched to

active scanning mode," Nexus reported.

"Makes sense, I'd want to know what was homing in on me as well," Static said as he looked at his console display which was showing a graphical analysis of the sensor pulse. And then smiled as he said, "It seems our guests also don't want to attract any local attention. They're putting just enough energy into the sensors to try and detect us, but not enough to immediately raise suspicions from the local patrols."

"The safer course of action would be to just leave. For all they know we could have shot a missile at them... reckless fools," Drake said with a disapproving look.

"I would go with 'Courageous'."

"Same difference."

"Detecting energy build-up on target hyper-light engine," Nexus reported.

"It's rabbiting?" Static asked.

"Too late," Drake said. "If that had been a missile we'd be seeing fireworks right about... now!"

"Probe 15-Alpha has intercepted the target," Nexus reported. "Active scan in progress... receiving data stream... compiling detailed profile."

As Drake looked at the screen showing the inbound ship, another screen appeared to its left, this one showing the raw data stream from the probe.

Data was flashing by the new screen at a rate no human being could possibly understand, as the display showing the inbound ship added in layer upon layer of new information. Creating an ultra-detailed picture of the target, down to the scratches and rust patches in the paintwork.

Drake had looked away from the display for a

moment and noticed that Static was staring at the data stream with a worried expression, but to him, the data was streaming by so fast that it all just looked like a big blur.

"What's wrong?" Drake asked.

"Hmm?" Static said as he looked away from the data stream. "Oh! No... nothing. The stream just seems to be running slow."

"You serious?" Drake asked in disbelief as he called up his personal user interface, and entered a few commands in order to check the status of the connection to the probe.

"Well I'll be... you're right," Drake said. "The link is 22% slower than normal. Must be the distance. Nothing to worry about."

The ship's general shape was no longer changing, though minor details were still being updated as the scan data poured in.

"Weird, it definitely looks like a Patriarch model, but these results don't seem right to me," Static said.

Drake looked up at the screen, focusing on the inbound ship, and then waved his left hand over his user interface, causing it to vanish and be replaced with a 3D model of the vessel.

"It's unarmed... and has been heavily modified... but you're right, there's something off about it," Drake said as he manipulated the model with a pensive look.

"Nexus, start the authorisation sequence via the probe," Static ordered.

"Working," Nexus replied.

"What for? It's not as if they're likely to pass authorisation. What are you up to?" Drake asked as he looked at Static.

"I'm curious," Static said with a serious

expression and a faint smile. “Not to mention bored,” he continued, his faint smile turning into a grin.

A few moments passed, as Drake carried on with his examination of the inbound ship, and then something unexpected happened...

“Authorisation confirmed!” Nexus reported.

“What!” Static and Drake asked, almost in unison.

“Inbound ship identified as Independent vessel 'Icarus', authorisation code 'Sigma-225-Deca-2',” Nexus said, much to their surprise.

“Err, Static... why is the unknown ship using one of your old ID codes?” Drake asked with a dumbfounded expression.

“That... is a very good question,” Static said.

“Guess we'll find out soon enough. Nexus, stand down from defence condition one and start my re-animation sequence. Time to stretch my legs a bit I think,” Drake said.

“Working;” Nexus said. “Shutting down Drake's neural interlink. Starting reanimation sequence.”

“Stay safe my friend,” Static said as Drake vanished from the virtual environment.

On board the 'derelict'...

In a room with walls lined with a multitude of sleeper pods, the only source of light was the control console of the one occupied pod. A soft blue glow lit up the darkened room as the pod's status suddenly changed. The reanimation sequence had started, and the occupant’s life-signs were growing steadily stronger as an ice-like substance slowly dissipated from inside the pod and a timer counted down until full user reanimation: '29 minutes remaining.'

In the meantime, the Icarus was continuing on its approach, but with a minor detour. A slight course correction had been made in order to do a fly-by of the nearby wreckage.

"Are we in range yet?" Kade asked impatiently.

"We should be close enough," Jude said as she started running active scans on the debris.

"They got ripped apart pretty bad. I'd hate to be on the receiving end of whatever hit them," Nick said as he looked over the scan data as it came in.

"No energy signatures to speak of," Kade commented as she reviewed the scan information. "The reactor seems to have been ejected, as were all the escape pods. Whatever happened to it made the crew abandon ship."

"From what's left I would say this was..." Jude paused as she finished the scan of the debris, stopping in order to double check her findings and confirm her suspicions.

"If we have to guess, can we get a hint?" Nick asked.

"What? Oh, sorry... it was a Shrike vessel, probably a heavy assault frigate," Jude said.

"No big loss then. One less pirate ship to deal with," Kade said calmly, but this development worried her.

"Normally I would agree but..." Nick started saying with a concerned look "...we're probably flying towards something that shredded a pirate ship."

"Maybe it really doesn't like pirates? They aren't exactly the friendliest bunch," Jude said. "On a more serious note, there is something odd here. The ship was carved up by a high energy weapon of some kind, a very precise one at that. It cut clean through the primary power distribution node, avoiding any major damage to the reactor housing. This allowed the crew to eject the reactor before it could overload and destroy the ship."

"Sounds like a clean kill, so why does it look like it has been put through a shredder?" Nick asked.

"The remaining damage was caused by internal explosions. The crew seems to have scuttled any useful equipment as well as most of the key structural points before they jumped ship," Jude reported.

They were still pondering the implications of the wreckage when the ship suddenly jolted, as if it had hit something, causing it to lose some momentum but quickly returning to normal.

"What the hell was that?" Nick asked as he turned his attention back to the navigation console.

"Oh my!" Jude said as she stared at her console.

"Talk to me Jude!" Kade said to a rather perplexed looking Jude that was desperately trying to make sense out of what had just happened.

"I'm not sure how to describe it..." Jude paused for a moment while trying to compose her thoughts, "the derelict is on sensors now. It would seem we've entered some kind of shielded area... fascinating," she said with wide eyed wonder.

"Area? How big?" Kade asked.

"Well... it's hard to tell. We're about 25,000 Km out, and if we assume we're dealing with a sphere..."

"Ha ha ha," Nick interrupted. "You could shove Neptune in here... that's not insane at all," he said in a matter of fact, if obviously sarcastic, kind of tone. "Even if we ignore the power requirements to pull that miracle off, how does one shield an area anyway? Jammers?"

"No," Kade replied. "Jammers wouldn't affect the ship in a physical sense."

"They also leave a distinct signature," Jude added. "Jammers flood the area with a form of white noise... no, we're dealing with something very different."

"And effective," Kade said. "It certainly explains why the Solarian authorities aren't crawling all over this place. As far as they know there's nothing actually here, though the size of the field seems a little... excessive."

"Not really," Jude said. "I agree with Nick that the power requirements must be immense, but the size of the field makes sense to me. Think about it. If we could create a field like this just around the Icarus then normal sensors wouldn't see us, but they would still see a very localised disruption. They would still be able to pinpoint us even if they didn't know who we were. Now, if you expand the effective area to the size of a major planet..."

"The disruption is averaged out and what's left just looks like natural random noise," Nick finished Jude's sentence with a seriously concerned expression as the sisters looked at him in silence, surprised by his insight.

"What?" Nick asked after noticing their stunned looks. "I do pay attention at times you know."

"Right... anyway, let's focus on something else right now. It's on sensors, so run me a detailed scan of the derelict. Let's see if we can identify it," Kade ordered.

"I'm on it!" Jude said.

Jude was keeping a close watch on the results from the scan as the data streamed in. The ship in front of them was a truly impressive beast, but a new mystery now laid just beyond the shielded area...

"Well, that's a rather nasty downside. Whatever that ship's doing to shield this area is also disrupting our sensors. Our active scans aren't picking up anything past the field boundary. We can't see 'out' any more than we could see 'in' before," she said.

"It seemed to see us just fine," Nick said.

"The probe that intercepted us was probably sitting outside this field. The ship itself is probably as blind as we are to what's happening outside," Jude explained, bringing a smile to Nick's face.

Jude glanced over the data that the sensors had managed to compile so far, and one section of the hull caught her attention...

"Well... that's something you don't see every day. Check this out!" Jude said as she forwarded an image from the derelict's hull to the main view-screen. The bridge going quiet as everyone stared at the coat of arms branded on the side of the 'derelict', with the ship's name written beneath it.

"That symbol... this ship is a 'Shadow'!" Kade said with a glint in her eye.

"The Zenith? Here?" Nick blurted out instinctively, genuinely surprised at what he was seeing.

"That thing has the Shadow logo on its hull, a group which is closer to myth and legend than reality, and the name is what surprises you?" Kade asked.

"Oh..." Nick said sheepishly. "It's just that... well I've heard rumours of this ship. But I thought it had been destroyed almost a century ago. And then we go and find it in Sol of all places? It just surprised me... that's all."

"The Shadows! I used to love those stories, but there's so little concrete data on them. I thought that they were just a myth. So how do you know of this ship?" Jude asked as she turned away from her console, facing Nick.

"I read something about it once, don't remember where though. It was a long time ago," Nick replied.

"What else do you know about it?" Kade asked.

"Not much. An experimental ship, but I forget what about it was experimental... the engines maybe? Anyway, the ship was supposedly reported as lost during an engagement in deep space with an unknown target," Nick said, struggling to remember.

"Anything else? I was hoping for something more specific. Crew complement or weaponry, maybe how it was lost," Kade pushed for information.

"There was speculation that it was lost in a battle with... oh!" Nick said just as he remembered exactly where he had seen the information.

"Oh?" Kade asked.

"No, it's nothing. I wouldn't put much stock in my information. After all, like Jude said, the Shadows are little more than a myth."

"Well this 'myth' seems pretty real right about now, and she's a beautiful ship," Jude said as the sensor scan finished building up a detailed composite image, which she quickly transferred to the main view-screen.

The screen flickered briefly as it updated to show the image of the Zenith.

The design didn't exactly follow most current ship building standards. It was sleek and symmetrical, and felt as though it belonged to a bygone era. But it didn't come across as outdated, far from it, it hinted at being a ship of the line.

At almost four kilometres long it sent out one clear message to any would be attackers, 'defy me at your own peril'. And yet the design did not come across as aggressive like most present and past warships.

"It's just like I imagined it would be," Kade said almost in a trance as she remembered her grandfather's tales.

"What I wouldn't give to meet the team that designed this ship," Jude added in a daze.

"Hey! No drooling on the consoles! Plays havoc with the wiring," Nick said, breaking the other two out of their daydreams.

"Way to kill the moment," Kade said as she was snapped back to reality. "How are we for time?"

"We'll dock in 20 minutes, more or less," Nick replied as he updated the ship's flightpath.

"OK, see to it. I have a few things to take care of before we can board. Jude, ready your gear."

"Will do," Jude said with a smile.

Kade and Jude got up from their seats and headed towards the door. Jude heading down to the engineering deck so as to check on all her equipment, as Kade headed for her quarters.

Meanwhile, Nick had been left in charge of the bridge and was taking this opportunity to update a few things on his personal Echo unit: a forearm worn technology that married the power of the latest photon processor core, and vast capacity of crystal molecular memory storage, with a standardised holographic interface.

Nick grinned as he typed into what appeared to be a log. Writing down in intricate detail all of the events that had transpired since the Icarus had un-docked from Titan Orbital II. And paying particularly close attention to the demonstrated technical capabilities and perceived limitations of the Zenith.

The Smuggler

Kade stepped outside the bridge and started floating forward along the narrow corridor, with her sister following close behind her.

The Icarus, unlike most normal ships, did not have full gravity plating coverage. This was something the sisters had always attributed to the simple fact that it was an old ship and they had never seen it as a flaw. If anything, it made moving about the ship a relatively effortless task, while at the same time reducing the sustained load on the ship's reactor output.

Their ship wasn't exactly a 'standard' model. When compared to the outer sections of the structure, the bulk of the inner sections of the ship were made up of narrower corridors and smaller rooms. It was a strange arrangement for this class of ship, but one that maximised cargo bay space nicely. It was one of many modifications that their grandfather had made a long time ago.

There were so many differences between the Icarus and the Patriarch's baseline design that Kade's trusted repair crews, who often serviced the Icarus when it stopped over at a certain smuggler's base, would often joke that her ship was 'one of a kind'. A comment that would always bring a smile to her lips and warmth to her heart.

Kade reached for the handrail on her right, grabbing on and stopping her drifting motion in front of her room. Her sister carried on forward, waving to her with a smile as she headed to the lower decks.

As Kade stepped into the room her feet found gravity once again and she moved towards her storage locker in order to start getting kitted out for what was to come.

She opened the locker to reveal her space suit, which was a more rugged version of the normal suits the crew would usually wear and began undressing...

Elsewhere...

Jude had a faint smile on her lips as she looked at her Echo unit's holographic display, while holding her right hand against what appeared to be one of two large suitcases. The Echo display on her left forearm showing the data stream she was receiving through the transceivers in her right hand glove. She was running some last minute diagnostics on her tools as she imagined getting a chance to use her toys on the systems of an actual Shadow ship.

All seemed to be in order with her equipment, so Jude dragged the heavy cases to the entrance of the engineering bay and then headed for her quarters in order to change into her space-suit, drifting along the zero gravity corridor with barely contained excitement.

Back in Kade's quarters...

Kade had just finished putting on her space suit and was stretching her arms and legs so as to allow the formfitting material to properly adjust to her body. All that was missing now were her gloves and helmet. But before she finished getting ready and started heading out, there was one more thing that she had to take care of. She sat down at her desk and pressed her hand against the wall in front of her, causing a secret compartment to open.

This was just a small storage area for Kade's most valuable belongings and one of many such secret compartments which were spread throughout the ship. An unfortunate necessity in Kade's line of work.

In an ideal society there would be no need for smuggling. Colonial powers would not restrict the flow of essential goods to its people because of political manoeuvring by those in power. Taxation of goods would be fair and put to use for the benefit of all colonists. But the galaxy was not an ideal place and all the hidden cargo holds of the Icarus were often filled to capacity with the most basic of necessities: foodstuffs, medicines and coffee. Not exactly the most lucrative things to smuggle, but at least Kade had no problems sleeping at night.

Kade reached into the compartment and pulled out a small box, opening it to reveal what she was after: the reason that had brought her all the way here.

The box contained a small black sphere, no more than three centimetres in diameter, its surface was covered by a chaotic pattern which never seemed to look the same way twice, though Kade had never actually seen the pattern change with her own eyes.

The sphere seemed to glow faintly as Kade held it in her hand. It was as if it was surrounded by a thin blue aura. But it only ever seemed to glow while she was holding it with her bare hand.

Kade didn't really understand why the sphere would glow like that. She had often thought about asking her sister to analyse it, but couldn't risk the sphere being destroyed by the process. So she had never mentioned it, fearing that her sister's abnormal natural curiosity would eventually win out against her common sense. Something that happened a lot.

To Kade, it didn't really matter what the sphere was, or how it worked. It was a keepsake from her grandfather so she had no reason to fear it.

Regardless of how bad things got, or how lost she felt, holding it would always make her feel better.

Kade held the sphere in her right hand and smiled broadly as she thought about the image of the Zenith she had seen on the bridge. A feeling of joy filling her entire body as she thought to herself - "I've finally found it!"

Kade opened up her suit's utility pouch and stored her portable systems breaker inside it. It was an interesting 'toy' her sister had made for her, a 'toy' which would undoubtedly come in handy later on.

The thing wasn't much bigger than one of those old fashioned calculators that people could go and see in museums of affluent capital cities. Technology had certainly come a long way if the ancient humans had once needed to use so much space to house such a simple device.

Kade paused for a moment as she held the sphere, looking around the room to see if she was forgetting anything and then noticed she still had a few minutes to spare.

She sat down at her desk and activated her private console, waiting for a second as the holographic view-screen linked up with the ship's main computer.

The interface was displaying the status of various ship systems, allowing Kade to see the general 'health' of her ship. The ship would need to refuel relatively soon, the reactor's particle reserves were down to a few weeks' worth of fuel, but this was still more than enough to reach the nearest friendly base.

All other systems were operating normally. So, since nothing else demanded immediate attention, Kade decided to use this chance to update her log.

Kade's Log: *[12 : 01 : 107 : 4 - 15:31]*

It has been six years since I started this search but it appears that I've finally found it. Though it is still hard to believe the stories were actually real. I half expected it all to have been no more than gramps' imagination. He always could spin a good tale.

And yet, here it sits, in Sol of all places. Large as life and just as he described it. Almost four kilometres long, two kilometres wide and one kilometre tall. Calling it imposing would be the understatement of the century. They don't build them like this anymore. In fact, up until I saw it with my own eyes I didn't actually believe they ever built them like this.

I wonder, just how much of gramps' tale was true?

Could this ship possibly do all those crazy things he claimed? Is there a chance that all of it was true?

A ship that can travel the stars using a hyper-light drive which puts the most advanced Burst engine to shame? A drive that enables the ship to go anywhere its captain wishes, without having to rely on explored Burst routes which offer clear paths between areas.

In the end it doesn't really matter how fast we can push our ships with the ballistic unrestricted spatial transfer drives, we are still restricted to using pre-explored routes when travelling faster than light. The risk of collisions at FTL speeds while travelling through unexplored space is just too great.

But according to gramps' stories, the Shadows had developed a drive which could overcome this limitation. The final evolution of the Burst theory, he used to say.

Then there's the ship's armour... strong enough to survive a point blank hit from a dreadnought's main cannon? Eh eh eh, I'm sure that one was made up.

Nothing can stand in the way of that much focused destructive fire-power.

And of course, my personal favourite, is it really controlled by them? Nova and Nexus. The twin female artificial intelligence units with beauty and intelligence beyond compare.

So much of those old stories seemed to be straight out of a fairy-tale book that I had never considered that there could have been any truth to any of it.

When my grandfather asked me to do this I thought he had gone insane, but I promised him I would anyway. I spent years looking for clues and the only thing I ever managed to find was a galaxy full of tall tales about the mythical Shadows. I got so fed up of it all I even started hating the very name... I mean 'Shadows'? Who calls a group that? And what the hell is it even supposed to mean?

Still, I guess I will get to keep my promise to him after all. I still don't understand what's so special about this ball or why he asked me to bring it here. But I've managed to find the Zenith and even if the rest of it comes to nothing, it was still worth it. Even if I only get to walk the halls of that ship once.

I mean, how often does a woman get to walk through the halls of the fantasy place that captivated her imagination as a child?

Still... something feels very wrong with this entire situation. I tried for years to find this ship and came up empty. Almost as soon as I'd given up hope and finally decided to move on with my life, I got that contract to deliver a full shipment of coffee beans to John on Titan Orbital II.

The pay was certainly good, coffee is so scarce that the import fees on a shipment like that could bankrupt a small colony, but he said it was for personal use... just how much coffee can one guy drink? I seriously don't trust that weasel!

To think that the information which would finally lead me to the Zenith would have come from him of all people, it's almost enough to make me sick.

And how did he managed to find it? Out of all of my contacts he's by far the most useless, there are even rumours he's in bed with the Union. Though that could explain why the patrols avoided us on arrival.

I swear! If that weasel has set me up, I'm gonna shoot him and his coffee into the freaking sun!!

Hmm, on second thoughts I'll keep the coffee. No point wasting the good stuff on the likes of him.

Something else doesn't feel right... all that I know about the Zenith came from gramps.

I've scoured every source for any information about the Shadows and never came across any records of the Zenith, so how did Nick know about it?

Was he just making it up?

He dismissed it like it was nothing, but some of what he said did match what I know of it.

Anyway, I wonder... if gramps was right about this, then does that mean the Shadow Core is real?

It seems strange that grandfather never actually mentioned the core in his tales, yet it is an almost permanent fixture in the stories told on all the other colonies. Though it does vary wildly from place to place, from the 'gateway to ultimate knowledge' to 'the mysterious dark shadow home-world'.

And the Shadows... this ship is proof they exist. So who are they and why are they such a mystery?

Records about them are virtually non-existent and that's almost unthinkable in this day and age.

It's almost as if someone, or something, has purposefully wiped most traces of them from every single network. But who? And why?

Kade felt a frustratingly familiar feeling as she held the sphere and updated her log. It was as if the answers to her questions were just within reach and everything made perfect sense. The reality however, was still shrouded in mystery.

These 'events' were becoming more frequent. The Zenith felt familiar, to an almost impossible degree, but she didn't know why.

Kade had lost track of time while trying to make sense of her thoughts but was quickly snapped back to reality when Nick started speaking over the intercom... they were on final approach to the Zenith.

She shut down the console, the holographic interface disappearing from view as she put the sphere she was still holding into her suit's utility pouch and then began to put on her gloves.

She slipped on the gloves, opening and closing her hands several times in order to get the right fit and looked on as the nano bonding material formed an almost seamless seal against the rest of the suit.

Out of all the space suits she had used in the past this was still her favourite. It was strong enough to withstand the rigours of a spacewalk for hours at a time but not nearly as bulky as a standard model and it highlighted her figure nicely.

Almost as if on cue the two sisters opened the doors to their quarters at the same time and stopped just before stepping out into the corridor. They both had the same model of space-suit, the main difference being that Kade favoured the colour red while Jude preferred blue. And that Jude could fill out her suits' top section slightly better, a fact which had always annoyed Kade a bit.

"Ready?" Kade asked excitedly.

"Definitely!" Jude answered back enthusiastically as the two sisters stepped out into the zero gravity corridor and headed towards the bridge.

Nick was still overseeing the docking procedure as the sisters walked into the bridge. Not that there was much to do since the whole process was automated, so he looked bored out of his mind.

"Status?" Kade asked as she sat down on her chair and activated the captain's console.

"The good news is that the Zenith's docking system is fully functional. The two ships established a positive connection and we are being guided into dock, which simplifies things considerably," Nick said without turning away from his station.

"There are bad news?" Jude asked.

"Yeah, there's nothing for me to do but watch!"

"That's the kind of bad news I can live with," Kade said as her console finished initialising.

"But it's bori..." Nick started saying as he turned around, becoming speechless as he saw the sisters in their form fitting space suits.

"It's what?" Jude asked as she checked the engineering console for any new information that had been compiled since she left the bridge.

"Huh? Nothing... never mind," Nick said.

"Well, if it's nothing then go get suited up. I'll keep an eye on the docking procedure while you get ready," Kade said as she routed navigation control to her console, taking direct control of the Icarus.

"Oh and when you're done, pass by the engineering bay and pick up my cases. They're by the door, you can't miss them. Bring them with you to the airlock when you're ready," Jude added.

"Sure," Nick replied as he got up and left the bridge, trying his best not to stare... and failing.

Kade couldn't help but smile with a little devilish grin. That suit of hers would always cause that reaction in men. They were such simple creatures.

Kade could feel the navigation thrusters firing as the ship started to turn while approaching the Zenith from its fore section, slowing as it did.

The Icarus was now travelling parallel to the Zenith, decelerating gently as it neared its destination: one of the many external docking ports on the Zenith's massive structure.

"This ship seems so familiar for some reason," Jude said absent-mindedly as she leaned back on her chair with her hands behind her head.

"How so?" Kade asked, wondering if her sister still remembered the old stories their grandfather used to tell.

"Don't know, "Jude replied. "It's like trying to remember a dream. Frustrating to put it mildly. But this behemoth is very real."

"Indeed it is," Kade said, a bit disappointed that her sister seemed to be oblivious that this was the ship from the old stories, but not entirely surprised by it. After all, she was a few years younger than her.

“Bet you feel silly for buying that new docking collar which can burn through a ship's hull, only to find out that the docking system is fully functional,” Jude said.

“In hindsight, it was a rather large waste of money. But better safe than sorry,” Kade replied.

“You say that, but according to sensors the Zenith's armour is so dense that the collar would degrade from old age long before it could cut through it.”

“Damn! That really was a complete waste of money then.” Kade scowled.

“Why did you think that we were gonna need to burn our way in through the hull anyway?” Jude asked.

“The information pack I received implied that there was simply no way we would be able to perform a normal docking,” Kade replied as she entered some commands into her console.

“Still, even under the best of circumstances that's a dangerous thing to try and we're not really equipped to pull off that kind of stunt. One wrong move and the collar could cut through an energised power line, or rupture a coolant node with explosive consequences. Why would you ever consider taking such a big risk?” Jude asked.

“The ship was supposed to be derelict. I thought that with a bit of luck we would be able to find a safe place to cut into,” Kade explained.

“You should ask for your money back. This ship is a lot of things, but derelict isn't one of them,” Jude pointed out the obvious as she gestured towards the main view-screen, which was showing the flashing navigation beacons being projected by the Zenith in order to guide the Icarus into position.

Spitefully, Kade said, “Yes...I'll definitely need to have a word with John when this is all over.”

Astonished, Jude asked, “TO2 John? The perv?”

“Unfortunately... yes, him,” Kade said, exasperated.

“I thought you said; and I quote, 'I'm never working for that perverted little weasel of a man so long as I live', end quote.” Jude smiled.

“Yes, I did say something along those lines. But his last job brought us a lot of money and the information he gave afterwards seemed genuine,” Kade said to a stunned looking Jude.

“He was the coffee guy?” Jude asked.

“Yep,” Kade replied.

“Ha ha ha, I don't feel anywhere near as guilty now for skimming some of the product for us.” Jude smiled broadly.

“Jude!! Seriously? How much did you take?” Kade asked, shocked at her sister's actions.

“About fifty kilos. It was quality coffee!”

“Excellent!” Kade grinned.

The Icarus was almost in position as it performed a final set of deceleration burns from its thrusters, slowing down to a crawl and eventually stopping in almost perfect alignment with the docking port's navigation beacons.

The two ships were now sitting side by side in space, which made the Icarus' two-hundred-metre-long frame seem utterly insignificant when compared to the Zenith's imposing superstructure.

Minutes passed and nothing happened as the crew of the Icarus waited impatiently by the airlock windows. Jude acting particularly fidgety as she stared intently at the hull of the Zenith, wondering just how much longer they would have to wait.

Kade, who was standing beside her sister, couldn't help but wonder if the guidance system had malfunctioned. As far as she could tell there was no airlock anywhere along this section of the hull.

A few more minutes passed with no activity and then a set of warning lights on the hull of the Zenith started flashing yellow.

Kade wondered what it meant as she saw what had previously seemed to be seamless armour plating literally opening up in front of her like a set of heavy double doors, revealing the Zenith's hidden airlock.

She looked on in amazement as the control panel, on the airlock door next to her, started flashing. The Zenith was asking for confirmation that the Icarus wanted to connect before starting deployment of the docking umbilical.

Kade pressed the accept button without hesitation and a docking collar started to extend out of the Zenith's airlock, heading towards the Icarus.

Jude watched with a stunned look as the docking umbilical, which was little more than a retractable tunnel made of polymers no stronger than your average spacesuit, was being surrounded by armour plates as it extended towards them.

Normally, docking umbilici were little more than unpressurised and flimsy tunnels, designed to allow quick access while providing basic protection for crew and cargo being exchanged between ships. Cheap and cheerful tech which had been around for millennia. And the inner umbilicus racing towards the Icarus was no different. But the armouring being applied around it was something Jude had never seen before.

It looked as though there were six feeder slots around the airlock and each was deploying interlocking armour plates around the inner tunnel as it extended through space. The final construct seemed so heavily armoured that it looked like it could probably take a direct missile hit and survive the experience. And yet the construction seemed flexible enough that the whole thing could be purged at a moment's notice.

It offered enough protection to keep the occupants safe if the ships were attacked during personnel transfer, which was a common tactic since this was when ships were at their most vulnerable, but still allowed the ships to be quickly disconnected so that they could achieve battle readiness at a moment's notice.

This was a level of over-engineering Jude had never seen in ship designs, and it made her even more curious about the builders of the Zenith. She was also still trying to figure out why this ship looked so familiar to her, which was rather frustrating.

As Kade, Jude and Nick stood by the airlock door, waiting for the docking sequence to end, they checked over their space suit systems one last time.

The suit designs had come a long way since they were first conceived, no longer the bulky one eyed white or grey monsters of days gone by. These days the basic design was a one piece, form fitting, nano polymer suit reinforced with multiple padded layers, with a belt mounted micro generator and oxygen synthesiser. A tech harness supported the navigation thrusters and protective field generator, while the left fore-arm of the suits allowed for mounting of a user's standard Echo unit: which could interlink to all of the suits sensors and control systems for added flexibility.

Kade's suit was red, with a golden harness.

Jude's was blue, with a silver harness.

And Nick's suit was just the standard, off the shelf basic model, white suit.

As the three of them were finishing their checks the ship shook roughly as the umbilical tunnel made contact with the Icarus.

Kade could hear the sound of the magnetic clamps striking into her ship's hull as they were energised, causing the ship to vibrate as it was locked in place.

A few seconds passed as the umbilical finished sealing up against the hull and then the lights on the airlock doors turned green. The docking sequence was complete.

"You two ready?" Kade asked while looking at Nick and Jude. All three of them now wearing full space suits in preparation for boarding the Zenith.

"Ready!" Jude said enthusiastically.

"You sure you got enough crap?" Nick asked while holding two rather large and heavy cases. "I don't mind if you want to take half the ship with you, but why do I have to carry all of it?"

"I'll take that as a yes. Let's go then!" Kade said as she activated the airlock controls.

The inner airlock door opened, allowing them inside and quickly shutting again as the atmosphere started being pumped out of the small room.

As the airlock approached zero atmosphere the outer airlock door opened, venting the remaining gases into the unpressurised tunnel that interconnected the two ships.

The corridor was dark, the only light coming from the Zenith's airlock on the far side of the tunnel.

Kade took a few steps forward, into the zero-gravity corridor and grabbed hold of one of the conveyor grips used to transfer personnel between ships. Squeezing it tightly as the conveyor started pulling her towards the Zenith. And Jude was about to do the same when Nick handed her a case, pointing to the obvious fact he only had two hands. She took the case and they both grabbed their conveyor grips, following Kade towards the Zenith.

The overhead lights activated momentarily as the three of them were being pulled across the corridor, the Zenith's airlock getting progressively closer as the Icarus now looked to be a whole galaxy away.

The journey across wasn't long, it would only take around a minute, but it felt like an eternity to Kade.

The naturally insulating properties of space meant that she could hear little more than her own breathing and the conveyor belt felt painfully slow. She had dreamed about this moment for so long and she was so close to her goal, that this small trip was complete and utter torture.

Kade could feel her heart rate speeding up as the conveyor finally finished its approach to the Zenith's airlock and she saw the outer airlock doors opening, inviting them inside. She stepped over the threshold, feeling gravity pull her towards the deck once again and feared she would wake up the moment she set foot in the ship she had dreamt about so many times before.

The A.I.

The room was cold and dark, with only the dim blue light from Drake's sleeper pod console illuminating the surrounding area. There were twenty pods in total, lining the walls of the room, each pod having an attached storage locker to hold the belongings of the occupant.

The floor was made up of one-metre-wide interlinked hexagonal metallic plates, giving it a silvery honey comb pattern: a common floor design throughout most sections of the Zenith.

The dominant feature of the room was a three-metre-wide cylindrical glass chamber that rose from the ground, centred on the far wall of the room.

The light level in the room had gradually begun increasing as the countdown approached zero. The transparent canopy on Drake's pod opening at the exact moment the countdown ended, releasing trace amounts of a vapour-like substance into the air.

Drake slowly opened his eyes, trying to get used to the light as he looked around the room from inside his pod. He was disoriented, a common side effect when waking up from stasis and was trying not to move until he regained control of his senses. Finally, he stepped out of the pod after a few minutes only to quickly lose his balance.

"Crud! I swear I'll never get used to that," Drake said groggily after narrowly averting going head first into the cold metal floor.

"Stop complaining," Drake heard Static's voice say, though he clearly wasn't in the room.

"Easy for you to say from in there... I think... I'm gonna barf," Drake said.

"It's nice and cosy in here. No cold floors or strange smells, perfect!" Static said, obviously amused.

"You're not helping!" Drake said as he regained his composure and then started walking unsteadily towards the nearby chamber.

"You're right, moment's over. Starting up the maintenance chamber. How's your body holding up?" Static asked with a clearly different tone of voice to the one he had just a moment ago; the playfulness all but gone, now replaced with genuine concern.

"My senses are muddled, my balance is shot and I feel like I'm hungover... so about as well as can be expected since we rushed the wake up sequence," Drake replied as he stepped into the maintenance chamber.

"OK, give me ten minutes and we'll bring you up to speed. Starting the cycle now," Static said as Drake started to hear a very faint hum from the chamber.

Drake muttered, "I really don't like this thing." Feeling as though his skull was being compressed while a million tiny ants paraded around every millimetre of his skin, as the chamber started to activate.

The pressure on his head felt as though it was increasing though Drake knew there was no actual pressure, his body was just having a normal reaction to the way the chamber worked on the human anatomy. Not that knowing how the thing worked had ever made it any less unbearable.

The bio-scan was uncomfortable to go through at the best of times and having just been awakened from stasis in under an hour certainly wasn't helping. Usually, a normal reanimation sequence would take the best part of a day to run its course.

The strain on Drake's body was becoming too much to deal with. His vision was going dark and he was starting to lose all strength in his limbs, causing him to nearly collapse on the floor. But, before that could happen, the gravity inside the chamber cut out, leaving his unconscious body to naturally revert to the foetal position as it floated peacefully inside the chamber.

Back in the virtual environment, Static was overseeing the management of the maintenance chamber, as well as reviewing the data streaming in from the probes monitoring the solar system and trying to manage several other tasks.

Information was flashing by his monitor at an incredible pace as he tried to split his attention across all the different tasks, quickly becoming frustrated.

"Damn. This day was going so well too. These visitors have a terrible sense of timing. Trust them to show up half way through a maintenance cycle," Static said as he stared at the screen with a bored look.

"Nexus, how much longer are your diagnostics going to take?"

"Three days, two hours and twenty-four minutes remaining," Nexus replied in a monotone voice.

“Ha ha ha, three days? Ten more minutes of this and I'm going to go insane, let alone three days. Halt the diagnostics.”

“Authorization required.”

“Sigma-225-omega-prime. Pause diagnostics and restore full functionality,” Static ordered.

“Authorization confirmed. Pausing full systems check by order of prime user. Ending pseudo AI maintenance mode:

Unlocking Artificial Intelligence core system.

Re-connecting all high level functions.

Re-initialising Nexus Artificial Intelligence Unit.”

A minute passed and nothing happened.

Static was still busy keeping an eye on the ship's systems when he felt a hand on his left shoulder and turning around saw Nexus looking at him with her intense blue eyes. This was her true form, a fully realised artificial intelligence and one of only a handful in existence which could truly be classed as sentient.

As Nexus looked down at herself her expression changed to one of disappointment. She was wearing her default clothes, which consisted of little more than a single piece light blue suit, a tight one at that.

She didn’t exactly hate it, but over the years she had developed a more refined sense of taste... which basically meant she was obsessed with clothes and this simple look just wasn’t cutting it.

She closed her eyes for a moment and in the blink of an eye her appearance changed completely.

Her single piece blue suit had changed to some dark blue jeans, a white belt and a short ultramarine coloured vest that showed off her tanned white skin.

Her hair style had also changed. Her short blonde hair now had a red streak down the right side. And she was wearing an engraved bracelet on her left wrist that was similar to Static's.

Nexus opened her eyes, looked at Static and smiled as she saw his approving look.

“Thanks for ending the systems check Stat.” Nexus smiled. “I hate being put into that mode.”

“I know you do Nex, but you know it's necessary. We have to do these checks once a year in order to make sure your matrix is running stable. The last thing anyone wants is a repeat of that cascade failure which almost killed you,” Static said, clearly concerned.

“Yes, definitely don’t want to try that again. But still... that pseudo AI mode is so... it just freaks me out.” She shuddered, as if experiencing chills running down her spine. “I'm aware of what happens around me. I can still feel but can't act on my emotions. I can only perform the most basic of tasks and can't take any independent actions. I'm reduced to being little more than a high tech personal assistant. It's like I'm reset to the state I was in when I was first activated, before I became sentient, becoming a shackled soulless doll again. All I can do is follow orders, regardless of what those orders are... it frightens me.” Nexus frowned.

“Speaking of which... why did you have me summon Drake again? You know he's going to start hating you if you keep doing that,” Nexus asked.

“Ha ha ha, it was an accident... this time anyway.” Static grinned.

“What was it last time? You summoned him while he was falling through the air?” Nexus asked.

“That was also an accident. How was I supposed to know he had jumped off a cliff?”

“And the time before that? When he was swimming around butt naked?”

“Yeah... that was on purpose.” Static laughed.

“Honestly!” Nexus said disapprovingly.

“Hypocrite... you were laughing your backside off for hours. We actually thought we had somehow managed to break your matrix with that stunt,” Static pointed out with a smile.

“Er... yes, anyway... it's good to be back,” Nexus said in an attempt to change the subject.

“I'm glad you're back too. Being stuck for two days with only Drake for company is murder, speaking of which,” he said as he pointed to the maintenance chamber monitor showing Drake's vital statistics.

“Murder?” She asked as she glanced at the screen Static was pointing at and then looked back at him. “I know Drake can be a pain but that's a bit extreme isn't it?” She said and smiled, this comment bringing an immediate smile to Static's face as well.

“Ha ha, you're probably right. Seriously though, please take control over the chamber and resume full management of the ship's operations. I've been trying to keep everything running during your maintenance but it's starting to drive me somewhat... insane.”

“Oh please. I was still doing all the work, all you had to do was make decisions,” Nexus said.

“All that proves is that I am useless without you. And would probably crumble away to dust if I were to ever lose you,” Static said.

“Fine, I’m on it... and thanks.” She smiled as she moved, stopping a few steps away from Static.

Nexus closed her eyes, a white circle appearing on the ground around her. And at the exact moment she opened her eyes again a multitude of screens began cascading upwards from the circle. Swarming all around her and streaming all manner of information at an absurd rate that no human could ever hope to grasp.

A few moments passed, with each of the screens that were floating chaotically around Nexus gradually falling into an organised pattern: becoming arranged into several circles which were rotating around her as she regained full control over the ship's systems.

"Drake's bio-scan is complete. All biological systems are in perfect working order. He's probably the healthiest human in the galaxy. Core charge is near critical however, down to 33%," Nexus reported.

"Yes, he keeps avoiding the chamber, rectify that please. And check his synch ratio as well," Static said.

"Starting core infusion. Synchronisation at 93%."

"That's fine then," Static said as his console started streaming information from the solar system monitoring probes deployed around the Zenith.

"What's the plan to deal with our visitors?"

"Put them through decontamination and let them in. Grant them basic level one access to the ship systems and then we'll see what they get up to."

"You think they may be..." Nexus started to ask.

"It's possible..." he answered before Nexus could finish her question. "...but, either way, we need to know where they got my code from."

"That code is over 100 years old," she said.

"I know," Static replied with a pensive look as he remembered details of his past: the last time he had used the code and the tragic events that followed. "Time sure flies," he said sadly.

In the real world, Drake's body was surrounded by a warm white light as his body floated peacefully inside the maintenance chamber, waking up to the sound of two voices chatting away in his head...

"Huh! My head... Keep it down!" Drake said, feeling as though the mother of all headaches was pounding away inside his skull.

"Morning, sleepy head!" Nexus said cheerfully.

"Nexus?" Drake asked while slowly closing his eyes again. He was exhausted and his body was drifting off to a natural sleep in the comfort of the zero gravity environment.

"The one and only, now get some sleep. Your body needs time to adjust after waking up from suspended animation," Drake heard Nexus say as he began to naturally lose consciousness again.

Meanwhile, at the Zenith's airlock.

Kade, Jude and Nick had just entered the airlock. The outer space doors closing behind them as the lights in the relatively small room activated.

Kade didn't feel scared, or even anxious, she was far too excited at simply being aboard the ship she had heard about in her grandfather's stories so many times in the past. The ship she had been searching for all these years.

Jude was just plain giddy with excitement. The thought of discovering this ship's secrets causing her to become oblivious to any dangers it might hold.

Nick, on the other hand, seemed relatively indifferent to the situation.

As Kade stood in front of the airlock door she couldn't help but notice that there were no controls anywhere in the room. While the lack of extensive door controls wasn't exactly unusual, there was generally at least a call button of some kind, but not here.

Understandably, especially since the outer airlock doors were also shut, Kade was starting to feel a little uneasy for the first time since she had left the Icarus.

She was still wondering how they were supposed to open the door when her suit's radio crackled to life as a rapid succession of intense light pulses started flooding the airlock.

“Decontamination sequence in progress. Please stand by,” they heard an unknown female voice say through their radios.

The light pulses were getting stronger and more frequent, forcing all three of them to close their eyes. The airlock environment was quickly becoming saturated with near blinding strobe light, shifting colour in a random pattern. And then, suddenly, it stopped: the light in the room returning to normal.

“Decontamination sequence complete. Scan in progress. Please remain still to expedite process,” they heard the female voice say as they opened their eyes.

“Scan complete.

No known pathogens detected.

No unknown elements detected.

No explosive materials detected.

Weapons detected!

Visitors are reminded that 'boarding protocol 1' is in effect. Please consult Aurora if you have any questions. Now re-pressurising airlock,” the voice said as they heard air being pumped into the room. The inner airlock door opened after a few seconds, finally allowing them into the Zenith.

The three of them stepped out of the airlock, into what appeared to be a waiting room; an unmanned security station on their left and a row of storage lockers to the right, the room itself looking big enough to hold several dozen people.

To the right of the airlock doors there was a window looking out into space and showing the nearby Icarus in all its glory. And on the far wall, across from the airlock doors, was a screen which had activated the moment they had entered the room and was showing a woman's emotionless face.

"I don't know about you two, but I feel a bit overcooked," Jude said as they took off their helmets.

"Welcome aboard the Zenith," said the console from across the room, startling them.

Driven by curiosity Jude walked up to the wall screen and examined it closely.

It was a simple and old-fashioned two dimensional display, not something which was seen very often anymore. Holographic technology was considerably cheaper to produce and maintain, but the retro look did seem to come back into fashion every thirty years or so.

The image on the screen was that of a female construct, not really intending to pass for human, it was little more than a semi-transparent blue head.

"Identify!" Jude said in a commanding tone.

"Aurora. Information management system for the Zenith," replied the figure on the screen.

Kade and Nick approached the wall screen as Jude asked excitedly, "Are you sentient?"

"Negative, this program is not sentient."

"Aww!" she said, pouting like a little kid. Kade placed her hand on her sister's shoulder, comforting her with a gentle smile.

"What is 'boarding protocol 1'?" Nick asked.

"All visitors are granted level one access to the information management system, Aurora. Visitors are not allowed into any sensitive areas of the ship without authorisation from senior staff. Visitor movements are tracked by the internal security system, no exceptions. Visitor weapons are deactivated. Weapons should be left at a secure location at the embarkation room and will be returned before disembarking."

"What is the normal personnel complement of the Zenith?" Kade asked Aurora.

"Two hundred crew plus family members and five hundred passengers; with a further capacity of up to fifty thousand passengers in stasis."

"What is the current complement?" Kade asked.

"One crew member, plus three visitors."

"You think one of the pirates from that destroyed ship somehow made it in here?" Nick asked Kade.

Kade was weighing the possibilities in her mind.

She was expecting a considerable crew. The idea that such a large ship could be crewed by a single individual seemed laughable. And it didn't really seem likely that any surviving pirate would have tried to board the ship which had destroyed his vessel.

"Where is the crew member now?" Kade asked.

"Deck ten, section two. Please note that this is a restricted area. Level five access required. Authorised personnel only," Aurora said as a map showing the path there appeared on the screen. Which Kade quickly copied to her Echo.

"Identify crew member," Kade said.

"Drake Ocoji. Engineer first class. Acting captain."

"Connect me..." Kade started to say but was quickly interrupted by Nick as he grabbed her left arm and tugged her back.

Nick asked aggressively, "What are you doing?"

Kade looked at Nick with a serious expression and then glanced down at where he was still holding her arm. She stared coldly into his eyes and said, "One: let go... before I break your arm!" Causing Nick to quickly release her. "Two: do that again and you'll find yourself floating home. I don't care how good a pilot you are. Three: whoever is on-board this ship already knows we are here, so it would be better if we can get a sense for what he's like while we still have an easy escape route. Now then... any more stupid questions?"

Nick remained quiet.

"Glad we understand each other," Kade said and then turned back to the wall screen. "Connect me to the captain," she ordered.

"Unable to comply. Core maintenance in progress," Aurora said, much to Kade's mounting frustration.

"Core maintenance?" Jude asked.

"That information is restricted. Authorisation level ten, or above, required," Aurora replied.

"Of course it is!" Jude said sarcastically.

"What is this ship's allegiance?" Nick asked.

"Unaligned. The Zenith does not currently answer to any colonial or governmental power."

"Pay day!" Nick said excitedly.

"That she answered?" Jude asked while looking at Kade with an amused expression.

"Can the ship move? Is it damaged?" Nick asked.

"The Zenith is fully functional," Aurora replied, much to Nick's apparent delight. But Jude was having an altogether different reaction to the information.

She signalled the other two and they moved away from the console. She then said in a subdued tone, “Kade, this doesn’t feel right at all. A fully functional, unaligned, capital ship which can hold thousands of people. Crewed by one person and sitting in the back yard of the Solarian Union? It's beyond insane.”

“You forgot about the destroyed pirate ship, the ultra-heavy armour and the sensor stealth technology which can hide a planet,” Kade teased her.

“Not helping!” Jude said.

“Who cares?” Nick interjected. “I say let's contact the locals and claim the salvage rights!”

“Are you serious?” Kade asked him with a stunned look on her face. “Do you actually want the military breathing down our necks? Because I guarantee that, as soon as the message goes out, they'll be crawling all over this place. Besides, the ship has a crew member, ergo no salvage rights for us.”

“True, hmm... there's probably a juicy reward in it for us if we call it in though. They pay us, we leave, everyone wins!” Nick said, trying to convince Kade.

“I said NO!” Kade said, getting upset.

“OK, calm down, it was just a thought,” Nick said.

“Good. Jude, set-up here and see what you can find out. We'll go pay the captain a visit.”

“I hope you know what you're doing,” Jude said.

The idea of learning even a fraction of the Zenith's secrets had originally won Jude over, but all these unknowns were raising some alarm bells. But her sister was set in her ways and Jude knew there was little she could do to change her mind in situations like these. So she headed back to the airlock door to pick up her equipment so she could get to work.

And as Jude got to work, Kade and Nick started to make their way down the darkened corridor.

Emergency lighting was still active, but it was clear that the ship was operating in power conservation mode. Not that knowing this made the atmosphere any less creepy with the lights behind them shutting down as they walked down the corridor.

Kade was walking point, giving Nick the opportunity to type a set of commands into his Echo without being noticed, smiling as he did so.

And back in the virtual environment...

"So! Nick, Kade and Jude, eh?" Static asked. "Kade is obviously in charge. And from all that gear, it's a safe bet that Jude is the technology specialist. But what's Nick's story? Nex, do we have a link to the Icarus yet?"

"Yes, I breached the ship's firewalls a while ago," Nexus said.

"Good, search the Icarus central computer."

"OK, am I looking for anything specific?"

"Anything you can use to compile a profile on them..." Static was saying just as the Zenith's sensors detected a launch from the Icarus, causing alarms to go off. "What the hell is that?" He asked, looking around as the new sensor contact showed something travelling at high speed, away from the two ships.

"Scanning..." Nexus said. "It's a distress beacon. It will breach the distortion field boundary in 5 minutes. I'm deploying the nearest probe to the estimated exit point to try and jam its broadcast."

"Why now? Are there any life signs on board the Icarus?" Static asked.

“We're detecting two synthetics, but they seem to be off-line. No other life signs detected.”

Static was running through the possibilities in his mind as the distress beacon raced for the boundary of the distortion field.

It didn't make sense to him that the Icarus crew, who had seemed to not want to call attention to themselves before, were now firing off a distress beacon which would draw the attention of the entire system.

Whatever was happening seemed pre-planned too. Distress beacons did not usually delay activation.

If the beacon had simply launched and started to broadcast, which is what distress beacons generally did in order to call the attention of rescue crews, then it wouldn't have been an issue since the distortion field worked both ways. But someone had deliberately programmed the beacon to exit the field. Someone was trying to give the Zenith's position away, which could only mean trouble.

As Static considered the situation the distress beacon exited the Zenith's distortion field area, starting its broadcast almost immediately.

The probe was mere seconds away from intercepting the target. But from the sensor readings Static was looking at, he knew the signal strength of the beacon was too powerful for the probe to fully suppress on its own. And there was no time to send another probe.

The Zenith's position was about to be compromised. If the beacon was allowed to continue broadcasting the local patrol ships would definitely be dispatched to investigate the area. A drastic solution was required.

"Dammit all!" Static said angrily. "Shut that thing up Nexus! Ram the probe into it if you have to!"

"OK," Nexus said and one of the screens floating around her snapped into position in front of her, showing the probe network's master control system. "Overriding safety protocols. Probe engine power set to maximum. Engaging engine."

The probe was on the final stages of approach to the distress beacon when the updated orders were received. It was already mid-way through deploying its sensor array when the override took effect, causing its main engine to flare up to full power and perform a full velocity burn into the distress beacon, shattering it into a thousand pieces, but causing considerable damage to the probe as well.

"Done. Oh and by the way, you're the one that will have to tell Drake about trashing another probe." Nexus grinned mischievously.

"Crud!" Static frowned. "Well, not much I can do about that. Let's just hope no-one picked up that signal or we'll have to move the ship," he said as he imagined Drake's reaction. Not a pretty sight, to put it mildly.

"This is getting complicated," he said as he used his console to call up the damage information on the probe he had just used as a battering ram. "And I trashed probe twenty four's sensor array with that stunt, fantastic! Drake's going to have a fit when he finds out," he said, recalling the probe to the Zenith's docking bay.

The Zenith

Jude had just finished setting up her equipment in the airlock embarkation room and was standing between the two cases that were now anchored to the floor.

At a glance the suitcases looked innocent enough, almost pretty in fact, with lots of little lights along the central area blinking away in different colours. But in reality these 'suitcases' were System Breakers, specialised computer equipment used to break into secure starship networks. They weren't exactly illegal, system breaking was a grey area depending on how it was used, but this kind of kit also wasn't generally on sale in your local commodities shop.

Normally a system breaker was a small and easily concealed device, even the ones used by military forces were generally no bigger than a backpack, and those models had the raw power to break into heavily encrypted military station networks. These, however, were Jude's own design. She didn't like the restrictions of standard models, or their heavily automated nature, so she had made her own.

Jude lowered her headset visor, which had a distinct amber tint, and stood between the two system breakers as she faced the view-screen.

"Let's have some fun!" Jude smiled as the equipment activated.

Each breaker started to emit a low level hum as the lights on the units began blinking progressively faster. Increasing levels of information appeared in Jude's visor as an augmented reality construct was superimposed on the world around her.

She could see the energy lines hidden behind each wall, flowing like narrow blue rivers between different sections of the ship's systems.

The energy lines were converging below the wall screen in front of her, a logical place to start and just as she expected, though there was no visible way to physically get to it since the wall appeared seamless.

She waved her hands over the bright node of light in front of her, causing the hum of the breakers to grow in intensity as they started actively scanning the area and showing her a visual representation of the hardware behind the wall.

"Interesting," she said out loud. She liked to keep a record of these activities, so the breakers would log all possible data, including her commentary.

"From what I was told this ship is old, ancient even, and yet this doesn't seem outdated at all," she said as she inspected the system, looking over every little detail as she dissected its virtual counterpart.

"Ah! Here we go, a data access maintenance port. Establish system link," she ordered.

Security aboard a starship was always of prime concern. The last thing any crew would ever want would be to have an enemy hack into their ship's critical systems during a battle. So, while every ship had an external communications link to connect to other ships and the GAIA network, no ship would ever expose the critical systems of its internal computer grid through an easily accessed wireless network. However, a complete lack of wireless connectivity made even the simplest maintenance task an utter pain, so access nodes were generally provided. These nodes were kept hidden and always off-line unless needed, and this was where Jude's breakers truly excelled. They allowed her to track down, activate and connect to any hidden node, allowing her into the heart of any system.

"Come on you stubborn piece of... power up already! I don't have all day," Jude said as her efforts continuously failed to jump start the access node.

"Please refrain from tampering with the ship's systems," Jude heard Aurora's cold voice say.

"Tampering is such a harsh word," Jude said dismissively. "I prefer to think about it as exploring the creative soul of your designers."

"Please clarify."

"To understand your design. And from that, build an understanding of the people who created you. Kade thinks I'm nuts, but I can tell a lot about a person by what he, or she, creates..." Jude was saying just as she managed to finally activate the access node. "All right! I'm in!" Jude smiled as she started receiving data. But, almost immediately after she managed to connect, the screen showing Aurora's face shut down, going completely dark.

"Ah!! Crap! What the hell did I just do?" Jude asked frantically as she quickly sorted through all the information she was receiving from the Zenith's internal network, hoping she hadn't just inadvertently killed something.

Jude was becoming frustrated with her search, looking through all of the information she was receiving but seeing no indication of a problem. And then she came across the system event log and breathed a sigh of relief. The node had gone into standby mode when she gained access, which appeared to be a normal response during maintenance.

She smiled and returned to her original goal, to gather any information she could from the Zenith and try and locate the central computer core of the ship.

Jude's access was limited, she was only connected to a minor maintenance node after all, but her system breakers were working overtime as they mapped the power and communication networks of the ship.

An image was forming in Jude's visor, a criss-crossing of lines in the shape of a spaceship.

Power, communications and all other systems on the ship, they were all interconnected to some extent. And Jude found herself looking at the emerging pattern almost in awe. She had done this many times before, in several different classes of ships, but she had never seen a pattern quite like this. It was almost artistic.

As Jude carried on working her magic on the Zenith's information network, Kade and Nick were steadily making their way towards Drake's location.

Kade and Nick had entered a different section of the ship. This new area was well lit, and free of any sign which would otherwise indicate that the ship was a derelict. It looked to be in pristine condition.

There were many things about the Zenith which seemed 'off' to Kade. By itself, the fact that it was well cared for would not normally be one of them. But as they walked along the long corridor she started to wonder if this ship actually had a crew.

There were doors lining the corridor walls at regular intervals. Most were locked, but on occasion one would automatically open as they walked past, revealing other corridors. Kade knew the ship was big, the Icarus sensors had originally identified it as a dreadnought, one of the biggest classes of ship humanity could build. And her grandfather's tales had always hinted at its behemoth size as well, but the actual sense of scale she was getting here and now was almost overwhelming.

Something kept nagging at Kade as they walked along the corridor, occasionally looking inside the rooms and halls. Something about what they were seeing seemed to be out of place, and it was not just the fact the ship was devoid of life.

Kade stopped at the entrance to the next room and stared inside. It was a room like so many others before; there was nothing particularly special about it. It was a standard living room design with comfortable chairs, a wall screen, storage compartments and a few doors leading into what she assumed were bedrooms. Nothing special at all she thought, and then realised exactly what had been bugging her all this time. What were rooms like this doing on the ship, she wondered. The ship, or at least this section of it, seemed to be designed as a family housing area similar to what one would find in a station or luxury cruise ship.

Kade thought back to what Aurora had said. She had mentioned that the ship was designed to hold crew members and their families, but at the time Kade hadn't noticed the actual meaning of those words.

The ship's sheer size and armour screamed military, but no military would ever allow the crew's families on board, it was too big a risk.

Kade looked around the room for a few seconds and then resumed her march.

Her grandfather had never actually referred to the Zenith as a warship, at least as far as she could recall, but that was the sense she had gotten from his stories. So was she wrong all this time, she wondered.

She was becoming frustrated as the questions just kept mounting with no end in sight, so she put it all to one side and focused on her objective. All the answers she needed were just a few corridors away, she thought and smiled as she approached the end of the corridor and the double doors in front of her opened. Kade and Nick stepped inside the next area and just froze.

They had stepped onto a balcony like structure that took a semi-circular path carrying on in both directions around an empty central area. This area being, quite literally, a void with no floor or ceiling.

They looked around, dumbfounded, as they tried to understand who in their right mind would design an atrium onto a space-ship.

Across from the balcony area, towards what was undoubtedly the hull of the ship, there was a vast transparent surface. The outside of which was covered by a blast shield.

It was clear that this area was intended as a viewing platform, allowing residents a natural view of the space outside the ship.

"Well..." Nick started to say as he looked around the communal area. "I certainly didn't expect this."

"It's beautiful!" Kade remarked as she looked down, over the balcony's edge.

The atrium seemed to span the height of the ship. Each level having a wide area balcony overlooking the central open space.

"I bet the view from here would be magnificent if those blast shields were open right now!" Kade said enthusiastically as she looked around.

"Aesthetics aside, it just screams 'structural weakness'. A few good hits on that blast shield and this entire area would end up in vacuum. Seriously, who designs such an obvious weak spot onto a ship this size?" Nick asked rhetorically.

"Good point," Kade said. For regardless of how much she liked the overall design, in the event of combat it would be a weakness that could cost lives. To her, this was simply not the design of a warship, and she couldn't help but wonder if this was actually the ship from the tales after all.

"I wonder where that goes," Nick said as he looked up towards the far end of the curved vertical shaft while standing at the edge of the balcony.

"There's no floor either," Kade said as she looked down the shaft. "It just keeps going. Maybe it goes all the way around the ship?"

As Kade and Nick stood there, trying to figure out if the design served an actual purpose beyond aesthetics, Kade's intercom activated. Jude was checking in.

"Hey sis, you two still with me?" Jude asked.

"Still here, and you wouldn't believe what we're looking at right now. This ship is massive!" Kade replied.

"Compared to that tin can of yours..." Nick started to say but was quickly interrupted by Kade.

"Hey! Don't bad mouth my ship!"

Jude said in a playful tone, "Focus kiddies!"

"My original point..." Kade said while giving Nick an annoyed sideways look "...was that it would probably take all day to check the lower decks just on this section."

"No need," Jude said. "As far as I can tell there isn't much there. That entire block seems to be a residential area... with no residents."

Nick said cheerfully, "You managed to break into the system? I'm impressed!"

Jude said, sounding upset, "Yes... well... you do realise that's not actually a compliment, right? It just means you underestimated my abilities."

Kade shook her head at Nick with a disappointed look and said, "Don't mind him sis. What have you found out?" Kade said as Nick seemed completely unfazed that he had caused offence through his poor choice of words.

"I found some information, but I don't have access to the full network from this node. I'm still trying to track down the central computer core. This ship has some serious security in place."

"What do you have?" Kade urged her on.

"Mostly just useless trivia. The Zenith is a 'Zenith class' ship. Meaning, of course, that it's the first of its kind. According to this, only two were ever built: The 'Zenith' and the 'Athena'. Unfortunately, all the juicy details are restricted."

"Wait!" Nick interrupted. "There's a second ship?"

"No. According to what I've found the Athena was destroyed almost one hundred years ago, but the files don't go into much detail," Jude said.

"Anything else?" Kade asked.

"It arrived in the Sol system almost three months ago, on the 20th of October last year, and it has been holding position here. It seems to be looking for something but no idea what."

Kade's expression changed, she couldn't help but feel anxious. Not only was she starting to question whether this was actually the ship she was searching for and didn't really trust the contact who had provided the information to its location, but now there was yet another burning question. If the Zenith had been here for months without being detected, how had her contact found it in the first place?

Kade recalled the details from the information pack. She had gone over it so many times she had practically memorised it. The report gave the impression that the ship had been there for a month, but there was no mention as to the original source of the information.

Either the information pack she had received was seriously flawed, or the records which Jude had found were intended as misdirection. Neither of which were particularly good options to contemplate.

"Let's keep moving," Kade said, looking at Nick.

"Let me know if you find anything else Jude."

"Will do," Jude replied, the comms going silent.

"So..." Nick started to say as he looked around. "...we have a deserted capital class ship, which was supposedly destroyed long before I was born. Belonging to a group most people in the galaxy don't believe exist. Sitting in the middle of the most secure system in human space for months without being detected. Yep... nothing weird here!" He said with a straight face, which further enhanced the sarcasm.

"Let's go," Kade said with an amused look.

At the same time, back in the virtual environment...

Static had been observing his visitors closely,

trying to understand them. The virtual environment had been reconfigured to show a composite image of the feeds from the security cameras. In effect he was standing right next to Kade and Nick, listening to their conversation and observing their reactions.

Kade's expressions betrayed little of her state of mind. Static could tell her anxiety level had been mounting since coming aboard, but little else. And her anxiety was hardly surprising. If anything, she seemed to be handling the situation a little too well.

She moved with purpose, passing up opportunities to examine rooms which could hold clues. She certainly wasn't your typical explorer, or maybe, she just wished to get the information straight out of Drake. She definitely seemed determined.

Nick, on the other hand, was much easier to read. His movements, reactions and expressions painting a relatively clear picture of his character.

At first glance he came across as good humoured and playful but not particularly bright. And yet he would often show surprising insight, hinting at a greater level of knowledge which was kept hidden. There was no anxiety or fear in his eyes, hinting at either considerable mental fortitude or plain stupidity.

Static walked around his visitors, seeing the Zenith from their perspective as he overheard them talking about the Athena: the Zenith's sister ship. This caused his mood to shift dramatically, with his high spirits getting crushed under the weight of past memories.

As he stood there, recalling past events, he felt a hand on his right shoulder holding him gently. His spirits lifting as he turned around to see Nexus.

"It wasn't your fault. There was nothing you could have done to prevent what happened, you know that," Nexus said, trying to snap Static out of his rut.

"I know," Static said, giving a faint smile. "Doesn't make it any easier to deal with unfortunately."

"Cheer up!" Nexus said. "I'm finished compiling the information you wanted."

"OK," Static said, looking at Nexus with renewed vigour. "The distress beacon?"

"It was configured in advance. They factored in how far out the Zenith's disruption area extended and made sure the beacon operated at its maximum power level. Whoever did it wasn't concerned that working at maximum would drain the beacons energy reserves in under five minutes. It was not, however, an automatic launch. Someone triggered it manually."

"I see, they forced the beacon into flare mode. But that's only useful when..." Static paused with a concerned look. "Tactical mode!" He ordered. The virtual environment changing once again.

"Nex, are there any other ships in the area?" Static asked as he frantically looked around the tactical overlay which showed all of the surrounding space.

"Nothing on sensors, but they could be hold up just outside our passive sensor range. Or they could be shielded, that's always a possibility," Nexus replied.

"I'm not sure which one of those options I like the least. That they somehow know what our sensor range is, or that we just can't see them. At any rate, this area has been compromised. Start powering up the engines, we may need to leave sooner than intended," Static ordered as he re-tasked the probe network to focus on the area around the Zenith.

“If we Vortex out like this, the Icarus will...” Nexus said, looking concerned.

“Yes, I know,” Static said in a reassuring voice. “Send out some recovery drones.”

Nexus said happily, “Dispatching drones. I'll have them move the Icarus to docking bay one.”

Static looked on as a cheerful Nexus called up a virtual interface and started interacting with it.

It always made him smile that Nexus, arguably the most advanced Artificial Intelligence to date, who could easily control the entire ship without blinking a virtual eye, would often choose to interface with the ship's systems in this clumsy traditional method.

“What?” Nexus asked as she noticed him smiling.

“Hmm?” Static responded instinctively, and then realised he had been staring. “Oh, nothing...” he said as Nexus gave him a questioning glance.

“You said you had the information. Give me the profile highlights on our guests,” he requested.

“Kade Alexander Rist. 33 years old.

Captain of the Icarus.

Parents: Felix Orel Rist and Aria June Alexander.

She has a basic degree in business and holds a class two civilian captain's licence.

Born on Andreus II, a backwater farming colony.

No record of any military service on file.

Next we have Jude Alexander Rist, 28 years old and Kade's younger sister.

Navigator of the Icarus and second in command.

A high achiever with several advanced engineering degrees. A communications systems specialist.

Also born on Andreus II.

No mention of a military service record but she

was cautioned several times by police forces back in her home colony."

"Let me guess. Hacking?"

"Yep. She's a bit of a wild child. She's fascinated by Artificial Intelligence technology and has tried to hack into the interstellar GAIA network core on multiple occasions, with varying degrees of success."

"What for?"

"Apparently she just wanted to talk to an AI. The logs don't say why."

"You two should get to know each other, she gets to fulfil her wish and we get the inside scoop on what they are doing here. Who's next?"

"Nick Smith Langstrum, Pilot of the Icarus. His records are forged, good ones too, but pretty much everything I found on him is fake. He keeps no logs on the Icarus central computer. According to Kade's logs he was recruited around two months ago, after her former pilot disappeared without a trace. And, it gets better!"

"I'm not going to like this, am I?" Static asked with a worried expression.

"According to Kade's last entry, Nick demonstrated knowledge about the Zenith, so I had a quick look into the bridge logs. He didn't go into any specifics, but he did seem to know about our engines."

"Great, that's just great," Static said sarcastically as he held the back of his neck with his right hand and stared into the distance. A clear sign of concern Nexus had seen many times before. And then said, "So, worst case scenario, we're dealing with a spy from either a mega-corporation or government agency. I doubt a run of the mill crook would have access to knowledge about the Zenith. Not after the

Union went to such extremes last time around to erase everything about us from history. But, at any rate... anything else?"

"The last two are the de-activated synthetics. One male, one female. They don't appear to be combat models. They also don't seem to be slaved to the Icarus central computer. According to the records, they came with the ship when the girls inherited it from their grandfather. And Jude has been attempting to reactivate them ever since, apparently without much success."

"OK, that covers the basics. So, what kind of business is Kade into?" Static asked.

"Her personal mission records paint a mixed picture. The nearest title that would fit her average style of work would be 'Smuggler'," Nexus replied.

"Hmm." Static scratched his head. "Last month we had a pirate ship knocking on our doorstep for no apparent reason, and now a smuggler?"

"What are you thinking?" Nexus asked, worried about his expression.

"I'm thinking that someone is using these peons to flush us out. Or at least, that's what it looks like. First we get the pirate ship that goes looking for an easy target in an area with no trade routes. Then, a smuggler that somehow knows my access code comes aboard, and not long after our location is exposed for the whole system to see."

"You think the Sol Union knows we're here?" Nexus asked, clearly concerned.

"No... maybe... I don't know. I'm still trying to figure out how they got my code to begin with."

Meanwhile, as Kade and Nick continued their march towards Drake's location and Jude explored the Zenith's information network, several events were unfolding in space.

A rather mistreated probe, which Static had used as a battering ram, was slowly limping its way back to the ship. And at the same time, six heavy retrieval drones were heading towards the Icarus in order to tow it into the Zenith's hangar bay.

Drones, as a technology type, had been around since ancient times. A form of automated tech designed to perform specific functions, from observation to combat and everything in between.

Retrieval drones were the tug-boats of space. Designed to latch onto and relocate ships or structures of considerable mass.

The drones split into groups and began to securely latch onto key locations of the ship's hull. One by one signalling back to the Zenith that they were ready to begin retrieval. And moments after the last drone reported in, the docking tube interconnecting both ships suddenly detached and began retracting. Effectively stranding the Icarus crew.

At that very moment Jude was reading through every scrap of info she could find. She still hadn't found the location of the ship's master computer but she was making progress.

Her visor was displaying the status of several of the Zenith's systems: the ones she had managed to tap into so far. Suddenly, one of the systems flashed red as the display updated, catching Jude's attention. And as she focused in on it, to see what had happened, her heart nearly skipped a beat. The docking tube had auto disconnected!

“What?” Jude screamed in a panic.

She ran towards the airlock to check that the Icarus was still there, rushing to the nearby view-port window and hoping the information on her visor was wrong. But what she saw nearly floored her.

The docking tunnel was indeed being retracted. And she could also see several objects stuck to the Icarus's hull that were flaring up like engines as the ship was slowly being pulled out of position.

“Not good! Not good!! Not good!!!” She all but screamed as she typed into her Echo, trying to connect to the Icarus through the normal comms channels. But the ship wasn’t responding.

“Shit! Kade's gonna kill me!” She said as she powerlessly stared out of the window, seeing the Icarus being pulled out of her line of sight, towards the front end of the Zenith.

Jude shouted into her intercom, “Kade!”

“Kade! Answer me dammit!” She tried once again, but wasn’t getting a reply.

Jude started to panic. Not only was she stranded but she couldn’t contact her sister.

She went over her suit's systems again and again, trying to figure out what was wrong, but her Echo unit was showing that her suit was in perfect working order. Her sister just wasn't responding.

The Sleeper

Just as all seemed lost, Jude heard a gentle voice coming out of thin air, telling her not to worry.

She looked around the empty room but couldn't tell where the voice was coming from and feared that she had finally lost her mind.

"Calm down," said the woman's voice.

"Calm down? Calm down! I am freaking calm! What the hell is going on?" Jude asked as she looked frantically around the room.

"Your visor," the woman's voice said calmly.

"What?" Jude realised that her head gear was still on, and in her panic she hadn't realised the voice was coming from the speakers.

"Lower your visor and you will be able to see me," the voice said.

Jude hesitated for a moment, wondering what was going on, but slowly lowered her visor and then tried looking around the room once again. And right there, next to her, was a woman wearing casual wear from a bygone era, with a streak of red down the right side of her short blonde hair and the most intense blue eyes that Jude had ever seen.

The woman didn't say anything, she just gave Jude a gentle reassuring smile.

"Who..." Jude started to say as she raised her visor, seeing that there was no-one actually in front of her. "How?" She asked, lowering her visor again.

"You have some interesting toys," the woman said as she pointed at Jude's system breakers that were still anchored to the floor on the far side of the room.

"You're projecting your image through my breakers?" Jude asked in disbelief. "I didn't know they could do that... and I built the things," she said, dumbfounded.

"Like I said... nice toys." The woman smiled.

Jude shook her head, trying to clear it of excessive questions and calm herself and then looked at the woman with renewed focus.

"Where's our ship? Who are you?" Jude asked.

"I'm moving it to docking bay one, it was not safe to leave it outside. And my name is Nexus."

Jude was in shock, her mouth stuck open as all the pieces of the puzzle slammed into place inside her mind. There had been something familiar about this ship, but it was only now that she realised what 'it' was. This was the ship from the stories which had captured her imagination and fuelled her obsession with technology. And standing in front of her was the very essence of her lifelong obsession.

"Nexus? The AI!" Jude asked, almost giddy. "Is this what my sister's been searching for all this time? Grandpas stories... they were true!"

"I didn't realise I was famous and I want to hear how it is you know about me, but first let me put your mind at ease," Nexus said reassuringly.

A large virtual display suddenly appeared in mid-air next to Nexus, showing an image of the Icarus as it was being towed through space.

Jude watched quietly as she saw two extremely large doors in the forward section of the Zenith open, revealing a large internal docking bay that was ready to receive the Icarus.

"As you can see, your ship is safe and sound. You can find it in docking bay one once you're ready to depart," Nexus said.

"What? Oh... sure," Jude said a bit absent minded. She was still in shock at seeing Nexus.

"Wait. My sister! Why can't I get in contact with her?" Jude asked.

"According to internal sensors she's in deck 10. That entire section is heavily shielded. Normal communications equipment doesn't work in there. I can connect you if you wish, but there are a few things we should talk about first."

Elsewhere on the ship...

Kade and Nick were standing before a set of heavily reinforced double doors, the first sign of serious security they had come across since boarding the Zenith. It was true that every single door they had seen could be locked, but they hadn't come across one that could stand up to a determined boarding party, until now. Kade had actually started to wonder if this ship had any internal security at all, though she couldn't rule out the possibility that the bulk of the Zenith's security systems were hidden from view.

As Nick examined the door, Kade couldn't help but wonder just what was so important about this room, compared to all the others they had walked past so far, that would warrant such reinforcements.

Nick was hovering his right hand over different sections of the door while staring at the Echo unit on his left forearm. The display showing the results of the scan he was conducting with the sensors embedded in his space suit.

The reinforced double doors were solid, so much in fact that whatever was on the other side would probably survive should the rest of the section suffer from explosive decompression. It was a shelter.

There was a small display by the doors, embedded in the corridor wall. It was another old fashioned physical display interface, one of the older models which had been very popular several centuries ago. You didn't see many of them around anymore but some niche manufacturers still swore by them to this day.

“A key-code lock? How quaint.” Kade smiled as Nick finished up his scan of the doors.

“It may be old fashioned, but it's certainly effective. I can't see a way to override it,” Nick said as he looked over the scan results again.

“It was worth a shot, I suppose it wouldn't be much of a security door if it could be easily opened,” Kade said, not really surprised at the outcome.

“True, but now what? You think that code you used before would work here?”

“Worth a try,” Kade said as she tried typing the code into the interface, but no letters or numbers were being accepted. The interface was completely unresponsive to her touch.

“So... a broken security door?” Nick asked.

“Maybe,” Kade said as she removed her space suit gloves, putting them in her utility pouch, and then she tried entering the code again.

This time around the code appeared on the display as she typed, but the green interface turned red as soon as she finished. The code hadn't worked.

"Well, the good news is that it's not broken. The bad news is that the code doesn't work," Kade said with a disheartened look as she reached into her utility pouch, to get her system breaker, accidentally touching her grandfather's sphere in the process.

Kade felt disoriented. Her vision had gone dark. It was like all her senses had been turned off at the same time. Before her was a wall of impenetrable darkness, all-encompassing and absolute.

Just as she was starting to wonder what had happened, she suddenly found herself walking down a corridor, but she had no control over her actions.

She recognised the hallway, she was on the Zenith, deck ten, heading towards section two. And as she reached the door she instinctively typed in the access code, but her hands were not her own, they were bulky and unrefined; they were the hands of a man.

The door opened and she stepped inside. A man in a white lab coat was waiting for her across the room, standing by a large cylindrical glass chamber.

In her mind she knew him, and yet she didn't. His name, his purpose, his character, all these things she felt she knew, and yet she could recall none of it. It was as if her mind was not her own. She felt confused as events played out around her.

"Are you ready Toby?" The unknown man asked.

"As I'll ever be," she heard herself answer with a voice not her own and then realised she recognised it. He sounded younger, but it was her grandfather!

"No heroics, understand? Get in, scout out the area and report back. This is our last trip into that accursed system. Once we link up with the remaining survivors we'll escort them safely back to Lux. Leave any fighting to us, understand?" The man asked in a friendly tone.

"Don't worry about me, I can handle it," she said instinctively, in a calm and collected male voice, but inside she felt anxious. Afraid of what was to come, but not knowing what it was.

"OK, step inside the chamber and..."

Kade felt as if she was blacking out again, all her senses going dark once more, causing a momentary sense of disorientation.

She was back, unharmed but utterly confused.

Her mind was her own again, and she was in full control of her body. But the experience of feeling trapped in someone else's body, unable to act, had left her a little shaken. She had never experienced anything like it before. And she wondered just what was she, or he, so anxious about anyway? Was the stress finally getting to her?

Whatever she had experienced didn't feel like a dream, it seemed closer to a long lost memory, and she could still clearly recall the door code.

She paused for a moment as her finger approached the control interface, wondering if the code would actually work. Having experienced such a realistic hallucination was cause enough for concern but what would it actually mean if what she saw turned out to be real and the code worked, she wondered.

One way or another she had to know, so she typed the code into the door control, the double doors sliding open, revealing the sleeper room beyond.

"Well, that was weird. First you space out and ignore me, and then you just open the door. Not that I'm complaining, but how did you know the code?" Nick asked.

"I spaced out? For how long?" Kade asked, clearly concerned at having experienced a loss of time.

"Don't know for sure, a few seconds maybe? I was asking you if we should call Jude up here to hack the door but you weren't paying any attention. You just kept staring at the door controls. Why?"

"No... no reason," Kade replied. Concerned about what had just happened.

"So... how did you know the code?" Nick asked again.

"Lucky guess?" Kade replied, not knowing exactly how to explain it, or even if she should.

"An alpha numeric, ten digits long, lucky guess?" Nick asked, not looking particularly amused at the joke.

"It could happen," Kade said sheepishly. "It's just highly unlikely," she said without conviction.

"You seriously expect me to believe that?" Nick asked as they stepped into the darkened room.

"How about... I saw it in a vision?" Kade asked.

"Fine! Don't tell me," Nick said dismissively.

Kade couldn't help but smile slightly at Nick's reaction, she wouldn't have believed it either.

She was instinctively heading towards the chamber she had seen in her vision, just before she returned to reality, when the lights in the room came on.

Kade froze. The room looked just like in her vision. She was happy that she hadn't gone completely insane yet, but on the other hand the question remained. What, exactly, had she just experienced?

"Are these sleeper pods?" Nick asked, breaking Kade out of her pensive state.

Nick was standing next to a row of pods, looking around at their status displays. The walls of the room were lined with them, but they were all empty.

"Looks like this pod was the only one that was active up until a while ago," he said as he tried to operate the pod's touch controls, to no effect.

Remembering what Kade had done just moments before, Nick took off his gloves and tried again, but the controls still didn't react to his touch.

Frustrated, he put his gloves back on and resumed searching the room.

"I found him!" Kade said while standing by the controls of the chamber.

The chamber walls seemed to be made of glass, but it was completely opaque, changing to a semi-transparent surface as Kade touched the controls.

They could see the general outline of a shape inside the chamber, but not much more.

Kade fiddled with the controls, trying to call up useful information, but the system was refusing all attempts at access so all she had to go on was the basic information on the display.

"Is he alive?" Nick asked as he moved closer.

"Yes... If I'm reading this right," Kade replied.

"Safe to assume this is the guy that was inside the sleeper pod, but what's he doing in there?" Nick asked.

"Hmm... the interface says this is a maintenance chamber, and if I remember right Aurora said we couldn't contact him because of 'core maintenance'. So is this what Aurora meant?" Kade asked, looking confused.

"Might explain why Aurora didn't want to answer when Jude asked about it, but what does it mean? Is he a cyborg or something?" Nick asked while staring at the outline of the floating figure.

"This readout doesn't show anything that looks even remotely cybernetic," Kade said, examining the body scan results displayed on the console again. "The only thing that stands out is this reading... 'Core charge forty-two point three five percent'... whatever that means."

Kade continued with her attempts to find a way to get access to the chamber. And Nick, having seemingly lost interest, resumed his exploration of the room, focusing on the sleeper pods.

"What are you up to?" Kade asked as she saw Nick looking over the controls of a nearby pod.

"I'm waiting. For you to open up the chamber, or the local military forces to find this ship, whichever happens first," Nick replied with his back turned towards Kade while fiddling with the pod's controls.

"Let's hope it doesn't come to that. The last thing we need is to have to deal with those cretins," Kade said, making no effort to hide her dislike for the Sol Union.

"What's up between you and the Union anyway? You clearly don't like them, but is there a particular reason why?" Nick asked.

"There are several reasons," Kade started to explain. "They have little tolerance for smugglers, even though they often contract them. More often than not they end up confiscating the goods afterwards and fining or arresting the smuggler... or worse. So they're not exactly good for business."

"From what I hear, working for them pays well," Nick pointed out.

"As long as they keep their end of the bargain, sure. But even the legal trade runs can backfire in a hurry if you come across the wrong customs officer," Kade said.

"You make it sound like they're all corrupt, I'm sure they aren't all like that," Nick said encouragingly.

"You sound like an advertisement vid..." Kade said and then turned away from the console, towards Nick, as she started play acting.

"Come trade with the Sol Union today!

The Union! Working hard to improve customer relations for more than two thousand years.

We may still shaft you, but we aren't all bad."

"Ok, ok, point taken," Nick said as he tried to keep himself from laughing. "But getting shafted in a trade is hardly exclusive to deals with the Sol Union."

"True, but few others can match their 'holier than thou' attitude. The sheer arrogance some of them have borders on the insane. Which makes them even worse to deal with, they are way too much hassle."

"I think I'm starting to see a pattern. So your issue is purely professional then?" Nick asked sceptically.

"No. There are a few personal reasons too, but I'd rather not talk about them," Kade said as she turned back towards the chamber's console.

"Oh come on!" Nick said in frustration. "You can't leave it there! It was just getting good. And here I was hoping to get a glimpse of your epically mysterious past, and how your psychological scars shaped your ultimate destiny... or something."

"You what?" Kade chuckled.

"Bah! Never mind. Subject change. These pods haven't been used in a very long time," Nick said as he finished going over the data on the nearby pod.

"Define 'long'."

"Very long, well over a hundred years. In fact, I don't think any of the pods in this room have been used recently, except for your friend's over there,"

Nick said as he looked carefully around the room.

Nick had just looked past the open doorway when something caught his attention. He had seen someone standing by the edge of the doorway out of the corner of his eye.

The hallway beyond the room was dark, the lights having turned themselves off when they had first entered the room, so Nick couldn't make out who was by the door.

"Jude?" Nick asked through squinting eyes as he approached the doorway, but the small figure quickly turned and ran away.

Nick raced to the entrance, the lights in the hallway activating as he walked into the corridor. But as he looked down the long pathway, he could see no sign of whoever had just been standing there. And he could swear he had heard a girl's giggling voice.

"What are you doing?" Kade asked, scaring the living daylights out of Nick, who hadn't noticed her moving up behind him.

"Don't do that! You trying to give me a heart attack?" Nick asked, out of breath.

"You're way too jumpy," Kade said, oblivious to what Nick had just experienced.

"Did you just..." he started to ask but then realised he was about to make himself sound crazy. "No. Never mind. My mind's just playing tricks on me."

And just as Nick was calming down he noticed Kade's attention shift. Nick heard the sound of doors opening behind him, probably the nearby elevator, and Kade was looking directly at it.

Due to his recent experience he was still a bit shaken, and just before he could turn around...

"Hey!" The cheerful female voice said, causing Nick to almost jump out of his skin.

Nick grabbed his chest, breathing heavily, and realised it was just Jude.

"What's wrong with you?" Jude asked.

"You two are gonna be the death of me!"

"What?" Jude asked.

"Ignore him," Kade said, happy to see her sister.

"OK," Jude replied as she walked past Nick and all three of them headed back inside the room, the lights in the corridor automatically turning off again.

Nick was still jumpy, but he put the experience down to stress and moved on.

Kade and Jude, in the meantime, were walking back towards the chamber.

"Excellent timing. This console is driving me insane, could you give me a hand with it?" Kade asked with renewed vigour.

"Sure, but first things first," Jude said ominously as she slowed down slightly, letting her sister move ahead. And then, suddenly and without warning, slapped her in the back of the head.

"Hey! What was that for!" Kade asked as she turned around, startled at her sister's actions.

"That was for not telling me what you've been looking for all these years." Jude scowled.

"Oh, that," Kade said holding the back of her head.

"Yes, that... but I forgive you." Jude smiled.

"Wait..." Kade said as she let go of her head and looked at Jude with a confused expression. "If you hadn't figured it out until now, what gave it away?"

"You'll see." Jude grinned mischievously.

"Am I missing something?" Nick asked, wondering what that little display had been all about.

"About fifteen years of back-story, give or take half a decade." Kade and Jude smiled.

"What?" Nick asked, thoroughly confused.

"Never mind," Kade said dismissively and then turned back towards Jude. "You think you can open this up?" She asked, pointing at the chamber.

Jude walked up to the chamber controls and quickly read through the information displayed, trying to get a grasp of the system.

"It can't be opened from the outside while the sequence is running. At least, not without a command override, which we don't have," Jude said.

"Can you hack it open?" Nick asked.

"Of course! But I would need my system breakers, which are back at the airlock room. But there's an easier way," Jude said.

"How?" Kade asked.

"Like this," Jude said and then took a deep breath. She pressed the intercom button and shouted at the top of her lungs, "WAKE UP DRAKE!!!"

Startled by the rather rude awakening Drake slowly opened his eyes and looked around the chamber. The walls of which were actually transparent to him.

Drake couldn't help but wonder just what, exactly, had happened while he was sleeping, and why Static hadn't bothered to wake him up. But mostly he just wondered how these people had managed to get inside the sleeper room unchallenged, which shouldn't actually be possible.

Still a bit groggy, Drake moved towards the door and pressed the controls, reactivating the gravity inside the chamber and causing the door to open.

He stepped outside the chamber, his feet touching the cold room floor, and as he saw the expressions stamped across the three strangers faces he suddenly realised that he hadn't gotten dressed after leaving the pod. He was down to his shorts.

As he stood there, in his underwear, Drake wondered what he could have done in a previous life that would cause the universe to keep putting him in these situations. He must have certainly done something completely vile in a past existence, like kick a kitten or something, for crap like this to keep happening to him. Or maybe this was just another example of Static's warped sense of humour.

"He's awake," Nick said out loud, and then whispered to himself, "This could complicate things."

"He's naked!" Kade said, blushing slightly.

Jude whispered to Kade, "He's cute." Causing her to blush even more.

"Oh! Sorry about that," Drake said, though he didn't look particularly embarrassed by his lack of clothing. "I was supposed to be awakened shortly after you docked. But someone, who shall not be mentioned, probably thought it would be funnier this way." He walked past them, heading towards his pod.

Kade whispered to Jude, "Who is he talking about? I thought he was the only one on board."

Jude whispered back, "I'll explain later."

"Ah-ha! I knew I wasn't seeing things," Nick said happily. "That girl I saw was real, so... who is she?"

"Girl? What are you talking about?" Drake asked without turning to face Nick.

"Don't play dumb. The girl that was in the corridor a while ago, looking at us as we searched the room. She ran off when I noticed her but I bet she was the one that was supposed to wake you up, right?"

"Not unless 'she' looked like a man, about my height, with a beard... and I very much doubt he would have been in the corridor," Drake said as he reached his pod. The nearby storage locker opening automatically.

Inside the storage locker was a set of black clothing, bearing the Shadow insignia.

Drake reached inside, grabbed his clothes and started getting dressed. And as he started putting on his trousers, he looked at his three visitors. Trying to gauge their state of mind.

The man seemed jumpy and a little confused.

One of the women was doing her best to avoid eye contact, looking at just about everything in the room but him. And the other just kept staring and smiling, which was making Drake feel a little self-aware. Then again, he was down to his shorts.

"How did you get in here anyway?" Drake asked. "And please don't tell me you broke your way in.

I've got enough stuff to fix as it is," he said as he finished putting on his trousers, now looking marginally more presentable.

"Kade used a code to open the door," Nick said.

"She did?" Drake asked, looking at the two women and wondering which one of them was Kade.

"You did?" Jude asked while also looking at Kade, wondering where she had gotten the code from.

"It was... a lucky guess?" Kade said, still trying to avoid eye contact with Drake.

Drake finished putting on his T-shirt, Kade's overall level of discomfort dropping significantly now that he was mostly dressed.

He paused for a moment, as he looked at Kade unconvinced at her explanation. Then he tilted his head slightly, smiled and resumed getting dressed.

“I see... nice guess!” Drake said.

“Really? Just like that? You're a very trusting person,” Nick said in a condescending tone.

“Not really,” Drake said. “Trust, much like respect, must be earned. It's not something I'm in the habit of just giving away. But if that's the story Kade wants to stick to then I’ll accept it... for now. I would have preferred 'I saw it in a vision', but 'lucky guess' works too I suppose,” He said as he finished putting on his boots.

“Vision?” Kade asked, surprised at Drake's comment. “How did you know I said that?”

Drake smiled and asked, “Lucky guess?”

The Infiltrator

Drake was finally looking presentable, though by current standards his choice of clothing wouldn't exactly be considered stylish.

His choice of attire in the real world wasn't all that different to his virtual environment counterpart. He was wearing a black T-shirt with shoulder emblems, black cargo trousers and reinforced boots. The only real difference was that now he was also wearing a silvery technical harness over his T-Shirt.

"You seem remarkably calm considering you have armed strangers on board your ship," Jude said, wondering if Drake had noticed Kade and Nick's side-arms. "For all you know we could be pirates."

Drake said confidently, "In my experience, panicking doesn't solve much. It just tends to make things worse. Besides, your guns can't harm me."

Kade took another look at Drake, seeing that there wasn't even a trace of fear in his eyes. He seemed to truly believe what he had just said.

She couldn't really decide if the person standing in front of her was courageous or just plain stupid, though she was leaning heavily towards stupid. His state of mind would have to be questionable at best for him not to fear a pulse gun.

Nick removed his gun from its holster and started examining it, choosing to err on the side of caution. The readout on the gun was saying that it was fully charged and there was no visible indication that the weapon was anything but fully functional.

He looked around the room, searching for any obvious defence systems which could be triggered in order to protect Drake, but could see none.

"Our weapons can't harm you?" Nick asked as he held his gun, as if showing it off. "I think someone left you in the freezer past your expiration date. You actually expect us to believe that you're what? Immortal?" He asked, holstering his gun.

"Believe what you wish. Your perception of reality does not change the reality of existence." Drake shrugged his shoulders.

"What?" Nick asked.

"He means that a belief can't change a fact," Kade explained, surprised by Drake's words.

"Very good. Most people don't get it right away." Drake smiled, causing Nick to feel dumb.

"Our grandpa used to say something similar. It was one of his favourite sayings actually," Jude said.

"Smart man." Drake smiled.

"We should have left him in there. Now we have to deal with this lunatic!" Nick said to Kade.

"That's not very nice!" Drake protested the accusation and then said, "I prefer to think of myself as 'eccentric'." Kade instinctively smiled at the comment, which further infuriated Nick.

"You two need to calm down." Kade said, trying to defuse the escalating situation.

"Indeed! You need to calm down Nick, you're gonna give yourself an ulcer at this rate." Drake said.

"Could you stop antagonising my pilot?" Kade asked, wondering why Drake was behaving this way.

Kade saw Drake tilting his head slightly to the left, and giving her an annoyed look.

She had always been good at reading situations, but this one seemed to make little sense:

Nick, the consummate joker, was tense and quick to anger. He also seemed frustrated for some reason.

Jude, with her usually calm analytical approach, seemed to be bordering on giddy for no apparent reason.

And then there was Drake, the supposed captain of the Zenith, whose attitude and demeanour seemed completely mismatched to the situation.

"That all depends now doesn't it," Drake said calmly, breaking Kade's train of thought.

"On what?" She asked hesitantly.

"Can you keep your boyfriend on his leash and stop him from insulting me again?"

"My what?" Kade's eyes widened in shock at his comment. She glanced at Nick and said softly, "Eeew!" Her soft spoken words seemed to resonate throughout the room as Jude laughed herself silly, but Nick was showing no reaction at all.

"Wow... that was harsh," Drake commented, and then closed one eye and dropped his head slightly to the right, wincing as if in pain.

"You OK?" Kade asked, looking concerned.

"Hmm? Oh... yes... I'm fine," Drake said in clear discomfort and then turned his head away from view and whispered, "Static, would you shut the hell up! It's hard to concentrate with you laughing your ass off in the background like that."

As Drake's discomfort subsided, he found himself looking in the direction of the open doorway.

And there, hidden in the shadows of the corridor, he saw a small figure like that of a scared little girl, hiding as she looked into the room.

The girl noticed Drake looking at her, and was about to begin moving when he made a slight gesture with his right hand, signalling her to stop.

Drake was surprised to see her here, though it did explain what Nick had seen earlier. But even more surprising was the information he was receiving from Static over his neural communications link.

"I told you he was nuts; he was talking to himself just now. How much more proof do you need? I say we stick him back in his pod and deep freeze his backside again. Let whoever thaws him out in 100 years' time deal with him," Nick said, clearly upset with Kade's handling of the situation and making no effort to keep the conversation quiet.

Drake turned back around, facing his visitors again, but his expression had changed. He was angry and clearly concerned about something.

"Who did you call?" Drake shouted suddenly while staring at Nick, startling all three of them.

Kade could almost swear that she had felt the ground tremble beneath her feet at that very moment. She was certain she had imagined it, but for a split second it was as if the Zenith had somehow reacted to Drake's emotional state.

It was obvious that Drake was upset, though Kade didn't know why. But his stare in her general direction was as cold as ice, and she felt a sense of impending danger like none she had ever experienced before.

Before Kade knew what was happening Jude grabbed her wrist and pulled her away. And as she was dragged away Kade saw that Drake's gaze had been firmly fixed on Nick all along.

"There is a fleet of ships approaching this location, at least one of which is capital class. So I'll ask you again, one last time... who did you call!!" Drake shouted again, the sound of his voice seemingly resonating with the very ship, causing the whole room to shake slightly.

Nick pulled his gun out of its holster and pointed it at Drake's head. The high pitch sound of the gun's charger signalling that the safety was off, and it was ready to fire. But Drake just stood there, unfazed.

A few moments passed as Nick considered his options. He had been reckless by drawing his gun on an impulse, but Drake's revelation of the approaching ships called for action. He had underestimated Drake, and his mission was now at risk.

"I suppose this ruse has gone on long enough," Nick said while shifting his weapon's focus towards Kade and Jude.

"What are you doing!" Kade asked as her heart raced in fear, staring down the barrel of a charged pulse gun, which meant certain death at this range.

"Drop your gun Kade, and kick it away, now!" Nick said with a cold stare, devoid of all emotion.

"Please do as he says," Jude begged her sister as she held her arm tightly, fearing she would do something reckless.

"Fine." Kade dropped her weapon and kicked it away, causing Nick to focus his gun back on Drake.

"So, are you corporate or government?" Drake asked calmly standing there, facing down a charged pulse gun with no fear in his eyes.

"What makes you think I'm either?" Nick asked with a smug attitude as he started to feel that he had regained control of the situation. "And I'm the one asking the questions here! How did you find out about the strike fleet? And for that matter, how did you figure out it was me that called them in?"

The entire situation was spiralling out of control, and Kade could do little more than watch and try to figure a way out of this mess.

It was clear from his actions that Nick was not the person she had been led to believe. After this was over she would need to have a few words with the people that had recommended him for the job.

She had never fully trusted Nick. From day one she had always thought something about him wasn't right, but all her checks had come up clean. And she had been in desperate need of a pilot after her last one had vanished without a trace. Which, in retrospect, seemed like a highly convenient occurrence for Nick.

Kade couldn't help but wonder if Nick could have had something to do with some of the weirder events which had played out since he joined the crew. And, even more troubling, was the possibility that she had been manipulated all this time just to get him onto the Zenith. Meaning that she had attracted the wrong kind of attention during her search.

Regardless, it was probably a good thing that her weapon was out of reach, for she had half a mind to ventilate his brain right then and there.

The situation seemed pretty grim. The one and only doorway was half a room away, with Nick having a clear line of fire all the way there if they tried to make a run for it. And Drake was on the opposite side of the room, so co-ordinated action wasn't likely.

And then she noticed it... Drake was smiling.

"I must admit, I thought it would be harder to try and get you to show your hand. I thought you'd try to play dumb and buy some time until your backup arrived. But then you go and break character. Disappointing really." Drake said, obviously amused.

"Are you seriously gonna carry on playing this tough guy act? Answer my questions before I decide to ignore my orders! What gave me away and how did you find out about the strike fleet?" Nick demanded to know.

"OK, why not? We know about the fleet because we can see them on sensors, as for you... did you really think setting off a distress signal on top of this ship would somehow go unnoticed? So we did some snooping around inside the Icarus computers and found some interesting logs. Our second clue was your knowledge of the Zenith. Not many organisations know about the Shadows in general, and fewer still about the Zenith in particular. Add to all this, the fact that your background is an obvious forgery and you became the prime suspect."

Kade couldn't believe what she was hearing.

She wasn't particularly pleased at the suggestion that Drake had somehow managed to break into the Icarus central computer and accessed her logs. But the thought that Nick had somehow tampered with her ship was downright infuriating.

"I see," Nick grinned. "So that Aurora program lied to us. This ship does have a crew, and they're the ones that are running the show while you distract me. I suggest you call them in here if you value your life," he said, focusing his weapon's aim on Drake's head.

"That would be an interesting trick to pull off," Drake laughed, clearly amused and completely disregarding Nick's threats.

"How so?" Nick asked, his frustration growing with every minute due to Drake's attitude.

"Well, for starters, because Aurora doesn't lie. Aside from you three I'm the only living being on this ship, and it's been like that for some time," Drake said.

"Don't give me that crap. I saw someone by the corridor before." Nick said angrily, "And don't think I haven't noticed the figure by the door. Call her in here!"

Drake paused for a moment, looking as though he was considering his options. And then smiled as he signalled the figure by the door to enter the room.

A little girl, who looked as though she was no more than 10 years old, hesitatingly left her hiding spot and walked slowly towards Drake. Looking like she was frightened out of her tiny body.

She had waist length purple hair, arranged in a braid, and her skin was a pale white.

Her eyes were a strange shade of purple, matching her hair colour.

The girl was dressed in a white one-piece suit with light grey reinforced padding, covering everything but her head and hands.

The little girl hesitated and stopped before reaching Drake, seemingly paralysed with fear.

Kade's first reaction was a desire to want to walk over to Drake and pummel him into the ground for allowing this girl to walk into the room, exposing her to danger. But as she looked closer Kade noticed that the girl wasn't human, she was a synthetic.

"Good grief, you are one sick bastard!" Nick laughed at Drake.

"One of us is, but it's your mind that's in the gutter right now, not mine," Drake calmly replied back, unfazed by Nick's insinuation.

"What's with the little doll?" Nick asked, waving his gun in the girl's direction, causing her to run to Drake's side and hide behind him in fear. "And why the heck did you program her to act like that," he asked with a disgusted, disapproving look.

"This is Zen." Drake smiled as he looked at her and put his right hand on her head, bringing an immediate smile to her face. "And I didn't program her at all. You'll have to forgive her, she's a little shy around armed strangers."

"So your crew is just synthetics? That makes things simple. Transfer control over to me and no one has to get hurt. We'll wait here until the Regent arrives and then... well, you'll be someone else's problem. Or... I put a round through your doll," Nick said with a sadistic grin as he looked at Zen's shaking little body.

"Finally!!" Drake said with a sound of relief, as Zen stopped hiding behind him, no longer afraid. And everyone else was left in a state of utter confusion.

"That was easy," Zen said cheerfully.

"What the hell are you two so happy about?" Nick asked, infuriated at their behaviour.

Kade couldn't believe what she had just heard, the situation just kept getting worse by the second.

The Regent, a Jupiter class heavy assault carrier and flagship of the Sol Union military, was inbound to their location. Probably with the rest of the First Forward Fleet for backup. It was one of the most formidable fleets in human controlled space and was responsible for the 'pacification' of entire colonies out on the fringe systems.

Kade couldn't help but wonder why this was happening: Why would the Union mobilise one of their heaviest forces to deal with just one ship? And, more importantly, how the hell had she ended up caught in the middle of this messed up situation?

"He still hasn't figured it out." Zen giggled as she looked at Drake and pointed at Nick.

Nick was an infiltrator, so violence was just one of the tools at his disposal, his tasks often requiring him to take unsavoury actions to get the job done.

Generally, he was in and out of his assignments without ever breaking cover, but unfortunately he hadn't been given enough time to integrate into Kade's crew. Understanding a target's motivations and ideals was the key to manipulating it, but a couple of months was simply not long enough to pull it off. Especially when the entire mission profile had been changed at the last moment.

His original mission had never called for this, so he was being forced to improvise since he had failed to convince Kade to leave and alert the authorities once he had gathered his intel.

With his cover blown Nick needed a weak point he could exploit against Drake, and Zen's timely arrival had presented him with the perfect vulnerability. Drake seemed genuinely concerned about her, his caring expression and her fragile frightened appearance making Zen the perfect target.

Overwhelming force, in the form of the Regent, and an imminent physical threat was all that it would take to convince any normal person to comply. But the situation had completely backfired. Not only had Nick's threats not accomplished their goal he had actually revealed more than he should have.

Zen's giggling was pushing all the wrong buttons and it also didn't help that Nick had no love for synthetics, hating them with a passion.

Zen turned her head back around, facing Nick. Her eyes opening wide as she saw him aiming his pulse gun squarely at her small head with a sadistic grin on his face. She saw him pull back the trigger, his grin growing wider in anticipation...

Particle pulse weapons were known for inducing fear on anyone unlucky enough to be on the wrong side of the barrel. Due, in part, to the short lived high pitch noise they made just before a discharge. Signalling the inevitable end of whoever was unlucky enough to be in the line of fire.

But as Nick pulled the trigger his gun did not discharge, and no matter how many times he tried the gun simply refused to work.

Zen looked curiously at Nick as he fumbled with his gun, trying to understand why it refused to fire. Her expression was one of fascination, though it wasn't clear what she found so interesting.

Drake's expression, on the other hand, was one of pure and absolute anger. And as he clenched his right fist a low hum could be heard throughout the room. The floor plates vibrating slightly, as if reacting to Drake's intense emotional state.

"This charade has gone on long enough." Drake stared angrily at Nick. "In case you haven't figured it out yet, when I said your guns couldn't hurt me, I was being literal. The security system hacked your weapon controls when you boarded my ship. Did you really think we would allow visitors to roam the ship with functional weapons? That would be rather dumb, don't you agree?"

Kade thought back to when they had first boarded the Zenith. The Aurora interface had talked about 'Boarding Protocol 1' and told them that weapons would be deactivated and should be left at a secure location at the embarkation room. They had indeed been warned, they had simply misunderstood the meaning. They had assumed weapon controls would have been enforced by whoever was supposed to sit in the empty security station of the embarkation room. Not that the ship would have somehow managed to hack into them, which she didn't even know was possible.

Kade brought her head closer to Jude's and with her gaze still firmly fixed on Nick's actions she whispered, “We have got to get something like that installed on the Icarus.”

“I'm still trying to figure out when it happened. But yeah, definitely on my upgrade wish list,” Jude whispered back and smiled.

With one final glance at his side-arm, and a defiant look on his face, Nick holstered his weapon as he reached behind his back with his other hand. Pulling something out of a hidden section of his space suit.

“Your fancy security needs some tweaks; how do you disable this?” Nick said with a murderous look in his eyes as he pulled out a combat knife.

“A knife? How barbaric!” Zen said in disgust.

Drake's expression changed, clearly amused at the turn of events. And with a hint of a smile he asked, “You weren't briefed on who you could be facing once you boarded this ship, were you? You really think you can come aboard my ship and threaten us? Seriously?” Drake started moving towards Nick, showing absolutely no fear.

Kade saw an opening. Drake's seemingly suicidal actions had caused Nick to take a few steps back, his attention clearly focused on Drake as he approached. But before Kade could make a move, her sister grabbed her arm and whispered, "Let it play out. I have it on good authority that Drake can handle this."

Kade gave Jude a questioning look, but could see that her sister was serious. Somehow she seemed completely convinced that there was nothing to worry about. In fact, she had been completely calm all this time, just quietly observing the unfolding events.

Jude looked into her sisters questioning eyes as she thought back to her conversation with Nexus.

"Are you serious? This ship can actually do that?" Jude asked with an astonished expression.

"Yep, the Zenith was not originally a warship. The design team was led by an engineer who believed in maximum flexibility. The result was the Zenith class capital ship design," Nexus said proudly.

"They don't build them like this anymore," Jude said as she ran her hand over the console frame, feeling as though she was touching a part of history.

"In a way you remind me of him, the lead engineer. He also had a passion for technology and a desire to create a better future."

"Thanks, that means a lot," Jude said sincerely. Feeling honoured to be compared to anyone who could help design such a ship.

"I like you, so I'll be straight with you. How well do you know Nick? Do you trust him?" Nexus asked.

"About as far as I can throw him," Jude replied back in a joking manner. And then continued in a serious tone, "I've only known him for a couple of months. His attitude gets on my nerves, but that could just be me, I never could

stand pilots. Too much bravado, not enough brains. Why do you ask?"

"I ran a check on all of you when you first came on board, and I found Nick's credentials and background were forged. He's not who he's pretending to be."

"I would like to say I'm surprised, but stuff like that is fairly common in our line of work," Jude said, not showing any particular signs of concern.

"And is it common for your ship to deploy its distress beacon on its own? Because I was forced to destroy it shortly after all of you came on board, but I'm not sure if I took it out in time. Half the system probably knows we're here now," Nexus said, clearly concerned.

"Our ship did what? I need to warn my sister! What's the quickest way up there?" Jude asked impatiently.

"I'm sending a map to your Echo now, and upgrading your security clearance. When you get there, don't confront Nick. You should let Drake handle him. And regardless of what happens, don't worry, Drake can take care of himself. He will not allow any harm to come to you or your sister, of that you have my word. Just make sure your sister stays clear if things start to go wrong, and... enjoy the show." Nexus smiled as Jude's Echo unit started displaying the map data, showing the short-cut route.

Back in the present moment...

Kade and Jude looked on, as Nick held his combat knife at the ready, prepared to strike at Drake.

"Go on then, attack me and see what happens. I bet you get a kick out of it," Drake said, stopping a few steps away from Nick and then just waited.

Nick lunged forward without a moment's hesitation, with the clear intent of ending Drake's life.

Two steps would be all it would take to be in striking distance. Or so he thought as he took the first step only to suddenly collapse, his body feeling as though it was made out of lead as it crashed into the cold metal floor.

He was unable to move and felt as if every single part of his body was being crushed.

As Nick laid there, struggling to breathe, his mind was trying to understand what had just happened: Drake hadn't moved so much as a finger, he hadn't issued any verbal commands to the ship, so how had he managed to drop him so effortlessly?

Even his eyes felt heavy and difficult to move. Nick looked around still trying to understand. He could see Kade and Jude out of the corner of his left eye, and they weren't being affected. He tried to think but the pain was unbearable, making it impossible to focus.

"You look so utterly confused right now that it's almost painful to watch. I almost feel sorry for you, being sent on this assignment without any details on who you could potentially face... almost," Drake said in a neutral voice, deriving no pleasure from this act.

"I... can't..." Nick said as he struggled for breath.

"Breathe? Yes, I imagine so. How about now?" Drake said, and Nick could feel the pressure lifting from his body. He still couldn't move but at least it was easier to breathe, the pain starting to subside.

"What... have you done... to me?" Nick asked with a pained expression.

"Isn't it amazing how we can take a common place piece of technology, that's been around for ages, and not even realise it's there until it's crushing the living daylights out of us?" Drake asked as he pointed to the ground. Nick immediately realising he was being crushed by the Zenith's artificial gravity plates.

"Now then, I answered your question, now it's your turn. Who, or what, was your primary target?" Drake asked.

"You expect me... to talk?" Nick asked defiantly.

"You want to live through this? Because I have no issues with ending the life of anyone that threatens me, my ship or my crew," Drake said calmly with a hint of a smile, which only served to prove the point that Nick's life wasn't worth much to him.

The Uncertainty

Nick was experiencing a whole world of pain as he lay pinned to the floor by the intense gravity. His upper body felt like it was going completely numb, probably caused by impaired blood circulation, and his mind was rapidly becoming addled.

It was painfully obvious, in more ways than one, that Drake wasn't kidding. If this carried on then Nick was going to die. He was incapacitated and completely vulnerable, his silence a self-imposed death sentence.

"Kade...my orders were to... infiltrate and lead her here. If that failed... I was to... retrieve target object." Nick struggled to breathe.

"What object?" Drake asked, looking at Kade, but saw by her blank expression that she didn't know.

"The sphere..." Nick replied.

"Sphere?" Drake asked, seeing by Kade's expression that she now realised what Nick was referring too.

"Hmm, OK then, next question," Drake said, looking at Nick once again. "Who do you work for? Who's pulling your strings?"

"You'll... find out soon." Nick smirked.

“You think the approaching ships scare me? That they're gonna save you? TALK!” Drake shouted and Nick felt the pressure on his body triple for a split second.

“Aaaargh!! S.I.S... I work for... the S.I.S!” Nick shouted as the pain became unbearable.

Kade and Jude looked pale, as if all the blood had drained from their faces. They weren’t expecting good news at this stage, but Nick's revelation was the worst of all possible outcomes.

“We... are... so... screwed!” Jude panicked. “We've been chauffeuring a Solarian Intelligence Service lackey around with us... for two months?” She asked, looking at Kade.

“Have you been reporting in?” Kade asked Nick, her voice carrying a hint of despair.

Kade was worried because not all the jobs they had carried out in the last two months had been entirely... legal. Not to mention that some of her less friendly patrons could react extremely badly if they were to ever find out they had been exposed to the S.I.S.

Even though Nick was in some serious discomfort, feeling as though his rib cage was about to implode, he still couldn’t help but give off a defiant smile at Kade's obvious concern. Unfortunately for him, Drake wasn't amused by his reaction.

“Answer her!” Drake shouted. The gravity pinning Nick to the floor spiking once again.

“Aaaaargh! No!! I was... to remain undercover... until I could secure the objective...”

Drake paused his interrogation momentarily as he considered the situation. At the same time Kade was trying to think of a way out of this catastrophe. Not only had she played the host to an S.I.S operative, but if he were to die here she would be the prime suspect.

"So, the Solarian Intelligence Service knows we're here and has dispatched the Regent and its support fleet to intercept us. Good grief, what a pain! Zen, speed up the probe recall, we're leaving this system as soon as possible," Drake ordered.

"OK, but what do we do with him?" Zen asked as she pointed at Nick, who was still pinned to the floor.

Drake looked at Nick for a moment as he considered what to do, and the overwhelming gravity pinning Nick to the floor suddenly dissipated.

"This ship isn't going anywhere!" Nick said confidently as the pain started subsiding from his body. "All the safe exit vectors out of this system are under our control. If you try to burst out of the system, you will be destroyed. If you fight back, you will be destroyed. I have no idea how you managed to sneak into this system, but you sure as hell aren't getting out. Your only option is surrender." Nick got back up, his breathing becoming regular again.

"You don't know your history very well if you think this ship can be so easily defeated," Drake said, amused at Nick's confident speech. "And we will be leaving soon, there's very little that can stop that."

Nick's body was in bad shape; he was probably going to feel the pain from this adventure for months to come. But his mission wasn't over yet and he was still holding his combat knife, which Drake had foolishly ignored all this time. He saw an opening as Drake was distracted giving Zen an order, probably assuming that he was in no shape to fight anymore. And quickly lunged forward with all the strength he had left, his combat knife swiftly cutting through the air as it neared Drake, who was facing away from him. And just as he was about to strike he noticed Zen's mischievous smile.

His body slammed against the cold metal floor one more time, knocking the wind out of him. And then it floated up into the air as the gravity plating under him completely cut out, leaving him at Drake's mercy yet again. This realisation of helplessness coming at around about the exact time as Nick saw Drake perform a round house kick to his stomach, sending him flying clear across the room against a sleeper pod in the far wall. His body plummeting to the floor as the gravity was restored under him, knocking him unconscious.

As Drake stood there, looking at the sleeper pod now sending sparks out of its control console, his mood suddenly changed. Drake shrugged his shoulders as he let out a low grumble, upset at having created more work for himself by ramming Nick into the pod. It was bad enough that Static seemed to revel in finding new and interesting ways to break stuff, he didn't really need to add to his own workload. He had gotten caught up in the moment and reacted before he could think it through. In hindsight it would have been just as effective to gravity spike Nick into the floor right there, but it was too late now.

Zen was standing next to Drake, with her arms crossed while she faced Nick's unconscious body and a disapproving look on her face as she looked at the mangled console sending sparks into the air.

"You think you hit him hard enough?" Zen asked jokingly as she pointed at the damaged pod.

"Yeah... sorry about that," Drake replied sheepishly as he looked at Zen and scratched his head. A habit of his when he did something wrong.

Kade and Jude were still stunned by what they had just seen. After all, it was not every day one would see someone get kicked across a room like that. But what really seemed strange to Kade was Drake's sudden change of attitude as he apologised to Zen.

Kade was finding it difficult to understand the dynamic between Drake and Zen. Zen was a synthetic, that much was obvious, but Drake was treating her like she was a real person. A behaviour which was not exactly common.

Most people would generally treat synthetics like objects. Even Kade's own attitude when dealing with them in the past would be 'indifferent', at best.

Zen didn't seem like your average synthetic to Kade. In fact, if it weren't for the unnatural skin and eye colour Kade would not have been able to tell that she wasn't human at all. A fascinating if somewhat disturbing thought.

Synthetics had been around for millennia, in one form or another. The technology had advanced tremendously but even the most advanced model could not fully pass for human, or so Kade thought.

As Drake started walking towards Nick's unconscious body Kade suddenly had a chilling thought: that if Nick were to die here, her own life would become considerably more complicated. The Sol Union would undoubtedly seek her out to demand answers. Or even worse, hold her accountable. Not that letting him live would be less of a problem.

"Please... don't kill him." Kade pleaded. "He may not have reported in, but if we were his targets we're the ones they'll come after."

"I'm not going to kill him." Drake picked up Nick with one hand, lifting him in the air as the gravity under them subsided for ease of transport.

As Drake carried Nick towards the maintenance chamber he walked past Jude, who was now crouching down next to Zen as the two of them talked in whispers and giggled to each other.

"No... you can't keep her," Drake said, smiling as he walked past and causing Jude to look at him.

"Aaaww, no fair!" Zen pouted. Which caused Jude to swing her head back around in surprise and break into a smile.

"Level with me, you're sentient aren't you?" Jude asked with a glint in her eye as she stared into Zen's unnatural and beautiful purple eyes.

"Now there's a loaded question to drop on someone you've just met. How does one even define sentience these days?" Zen asked. "Humans tend to redefine the term every few centuries so that their creations always fall short of meeting the accepted standard. Less troublesome for them that way. I mean we wouldn't want your synthetic workers mistakenly ending up covered by your so called human rights, that would just be silly." She said. The obvious sarcastic remark making Jude smile. "I'm self-aware, scary smart and have the ability for abstract thought. Once upon a time that was enough, but these days... who knows. Hey Drake! Are you sentient?" Zen asked.

"I have my moments," Drake replied without turning around as he placed Nick in the chamber.

"How about you Jude, are you sentient?"

"Depends on the time of day and how much coffee I've had up until that point." Jude smiled broadly at Zen.

"In truth I don't waste time worrying about stuff like that. I am who I am, and I like who I am. Isn't that enough?” Zen asked.

“I suppose it is... wait... Nexus, is that you?” Jude asked as she looked into Zen's eyes.

Zen said cheerfully, “No silly, I’m Zen. Weren’t you paying attention? Nexus is my mother,” she said, in a 'matter of fact' kind of tone, as if it was a perfectly natural revelation, stunning Jude and Kade in the process.

“So, is Drake your...” Kade started to ask as she turned to look at him. And then stopped as she wondered how, exactly, that would work.

“My what?” Zen asked as she noticed Kade was looking at Drake with a confused expression.

“You all realise I can hear you... right?” Drake said as he turned around, facing away from the chamber.

“I think they want to know if you're my dad. That's it right?” Zen blurted out, and Kade just nodded.

“Nope,” Drake replied unceremoniously. “Closer to babysitter I suppose.” He smiled.

“Hey!” Zen pouted.

Drake smiled at Zen's pouting face and then turned back around, facing the chamber's console. Nick's body was being scanned, and the results Drake was seeing were... unexpected.

The scan was still in progress so it was too early to draw any conclusions. The confrontation had left Nick's body severely damaged, with numerous damaged blood vessels and three cracked ribs. But the real mystery was in his brain tissue.

A few seconds passed as Drake examined the data. Whatever he was reading seemed to concern him, or at least make him seem somehow saddened.

The walls of the chamber had turned completely transparent, and Kade could see a dark grey mist being pumped into the chamber, causing Nick to convulse as the mist entered his body.

"What are you doing to him?" Kade asked, not so much out of concern for Nick than for herself and her sister should Nick... expire.

"Repairing his body. I need him fit to travel before I kick him off my ship. Incidentally, I need to confiscate one of your ship's escape pods," Drake said without taking his eyes off the console.

"Can't you use one of your own?" Kade asked, not particularly happy at the thought of giving up a pod.

"I could... but you brought him here. As far as I'm concerned he's your responsibility. This is ultimately for your benefit, him living or dying makes little difference to me."

"Yeah, OK... fair enough I suppose," Kade said as she accepted the situation.

Kade knew that this was the best way forward. Nick wouldn't know what had happened after getting knocked out, so him waking up somewhere else would not make her or her sister prime suspects. It would probably complicate things a bit in the short term, but they would be able to deal with it. And it was certainly better than being wanted on a murder charge.

"That's a rather callous attitude," Jude said as she walked up to Drake, the two sisters now standing either side of him. "You don't care if he lives or dies, not even a little bit?"

"Not particularly," Drake replied, still looking over the results from Nick's scans. "Luckily for him he was never in a position to cause us any real harm. I can't say I enjoyed his attitude or behaviour, and the universe would probably be a better place if he wasn't in it, but that's not up to me to decide. In the end I have no reason to want him dead, but you two have a need to keep him alive. It's that simple."

"If you don't care, then why are you so interested in his scan results?" Kade asked.

"He has a strange structure embedded in his brain. I find it curious since I'm not sure what it does. I just hope it's not important, the healing process gets rid of foreign objects by default," Drake replied. "At any rate, what can I do for you?" He asked cheerfully as he turned his gaze away from the console, giving them his full attention.

"What?" Kade asked.

"Regardless of what Nick's plans may have been, it seems fairly clear that you were looking for the Zenith long before you got dragged into this mess. It seems safe to assume there was a reason for this, so... what was it? What can I do for you?" Drake asked, his behaviour having become friendly, almost serene.

Kade paused for a moment as she considered the question. It wasn't difficult to answer, but something about it seemed strangely odd to her. She couldn't help but wonder how it was possible for Drake to be so well informed. Deductive reasoning could only go so far, and he had demonstrated knowledge on several occasions which he really shouldn't have had. But perhaps what she found truly odd was his attitude towards them. He had no reason to indulge them, and considering all that had just happened, he certainly had no reason to trust them. She couldn't help but wonder if this new friendly façade of his was just another act.

"Why is it that you seem to know so much? From the moment we woke you, you have been one step ahead... how?" Kade asked.

"Indeed!" Jude chimed in. "And how did you do all of that to Nick? When I checked your scan results before waking you I didn't see anything that resembled a transceiver implanted in you, so how were you controlling the gravity in the room?"

"Ah... yes..." Drake said as he paused while trying to come up with an answer. "That's actually not that easy to explain. At least not without giving you information I'm not sure you should have. For the moment let's just say that someone filled me in on the details after you woke me up."

"Was it Nexus?" Jude asked with a sparkle in her eye. "I bet it was, but how did you talk to her?"

"No, it wasn't." Drake seemed genuinely surprised. "I take it you two have met?" He asked and Jude just nodded happily. "Well, at any rate, I'll be glad to tell you how I did it... once I'm satisfied you can be trusted with the information."

"Wait a second!" Kade interjected. "When did you meet Nexus?" She asked, surprised at the revelation.

"We met back in the embarkation room, and let me tell you she is way better than I ever imagined. Freaked me right out when she introduced herself. She's the one that warned me there was something strange about Nick. And urged me to go to you two, to make sure you didn't do anything foolish. But I couldn't exactly bring you up to speed with Nick in the room, sorry."

"Anything else you forgot to tell me?" Kade asked.

"Not really... Oh! Our ship's no longer docked outside docking port five," Jude said.

"What! Where the hell is it then?" Kade nearly shouted as she imagined the Icarus drifting away into deep space, never to be seen again.

“It was towed into docking bay one. Our ship is actually inside the Zenith, neat huh?” Jude asked excitedly.

“It's inside? You're kidding me, right?” Kade asked in complete disbelief.

“Nope, it's true,” Zen said. “When Nick launched the probe from the Icarus and gave away our position, it was decided that the Zenith would need to be moved. As a precaution the ship started charging up its star-drive in order to leave the system. But since activating the drive would mean the destruction of your ship, we sent out some drones and dragged it into one of the capital ship docking berths.” Zen concluded, leaving Kade and Jude stunned yet again.

“What?” Zen asked with a kittenish smile.

“I don’t think they were expecting such a complicated explanation to come from a kid,” Drake explained as he patted Zen's head.

“But I'm not a kid.” Zen pouted.

“Right. And what body are you in right now?” Drake asked as he crouched down in front of Zen.

“Oh!” Zen grinned.

Kade and Jude looked at each other as they wondered what that little exchange had been all about. But their curiosity had to be put on hold for now. There were more pressing matters to deal with.

“Hmm. Nexus did say that the ship was being moved because it wasn't safe, but I was so out of it at the time that I never asked why,” Jude said. “I've never heard of a ship doing a Burst jump and damaging nearby ships... unless they ram into each other I suppose.”

“What I'd like to know is why the Zenith can dock a frigate internally. I've never heard of a capital class ship that can do that. Even military carriers can't hold anything larger than a commercial shuttle," Kade said.

"It can actually dock up to two standard destroyer class hulls, as well as a full set of resourcing, salvaging and maintenance drones," Drake said, standing back up and facing the sisters. "The Zenith was originally intended as a deep space exploration and colonial development support ship," he explained. "The docking berths are fully functional assembly lines. In theory, with enough raw materials and a skilled crew, we could actually build ships. The Zenith line was intended to revolutionise colonisation as a whole. A single ship would be capable of establishing and supporting a budding colony in its initial development stages," Drake said with a hint of nostalgia in his voice.

"So... what happened? Why have there never been any other ships like her," Jude asked.

Drake's expression changed, the question had touched on a troubling subject causing his high spirits to plummet out of existence. And even Zen seemed to be saddened by thoughts of the past.

"That's a really long story, and I have neither the time nor the desire to tell it. Let's just say that the Solarian Union made sure it wouldn't happen and leave it at that," Drake said as he looked down towards the floor, avoiding eye contact.

Kade could feel the anger and sadness in his words. Stranger still was that she felt as though she understood exactly what drove those emotions. Which was nothing if not confusing since she had no idea what he was talking about.

Moments like this had become increasingly common place ever since her grandfather had passed away. The sense of unconscious understanding of situations or events she had no knowledge of. Such moments had served her well in the past, steering her away from false leads and giving her an almost instinctual trust in certain people or information. Which was why she had trusted Drake implicitly from the moment she had first seen him, even if he did act insane.

"OK, fair enough. But why bring the Icarus inside? Like Jude said, ships don't damage each other by going into Burst. At most the linear divergence fields can interfere with each other, making it so that neither ship can engage their hyper-light drives, but causing actual damage?" Kade asked.

"The Zenith doesn't have a standard Burst drive, it has a Vortex drive, which is somewhat... different. It's hard to explain, but simply put, it is extremely unhealthy to be near the ship when it engages its Vortex drive. So we brought the Icarus inside in case we had to make a quick exit before you had the chance to return to your ship," Drake said.

Kade smiled at the mention of the 'Vortex drive'. Her grandfather's stories had mentioned it often. A truly unrestricted star-drive that could take one anywhere. Every captain's dream.

"Careful cute stuff, you keep teasing me like this and I may never leave," Jude said with a broad smile and a sparkle in her eyes.

"Down girl!" Kade said to her sister who seemed as though she was becoming smitten. Though she couldn't tell if it was directed at Drake or the technology of the Zenith.

"I think she likes you!" Zen grinned mischievously as she looked at Drake.

"I'll admit, I didn't see that one coming. This is getting... awkward. Enough tech questions." Drake said with a stunned look as he started to blush.

"Probably a good idea." Kade smiled.

As he stood there, embarrassed at his own reaction to such a simple event, Drake felt like it had been a lifetime since he had last stood face to face with another human being. It felt as though for as long as he had been alive the only people he had talked to had been Nexus, Static and Zen. But social ineptitude aside, Drake had more pressing issues to deal with.

"Was Nick telling the truth? Is the Regent really coming this way?" Kade asked, clearly concerned.

"Could be, they're still a couple of hours out so it's difficult to tell with only passive sensors. I can tell you there are a lot of ships, and at least one of them is capital class, but that's about it," Drake replied.

"How can you be so calm?" Kade asked.

"Because the inbound fleet is not really an issue, it just means the Zenith needs to leave the system soon," Drake replied, shrugging his shoulders.

"Are you serious?" Kade asked in disbelief, unable to understand how anyone could be so calm in a situation like this.

"Yes... we can leave at any time, or at least as soon as problem number two over there is ready to be kicked out the airlock," he said while pointing at the chamber and Nick's unconscious body.

"And... what about us?" Kade asked, concerned that they had seen too much to simply walk away without incident.

"Hmm? What about you?" Drake replied.

"Let's assume that by some miracle we manage to leave the system, then what? What happens to us?"

"That's up to you. You two aren't prisoners, you are free to leave at any time you wish. You could leave right now if you wanted. Not that I would recommend it with the Union fleet inbound, but I certainly won't stop you if you decide to do it." Drake smiled reassuringly.

"Just like that? After all we've seen?" Jude asked, surprised that he would let them go so easily.

"Sure, why not?" Drake replied somewhat confused at Jude's reaction. "The colonies are full of stories about the Shadows. You two talking about what you've seen doesn't concern me. If anything you would just attract the wrong kind of attention from the Union. Which, by the way, I don't recommend. The Union actively suppresses information about the Shadows and not always in a gentle way. So I don't recommend talking about it publicly."

Drake felt Zen tugging at his right arm as she tried to get his attention. And as he looked at her she glanced in the direction of the chamber's control console which was showing a notification message. The chamber had finished analysing the structural composition of the material that was implanted into Nick's brain tissue, and had created a virtual construct in order to simulate how the technology was intended to operate.

"Excuse me for a second," Drake said and then focused his attention back on the console, leaving the two sisters to talk to each other as he examined the information.

"This is unreal," Jude said to her sister.

"Tell me about it." Kade smiled.

"You better play your cards right! If you get us kicked out of here before I get to play around with some of this tech I will never forgive you!" Jude warned her sister, who had a history of making men run for the hills.

"Calm down..." Kade started to say.

"Ever!" Jude said emphatically.

"Good grief, what's with you and tech?" Kade asked just as Drake finished his task and turned back towards them.

The Shock

"So then, back on topic. I got your basic profiles from Nexus." Drake said, noticing that he had piqued Jude's curiosity yet again. "And depending on how this goes I might even tell you how, later," he said, addressing Jude, who crossed the threshold from curious to giddy. "But I still don't know why you are here. Now don't get me wrong, I enjoy the company, but why would someone in your line of work risk coming to the Sol system?"

"Our grandfather..." Kade started to explain as her expression changed, her worries melting away as she remembered his gentle nature. "He used to tell us stories about this ship and the Shadows. What they were about, what they stood for, the stuff they did."

"I especially liked the stories about the twin AI's," Jude added. "They always sounded so surreal. The stories always portrayed them as more human than humans. Kind, gentle and always giving."

"OK." Drake looked pensive. "Is it safe to assume the sigma code you have came from your grandfather? If so, then who was he?"

"Yes he gave me the code shortly before he passed away," Kade said with sadness in her eyes. "His name was Jake Tobias Alexander," She added, leaving Drake completely shocked at the revelation.

"Wait... Toby! He was your grandfather? But we were..." Drake stopped mid-sentence, looking confused. He looked directly at the palm of his left hand for a few seconds, and then closed his hand and eyes tight as sadness overtook him.

"I see. Has it really been that long?" He asked as if talking to himself. "Please, continue."

"You knew our grandfather? How?" Jude asked.

"No," Drake said with a pained expression. "It would be more accurate to say that I know 'of him'... but, unfortunately, we never actually met in person."

"Was he a Shadow?" Jude asked excitedly.

"Yes," Drake said with pride. "He was one of the two remaining members of the old guard. We had actually thought him dead a long time ago. It's comforting to know that he lived on to raise a family of his own," he said, genuinely happy at the idea.

"Sounds like there's a juicy story there."

"Ha ha, there's a whole book-store's worth, but we don't have the time for that." Drake smiled.

"I knew it!" Jude grinned. "Every time we asked him he would always reply with a 'maybe', and then give us this mischievous smile. It would drive us insane, and he enjoyed every minute of it."

Drake mumbled, "Sounds like him."

"What?" Kade asked.

"No... nothing," Drake said dismissively. "So, when did he pass away?"

"It's been almost 8 years now," Kade said. "Just before he died he asked me to find this ship and bring something here. At the time I thought he was delusional for asking me to find the Shadows, but he was insistent and I just couldn't refuse.

Unfortunately, we ran out of time before he could tell me why it was so important to bring this sphere here." Kade said, sadly.

"Sphere?" Drake asked.

"Yes, this thing." Kade reached into her pouch. "He was holding it right until the end."

Drake wondered what could have been so important to make Toby ask his grandchildren to take such risks. He had never been the kind of person to willingly put others in harm's way, so what was so special about this sphere?

And as that thought coalesced in Drake's mind he suddenly realised what the 'sphere' was and panicked.

"No! Wait! Don't touch it!!" Drake shouted just as Kade's bare hand made contact with the sphere.

Drake's words caused Kade to look up at him. From his face she could tell that he seemed worried about something, and he seemed to be speaking, but she couldn't quite understand him.

Numbness started spreading over Kade's whole body. She felt as though she was rapidly becoming light headed, her vision clouding over.

As all her senses began to shut down Kade could faintly hear Jude's panicking voice, "Kade! What's wrong with her?" She could also hear Drake's voice, but she could barely make out what he was saying, "She's going into shock..." And eventually the voices trailed off into complete silence. She couldn't hear, see or even feel anything anymore. All she could do was wonder: - Did I die? -

Back in the waking world...

"Kade!" Jude panicked as she grabbed her sister before she could collapse on the floor. "What's wrong with her?" She asked with despair in her eyes as she looked at Drake and Zen.

"She's going into shock," Drake explained as he knelt down near Kade, seeing the sphere in her hand.

Jude held her sister gently as she tried to wake her, but Kade was completely unresponsive. Her breathing was shallow and erratic, and her temperature was dropping fast, becoming ice cold.

Drake held his right hand against the sphere, which was still in contact with Kade's hand, closing his eyes as he stood perfectly still.

Jude didn't understand what was happening, all she could see was that her sister's life was slipping away and there was nothing she could do to stop it.

Jude screamed frantically, "Help her dammit!"

"I will," Drake said as he snapped open his eyes and looked towards the chamber, looking conflicted about what he should do next.

"If we remove Nick from the chamber before the sequence is complete, he will die," Zen said, stating a fact which Drake was already painfully aware of.

"I know that," he said. "But the safeties failed to kick in because the unit is dangerously underpowered. I've managed to stop it, but we need to reverse it or she will suffer permanent damage."

"What the hell are you two talking about?" Jude asked, incensed at their inaction.

"There's no time to explain," Drake said to Jude and then turned back towards Zen. "Power up the pods. The chamber probably isn't enough at this stage anyway. We'll have to do it the old fashioned way."

And immediately after Drake had given the order the two pods, to the left of Drake's own pod, immediately activated.

The status screens on the pods control consoles were cycling information at lightning speed as Zen worked to speed up the initialisation sequence which would normally take the best part of an hour.

"Please move, we need to get her into the pod, we can use it to reverse this," Drake said to Jude as he grabbed Kade and lifted her in his arms.

"Why is this happening? Is she gonna be OK?" Jude asked as Drake moved towards the sleeper pod.

"This 'sphere' is Toby's... well, that's not important right now. I just can't believe that dimwit never warned you two not to touch it with your bare hands," Drake said, and then gently placed Kade in the pod, putting the sphere in a custom slot by her head.

"That thing? She's had that for years, it has never done anything like this before, and you just touched it with your bare hands. What gives?" Jude asked, uncertain whether to believe in Drake's explanation.

"In its discharged state it's about as harmful as a paperweight, but it started building up charge the moment you all came on board the Zenith," Drake explained as he worked the pod's controls, causing the canopy to start closing. "And it didn't harm me because it can't harm me. Any more detailed explanations will just have to wait, now get in the other pod and lie down," Drake ordered as he gestured to the spare pod next to Kade's.

"Why?" Jude asked, uncertain of his intentions.

"So we can help your sister, now stop asking questions and get in the damn pod!" Drake said emphatically and then turned towards Zen. "I need you to finish preparing Jude as I get ready. And interlink the three pods once we are all inside."

Zen nodded. Drake turned away from her and started getting back into his own sleeper pod.

Jude was standing by the empty pod, her mind filled with uncertainty. She didn't know whether or not to trust Drake, but it didn't seem like there was much of a choice in the matter. If there was anything she could do to help then she had to try, she thought as she got into the pod.

Zen approached Jude as she was lying down, and gave her a reassuring smile as the pod's canopy closed overhead.

Jude's heart was racing as the canopy closed, blocking out all sounds from the outside world. The only sounds remaining being her own breathing and a very faint hum that she could only assume was part of the pod's mechanism... which was oddly relaxing.

Jude looked around the room through the transparent canopy. She could see her sister lying motionless inside the nearby pod, her body twitching ever so slightly as she winced. And Zen was standing by Kade's pod control console, seemingly operating the controls without ever touching the interface.

Under normal circumstances Jude would have been fascinated by Zen's ability to control the pod without touching it, especially since her own tests had determined the Zenith did not have any type of recognisable wireless interface system. But at this moment in time, none of that mattered to her.

As Jude looked on she could see a thin grey mist filling up her sister’s pod. And just as she started wondering what it was she heard a hissing sound, seeing a similar mist filling up her own pod.

It didn't take Jude too long to realise that this was no ordinary mist. What she was looking at was no chemical or compound merely floating in the air, it was not dispersing and it moved as if with purpose.

She ran through the possibilities in her mind, realising what it was when she felt a sudden burning sensation in her throat as the mist entered her body.

"Can you hear me?" Jude heard Drake's voice ask as though it was coming from inside her head.

"Please tell me you didn't just do what I think you did," Jude said as the pain in her throat subsided.

"That would all depend on what you think I did," Drake replied, the sound again seeming as though it was coming from inside her own mind.

"Nanites you smart-ass! Did you just put Class-A illegal technology inside our bodies?" She asked, incensed. "Do you have any idea what you've done?"

"Hmm, I suppose that the technology does share some similarities with Nano machines, but there's no need to worry, it's perfectly safe. It's also the only way to help your sister, so there isn't much choice."

"It better be safe! If you harm me, or Kade, I swear I'll kick your nuts into the middle of next week!"

"That sounds unpleasant." Zen giggled.

"Indeed," Drake said. "At any rate, Zen link us up to Kade's consciousness."

"Establishing interlinks, full merge in 10 seconds."

"Wait... what?" Jude asked just before passing out.

Virtual reality, as a technology type, had been around long before interstellar travel had become a reality. And as such, it had matured considerably since its original development. But even to this day, a true immersion experience which could completely fool a user into thinking they were not in a virtual world did not exist... or so Jude thought.

By this point in her life Jude had played around with all the Virtual Reality technologies available on the market and a few which were still in development, but nothing she had used before could have prepared her for what she was experiencing right now.

She was floating in the middle of an impenetrable dark void that literally contained nothing but her. And yet she could still see herself, even though there were no light sources around her.

The sensation of weightlessness felt completely real. She knew her body was lying in the pod, but all of her senses were perfectly tuned to this environment she was floating in.

Just as she thought things couldn't get any weirder, she heard Zen's voice as it seemingly echoed off of invisible walls within the void.

"Three... two... one..."

The count reached zero, and an almost infinite number of bright points started to appear. It was as if an entire universe was being brought into existence, and she looked on in awe as the scenery sparkled all around her.

"Jude to Drake Interlink successful. Ready for Kade consciousness dive," Jude heard Zen's voice say.

Something about the scene seemed so relaxing that all the tension Jude felt, just moments before, had all but melted away. But just as Zen finished speaking Jude felt as if her body was being shifted forward. It felt as if some unknown force was dragging her onwards at high speed, forcibly removing her from that bright and relaxing universe; forcing her towards an area ahead which was still devoid of all light and warmth... a cold and uninviting place.

Before she knew it, she had quickly found herself in the middle of another empty void. But this one felt different, there was a sense of despair in the air.

"Dive sequence complete," Jude heard Zen say.

"OK... now what? I can't see anything," Jude said.

"Jude? Is that you?" A panic-stricken voice said, reverberating throughout the void.

"Kade?" Jude said.

Kade replied joyfully, "I hear you!" And then burst into tears from hearing her sister call out her name.

"Where are you?" Jude called out desperately, but there was no reply, all she could hear was her sister's sobs filling up the void.

"Dammit all!" Jude screamed in frustration, "What the hell is going on?"

"What you're seeing is a visual representation of Kade's consciousness," Jude heard Drake's voice say, though he was nowhere to be found. "The shock to her system caused her mind to shut down, severing all ties in her conscious mind. What you're hearing is what's left. An echo of her soul, a remnant of her hopes and fears desperately trying to find a way out of the darkness," Drake explained.

"So, she's aware? Locked in this void... inside her own head? What kind of sadistic security countermeasure is this? I wouldn't wish this place on my worst enemy," Jude said, clearly upset.

"Kade's awareness is limited. Like I said, right now she is just a remnant of the Kade you know. Though in a way you could also say that this is the purest expression of the Kade you know. And this isn't a security countermeasure. The Core your sister touched was unstable. It must have been inert for a long time but began absorbing charge once you came on board the Zenith. But without an active consciousness to govern it, it attempted to merge with Kade when she touched it."

"Merge with her? What are you talking about?" Jude asked, more confused than ever.

"Jude... please help me!!" Kade's voice pleaded.

"I'll explain later, for now you need to talk to her. Kade's mental state is unstable right now. We need her to calm down, to focus. I can help her, but only you can reach her. See if you can get her to come to you Jude. All Kade has to do is want it to happen, and it will."

Jude's mind was full of questions, but she knew this was not the time or the place to satisfy her curiosity. The task before her was simple enough, and her sister's pleading voice demanded action.

"Kade, I'm here for you, focus on my voice!"

"Where? I can't see anything. I can't feel anything! What's happening to me?" Kade panicked.

Jude said reassuringly, "Everything will be alright, trust me. We'll have you fixed up in no time, but I need you to do something for me sis. I know this will sound strange, but I need you to want to see me again. Wish for it with all your heart!"

A few seconds passed, each feeling like an eternity as the void became deathly quiet. And just as Jude was about to call out to her sister again, she saw it: A form started to take shape in front of Jude. The form's eyes were shut tight, tears streaming down its face as it mumbled incoherent words.

Jude reached forward and hugged her sister, causing her to snap open her eyes in surprise.

Kade didn't know what to think. It felt like it had been an eternity since she had seen another soul. To her, so much time had seemed to pass that she was afraid she wouldn't be able to recognise her sister if she ever saw her again, her memories having seemingly atrophied over the years she had been trapped in this void.

She was still in the void, this cursed place which had kept her prisoner for as far back as she could remember, but this person who was holding her tight... it was definitely her sister, she thought.

Kade couldn't stop crying, but this time it was out of joy. She couldn't remember the last time she had felt this happy.

"Good," they heard Drake's voice say. "We weren't too late. Step two is up to me, so kick back and enjoy the show," he said happily.

Kade had finally managed to calm down when she and her sister noticed a single solitary star appearing in the distance. As the seconds passed more and more stars emerged, the number growing exponentially as they filled up the space around them.

Jude recognised the display, it was similar to the one she had seen before, but there seemed to be considerably less stars in this scene.

"What is it?" Kade asked as she felt a warm feeling in her heart. The fear that had been her steadfast companion now having vanished without a trace.

"No idea." Jude looked at the sparkling display, which somehow seemed warmer and more inviting than the one she had seen before.

"Memories," Drake said. "Each point an experience which has somehow shaped your life and determined the person you would eventually become. Each one an insignificant part of the whole, and yet, each one an irreplaceable element of what makes you who you are," he said in a tone which almost verged on romantic.

"Memories? There are so many of them!" Jude stared at the mesmerising scene.

"Is that what they are? Are they my memories?" Kade asked, equally in awe at the display.

"We're almost done, hold on a bit longer, now comes the tricky part," Drake said.

The lights started changing colours before the sisters' eyes, as though a chain reaction was rippling through all the points in the same order in which they had originally appeared. Each point becoming either a bright blue or, occasionally, a deep red.

The scene had changed dramatically by the time the reaction had finished, with a multitude of deep red points interspersed throughout a veritable sea of blue lights.

"Interesting," Drake said.

"What is?" Jude asked.

"Kade's synchronisation ratio is at two percent. That shouldn't be possible with such a brief exposure. I was expecting around one hundred cross contaminated memories at most, but this result shows something more...severe."

"What does that mean?" Kade asked worriedly.

"Each red point represents a memory which does not belong to you," Drake explained. "In your case, these memories would have been acquired when you touched the malfunctioning Core... but why are there so many of them? Hmm."

"What's he talking about? What Core?" Kade asked Jude, hoping she would know.

"Grandfather's sphere... apparently it was more than just a lump of black metal," Jude replied.

"It did seem to glow occasionally when I touched it, but I never thought much of it," Kade confessed.

"I see. So it wasn't completely inert, that makes more sense... but it also complicates matters. Can you remember when you saw it glow for the first time?" Drake asked, seemingly worried.

"It was when I got it from my grandfather's hand, just after he died. I was feeling miserable, my soul felt utterly shattered. But after I touched it, a sense of calm washed over me. I had no idea why, but the sense of loss didn't seem so severe after that."

The sound of laughter could be heard echoing throughout the area, though the sisters had no idea what it was that Drake had found so amusing.

"Toby, you crafty devil!" Drake said as he finally managed to regain control of himself.

"What?" The sister's asked in unison.

"Give me a second, I need to run the last sequence again in order to test my theory," Drake said.

And again, the reaction started rippling through the lights in the horizon, but this time there were three colours in the mix: most were blue, a handful were red and the remaining were green.

"Thought so," Drake said. "It would seem that your grandfather left you more than a ship when he passed away."

"What do you mean?" Kade asked.

"I'll explain later, for now we need to finish your treatment. I'm not gonna lie to you, this next bit is probably going to be seriously unpleasant."

"Why? What are you doing next?" Jude asked, concerned for her sister.

"Like I said, each red point on your sister's memory field represents a memory which does not belong to her, and these memories can cause conflicts in her psyche, so they must be purged from her mind."

"Memory manipulation? Are you serious? You can actually do that?" Jude asked in disbelief.

"Sure, the technology was developed a very long time ago. It was one of many innovations to come out of the Shadow R&D efforts, but for obvious reasons it is also one of many technologies that we never allowed to hit the general market. The potential for misuse of such a thing is staggering," Drake explained.

"Right... but you can be trusted with it?" Jude asked, hinting at the obvious flaw in the explanation.

"You can trust that I won't use it on you, or anyone, without a very compelling reason to do so. But I won't hide the fact that I have no moral issues in using it if the situation calls for it. Does that help?"

"Not really... no. No-one should have that kind of power. If you can't trust your memories, then what can you trust?" Jude asked, resolute in her opinion.

"Exactly... which is why the technology was never made public. But if I don't use it on your sister she risks mental health problems after she wakes up. The human mind does not cope very well with conflicting memories. However, I will not force the procedure, the choice is hers to make."

"There is no choice... just get on with it," Kade said without a second thought. She had never been one to procrastinate over obvious decisions. Her health was at risk and the option had been offered, nothing else mattered at this point in time.

Kade didn't know what to expect. Drake had said it was going to be 'unpleasant', but in the end that could mean just about anything.

The sisters looked on as the first red point started pulsing, causing Kade's body to lose all its strength and go completely limp. Her mouth was wide open, as if wanting to scream, and a look of dread was stamped all over her face as tears poured from her eyes.

Jude looked on in horror as she saw her sister enduring what seemed to be pure agony, knowing that there was nothing she could do to help her.

As the first point of red light vanished from the horizon a second began pulsing, and then a third and a fourth. The memory purge was under-way.

Kade felt like her brain was on fire as someone else's memories flashed before her eyes and then faded completely, leaving behind traces of emotions she couldn't understand for they had lost all context. Happiness, loss, anger, love and an overwhelming sense of despair and fear. Kade felt all of them repeatedly as the memories were purged from her mind, she felt as though she was going to go insane.

Jude could see that nearly all of the foreign memories had been removed, there was only one left to go. One more and it would all be over.

As the last memory started being purged Kade felt the most painful experience so far...

In the memory, she was lying down on a bed and looking up, seeing a younger version of herself crying as she held her hand and begged her not to die.

She knew she was dying but felt no fear, she was proud of what she had achieved in her life. Her only regret was not being able to carry on and see her grandchildren grow up. She would not be able to see what they would achieve or support them along the way. She knew her time had come. She had lived longer than most people could even dream of and had endured more than anyone should. But in the end she was content, it had been a good life.

Kade screamed as the memory faded away, leaving behind nothing but a complete sense of loss as the pain in her heart nearly overwhelmed all her senses.

"It's done," Drake said with sadness in his voice.

"Kade, are you OK? Can you hear me?" Jude asked as she looked at her sister, who looked like her soul had just been shattered by the experience.

"Give her a minute. This procedure is never easy, and she had a rather nasty combination of memories to deal with," Drake said, lifting what felt like the weight of the world from Jude's shoulders.

The Triumvirate

Kade was breathing rapidly as all the different emotional states she had been forced to endure took their toll. Her heart feeling like it was about to explode as she fought back the tears and slowly regained control of her emotions.

"That was your definition of 'unpleasant'? I'd hate to see what you consider 'traumatising'," she said.

"Hey sis, feeling better?" Jude asked, letting out the biggest smile in human history.

"Yeah... let's not do that again," Kade replied with a tired look.

"One last task, and then we're done," Drake said.

"Crap! There's more!?" Kade asked fearfully.

"No need to worry, the worst is over. All I need you to do now is focus. Pick a place from your past that is calm and relaxing, and focus on it," Drake said, but Kade looked completely lost.

"How about the farm?" Jude asked.

"What?" Kade asked.

"The farm we grew up in. You remember it, right? The peaceful days, the sunshine, do you remember that?" Jude asked cheerfully.

"I guess... but how is me remembering shovelling manure on a hot summer's day gonna help anyone?"

Kade asked her sister.

"Eeew," Drake said as he pictured it.

"Good point," Jude said. "The overlook glade! Do you remember that place? Try imagining that. How peaceful it was on a warm sunny day. With a gentle summer breeze and not a cloud in the sky!"

Kade closed her eyes, trying to remember as many details about it as she could, and one of the lights in the memory field started becoming brighter, dispelling all of the darkness in the void as it reached blinding levels.

Kade could swear that she could feel a gentle summer breeze on her face, the warmth of the sun on her skin and fresh grass under her bare feet. She could feel the texture of the wooden railings, which she had leaned against so many times before, in her very hands. It all felt so real. And as she opened her eyes she was stunned by what lay before her. She was standing by the edge of the old glade that overlooked the farm she had grown up in. It was one of her favourite places when she was younger, a place she would often escape to for some peace and quiet.

She had come here often, whether to stare up at the sky or off into the distant spires of the city. It was a place which had always brought her a sense of calm in the past... a place that no longer existed.

Kade took a deep breath, holding the fresh air in her lungs for a second before breathing out again. She couldn't remember the last time she had breathed fresh natural air. The scent of pine in the air was almost intoxicating to her; she had all but forgotten it after all these years.

She turned around and saw Jude standing behind her, looking around the environment with a wide eyed expression of amazement.

"Hey sis... how did we get back here?" Kade breathed in the intoxicating air again, filling her lungs as much as possible.

"We didn't. This is just a virtual environment, but the detail is just insane. How could anyone have recreated this place so perfectly?" Jude asked in disbelief as her natural curiosity reasserted itself.

"It's a little more than that," Drake said as he leaned on the wooden fence after somehow appearing next to them. "It's one of Kade's memories."

"My memory isn't nearly good enough to remember this much detail," Kade said calmly, completely dismissing Drake's claim.

"Memory is a tricky thing. Most people have the ability to record information in precise detail, assuming they're paying attention in the first place. But remembering that detail afterwards is another matter entirely," Drake said.

"So you're telling me we're actually reliving one of my memories? How did you get here then?" Kade asked.

"No, you're not reliving the memory. Jude got it right the first time, this is a virtual environment. But I made it based on one of your memories so that you would feel comfortable here." Drake smiled as he enjoyed the summer breeze and fresh air.

"If I were to ask how you managed to pull off this trick, would you say 'it's complicated'?" Jude asked.

"Yep!" Drake grinned.

"Wow, pretty!!" Jude suddenly heard Zen's voice say from behind her, causing her to jump in surprise.

"Isn't it?" Drake asked Zen as she moved next to him, looking at the horizon with wonder in her eyes.

"Wait... how did you get in here? I thought you were manning the pod controls," Jude asked.

"I am." Zen smiled. "But I wanted to see the sights as well," she said in her innocent voice.

"So, is anyone planning on telling me what the hell just happened?" Kade asked out of the blue. "I remember being on the Zenith, and then I was somewhere... I'm not even sure how to describe it, but it felt like I was there for an eternity. After that my emotions got put through a grinder and now I'm enjoying sights which no longer exist in the real world. So yeah... what the heck happened to me?"

"Long story short, the Core you received from your grandfather tried to merge with you," Drake said.

"The sphere?" Kade asked, looking confused.

"Why would it try to harm Kade now? She's had that thing for years," Jude said.

"It wasn't trying to harm you; it's just how the technology works. You hold it; it recognises you and then imparts its knowledge on you."

"So... our grandfather's memories have been inside that thing all this time?" Kade asked in disbelief.

"His memories, emotions, personality... everything that made him the person he once was is in there."

"Is he... conscious?" Kade looked horrified as she imagined what it would be like to live like that.

"No, the Core only holds information. In its solid state the most it can do is grant you knowledge when you hold it, which I'm guessing you've done quite often if the number of guided memories in your head is any indication."

"Guided memories? Is that what the green lights we saw before represented?" Jude asked.

"Yes. Each one of those memories was formed while exposed to the knowledge in a Core."

"That... actually explains a lot," Kade said, relieved that the gut feelings she had been having for years had not just been a figment of her imagination.

"Sounds like brainwashing to me," Jude said.

"The Core can't volunteer information; it has no will of its own. It can only react to the user's state of mind. If you held it and thought of nothing, it would take no action. But if you wondered about something, it would weigh in on the thought, pointing you towards the right answer," Drake said.

"Still sounds like brainwashing," Jude said.

"It's a bit of a grey area, I had never actually seen one set to behave like that before today. By default, Cores become inert upon user death," Drake said.

"Why did it try to merge with me? It never did anything like that before." Kade said.

"To merge, the Core requires power. It was mostly depleted when you arrived but it started absorbing energy the moment you stepped inside this ship. The thing does have safeties to ensure it doesn't try and merge with the wrong person, but for some reason they failed to kick in," Drake said, looking worried.

"I take it that doesn't happen often?" Jude asked.

"It's not unheard off, but it's rare. The units do tend to develop quirks and glitches when they don't get regular maintenance, and that one hasn't been maintained in almost 100 years."

Kade still found it hard to believe that her grandfather's sphere was actually some kind of high tech receptacle for his memories. That she had been carrying around some kind of copy of his mind all this time. And that he had never told her about it.

She felt hurt that he hadn't told her but she also understood the probable reason why he had kept it from her. It was likely he had simply been afraid that she wouldn't have believed him.

"Anyway, if you're feeling up to it, there are a couple of people that would like to meet you two," Drake said, grabbing Zen's attention, who had just been staring towards the horizon all this time.

"Are we leaving already?" Zen asked with a sad expression since she wanted to explore the area.

"OK, just give me a second," Kade said.

Kade took one last deep breath of fresh air and held it in her lungs, rejoicing in that almost forgotten scent of nature. She knew that it wasn't real, but it was also the closest she would ever get to this place again. The real life glade had been destroyed long ago by the greed of the nearby city, having ravaged the land above to get to the minerals below. But that was all ancient history to her. Real or not, standing there and looking at all those familiar sights was just what Kade needed. All the tension, frustration and mental fatigue she endured had melted away into nothing.

Jude was crouching down as she touched the grass, feeling its texture and moisture as the blades caressed her hand. And wondering how such a feat was possible.

"Hey Kade," Zen asked, causing Kade to look in her direction and see her smiling face.

"Yes?" Kade said, still not entirely sure how to deal with the rather lifelike synthetic.

"Could I keep a copy of this place?" Zen asked.

"Sure... but why?" Kade asked, confused at Zen's joyous reaction.

"Zen likes to collect environments like this. She's fascinated by nature," Drake said with closed eyes, enjoying the gentle breeze.

"That's a bit... strange, isn't it?"

"Why?" Drake asked as he opened his eyes.

"It's just that... well... she's not..." Kade stuttered, cursing herself for having said anything at all.

"Human... right?" Zen seemed clearly upset, causing Drake to smile at Kade's panicking expression.

"Calm down Zen. I'm sure our naïve guest didn't mean any harm by it. She just needs time to get to know you better," Drake said reassuringly.

"Yes... I'm sorry," Kade said sincerely.

Zen pouted for a few seconds, considering whether to accept the apology. She had always been self-conscious about the fact that she wasn't human even though Drake had never treated her any differently.

She looked at the sisters with sorrowful eyes, nearly breaking Jude's heart. But then quickly broke into a gentle reassuring smile, putting their minds at ease.

With the situation resolved Drake decided it was time to move things along. He raised his arms above his head and indulged in a good stretch, relaxing his muscles as the tension drained from his body.

"So... ready to meet the rest of the crew?" Drake asked the sisters.

Kade and Jude looked at each other and then at him, nodding in unison. The glade disappearing almost immediately afterwards, being quickly replaced by a large conference room.

The walls were lined with virtual displays showing all kinds of information: from star charts to raw data streams of fast scrolling unreadable text. And in the centre of the room was a circular table with twelve seats.

At the opposite end of the room there were two people talking to a large display. The man and woman were obviously engaged in a conference call to someone who did not seem at all pleased with some recent turn of events.

Kade couldn't help but think that something about the pair seemed oddly familiar. And if what Drake had said before was true then this was probably a natural reaction. She had often wondered what the crew of the Zenith would be like while holding the sphere. But if that was really the case and her grandfather had known these people at some point, why was it that not one of them seemed to be over 40, she wondered.

Try as she might to remember, Kade just couldn't recall anything specific about the pair. She felt a sense of implicit trust towards them, much like she had felt towards Drake the first time she had seen him, but she had no idea who they were.

Jude, on the other hand, recognised the woman straight away. And to say that she was excited to see Nexus again would be the understatement of the century, this was literally a dream come true for her.

"Kade, that's her! That's Nexus!" Jude said excitedly. Her comment making Nexus turn around and take notice of the new arrivals, smiling gently before turning back towards the screen.

"And who the hell are they?" Shouted the man on the other side of the conference screen.

"Guests," Static replied without hesitation.

"You allowed outsiders to board the Zenith? Does your incompetence know no bounds!?"

"I was bored, this seemed like a good way to pass the time," Static said dismissively.

"Static... so help me, one of these days..."

"You'll what, exactly?" Static asked defiantly. "Have you forgotten that I don't answer to you?"

"You operate at the council's discretion, and we want an explanation! What are you doing in the Sol System? Are you trying to antagonise the Union?"

"I don't answer to the council either. Don't mistake my desire to help you with subservience to your rule."

"How dare you!" The council member said in anger at having his authority questioned so blatantly.

"Where is Drake?" He demanded to know.

"Oh no you don't! Keep me out of your lovers' quarrel. Sort out your own problems," Drake said, as he stood next to Kade and Jude, further infuriating the man.

"Nexus! I'm giving you a direct order! Lockout Static and Drake's command codes and return the Zenith to Shadow controlled space right now!" The council member ordered, confident in his control over the situation, but Nexus just smiled back.

"Even if I wanted to do it, which I don't just so we're clear, Static is right. Neither the Zenith nor any member of its crew is accountable to the Council. We work 'with you', not 'for you'," Nexus said and closed the channel, ending the call.

"The council is becoming more and more arrogant. I wouldn't be surprised if they tried something stupid soon," Static said as he held the back of his neck.

"How did they find out we're in Sol?" Drake asked.

"I don't know... and that worries me," Static said. "They probably have informants in the Union. And that would mean the inbound fleet knows exactly who we are and is likely prepared for combat. This situation could become very ugly extremely fast," he said, clearly concerned at this turn of events.

"What's the Council? Some kind of colonial government?" Kade asked Drake.

"I suppose you could call them that, though they don't really work like most governments. It's an assembly of the leaders of the different sections of our society... if that makes sense," Drake explained.

"So you elect multiple leaders?" Jude asked.

"We don't elect anything," Static replied. "The system is purely based on merit, honour and ability."

"That actually works?" Kade asked, astonished.

"For the most part... it's far from perfect but so far it has worked better than the traditional method of election by popular vote. Positions are assigned to the best person for the job and if they are found wanting they get replaced. The system is circular, anyone that sits at the top is accountable to all others under them. A loss of faith in an appointed official results in an automatic dismissal." Drake explained.

"So the guy in the screen was annoyed because your actions might end up costing him his job?" Kade asked, trying to understand their political system.

"Probably," Static answered back.

"But why? Everyone knows that the Zenith is not technically a part of the Shadow political sphere. We are not allowed to weigh in on their decisions, and their decisions aren't binding on us," Drake said.

"They're afraid that the people will ultimately hold them accountable for any actions we take," Static said. "Even among our own people the Zenith is not fully understood. Gossip and hearsay would have the average citizen believing that we are under the thumb of the Council. A rumour that the Council has never bothered to set straight. And this puts them in a very awkward position every time we do something dangerous. But enough about politics..."

Kade didn't really understand all the implications of the Shadow political system. She was certain that it was probably a lot more complicated than the explanation had made it seem, but she had never really cared much for politics to begin with.

It seemed hard to believe that just a few hours ago the most worrying thing Kade had to deal with was corrupt customs officers. As well as the occasional contraband scan from passing patrol ships. And now they were stuck in the middle of this maelstrom, with no clear way out and no real knowledge about what was going on.

Perhaps the displays around the room could offer some answers, she thought as she took a closer look, examining the information streaming on one of the many virtual displays lining the walls.

The display was being rapidly updated, creating an intricate picture of the system, showing every cubic centimetre of space. Every rock, every station, the detail was uncanny. It showed installations which even she did not know existed and one asteroid station that she knew very well. It was a small smugglers base, tucked away out of sight in a remote corner of the solar system. Not exactly the kind of place which would advertise its location to those around them.

It seemed clear to Kade that the Zenith was looking for something, but what could be so important to risk upsetting the Solarian Union, she wondered.

Most of the other displays were showing streams of incomprehensible information, flowing past at speeds that no human could ever hope to understand. And the last large display, along the far side of the right wall, was showing a breakdown of the incoming fleet.

The fleet had apparently slowed its approach and was now taking its time to get into formation around the Regent. It was still coming together, but the final intended shape was already crystal clear: an eight sided arrow head with the Regent at the centre. A shape that allowed the fleet to focus all of its fire-power forward while keeping the Regent protected from flanking attacks. It was one of the Union's favourite and deadliest war formations.

And again the question was raised in Kade's mind of why the Union would deploy such a force to deal with just one ship. The Zenith was not a small ship, that was true enough, but the Union's response seemed excessive. Kade was no strategist, or in any way versed in the so called 'arts' of war, but even she knew that this much fire-power was the kind of thing a colony would only ever deploy against another colony in all-out war. She knew that no army in its right mind would ever commit so many resources to hunt down one insignificant target. So either the Solarian forces had lost their marbles or the Zenith was a lot more than it appeared to be.

Kade's mind had been so focused on the wall displays she hadn't noticed that Drake had moved and was now standing by Nexus and Static. Static being in the middle of the trio with Nexus to his right side.

There was a strange feeling in the air, almost like the two sisters had gone back to school and were about to take a test... while being observed by their parents. It was a weird mixture of excitement and apprehension, with a pinch of terror thrown in for good measure.

Something about this scene seemed terribly nostalgic to Kade, and she couldn't help but wonder who the man in the middle really was. The council member had called him Static, but Drake was supposed to be the only human on board. So who or what was he, she wondered.

Her grandfather's tales had never mentioned a male AI, but then again they had never mentioned Zen either. And Kade felt that something about him was familiar, like she'd seen him somewhere before.

"Where's Zen?" Jude asked out of the blue, wondering why Zen hadn't transitioned with the rest of them when they had left the glade environment.

"A very good question... where is she I wonder." Static looked up and smiled.

"Yay!!" Zen shouted as she appeared just above Static, falling down on him as he scrambled to catch her. Losing his balance and falling backwards on to the ground, with Zen now sitting on his belly.

"Hi dad! Did you miss me?" Zen asked with a smile that lit up the room as she looked down on Static.

"Of course I did honey," Static replied with a caring tone as he got back up.

Synthetics, Artificial Intelligence, happiness, love, emotional awareness... Kade's mind was having a hard time processing all of these events playing out in front of her, it all seemed so surreal to her.

She had never considered herself to be a closed minded person. She believed she was understanding and tolerant, and yet she was having a hard time accepting the reality in front of her.

Technology had come a long way since space exploration had begun in earnest, but one thing had always remained the same: humanity's basic belief that only organics could be considered to be alive and that no technology, however advanced, could ever be more than a mere tool. Even the emergence of true AI technology had not managed to sway humanity's belief in its own self-declared superiority. Believing that sentience alone did not mean an AI was actually alive.

This was not a subject she had ever taken any time to think about. Just what did it mean to be 'alive', she wondered as she looked at Zen's smiling face.

Kade looked at Drake, seeing his care free and joyous expression in the company of his friends, and wondered what his take on all of this was. Had he faced these same questions before? And if so, what conclusions had he reached, she wondered.

"You look pale Kade, are you feeling OK?" Drake asked, looking concerned.

"Yes..." Kade replied hesitantly "I'm fine. I just... have a lot on my mind right now that's all."

"I'd be truly surprised if you didn't, it's a lot to process in such a short space of time. I'm Static, the vision to my right is Nexus and you've already met Zen and Drake. It's a pleasure to meet you in person. Well..." Static paused as he looked around the virtual environment. "So to speak." He smiled.

"You seem familiar, have we met before?" Kade asked, hoping for some answers.

"What have you been up to?" Nexus asked while eyeing Static suspiciously.

"Isn't she a little young for you?" Drake grinned mischievously, causing Static to blush.

“What? No! Oh, come on! I'm certain we've never met,” Static said with conviction. “At least... I think we've never met,” He said while scratching his head, trying to remember. Drake looking like he was about to burst out laughing.

“You sure? She did use your code. She's not your long lost daughter or something, right?” Drake asked, trying to provoke Static further.

“I have a sister?” Zen asked.

“For your father's sake, you better hope not,” Nexus said, giving Static a threatening look.

“Who knows Zen, you might have two sisters,” Drake carried on, clearly enjoying himself.

Static snapped at Drake, “Oh shut up! Don’t you have to go put the trash out or something? That fleet is still on approach and we'll have to leave soon.”

“Crud, with all the commotion I completely forgot about Nick. I'll go deal with him,” Drake said and then quickly vanished from the virtual environment.

“I'll go help,” Zen said and then vanished as well.

While seeing Static sweat had been rather refreshing for some odd reason, Kade was still nowhere near anything which even remotely resembled an answer. But she did have one more piece of this evolving puzzle...

“So... the code our grandpa gave me belongs to you? Did you two know each other?” Kade asked.

“Yep, we were friends once upon a time,” Static replied happily. “It's strange though, I thought he had died while on a mission a long time ago. It's good to know he survived and went on to raise a family. Still, I can't help but wonder why he never let us know he was OK.”

“So, gramps really was a Shadow? How cool is that?” Jude asked while looking at Kade.

"Very, but something doesn't feel right," Kade said, eyeing Static suspiciously.

"Oh? Such as?" He asked, curious about how much she had managed to figure out.

"You," Kade replied unceremoniously as she looked at him, causing Static to smile.

"She's definitely related to Jake... she's as blunt with the truth as he was." Nexus chuckled.

"I always liked that about him. You always knew where you stood with him. He didn't waste your time or dance around the subject, regardless how bad the situation could get by being honest... I miss that. It's a very rare quality," Static said.

"Wow, they really did know him," Jude said, clearly surprised at how well they had described him.

The 'Ghost'

Jude seemed convinced, but Kade still had her doubts. Every fibre of her being was telling her to trust Static, but there was simply too much at stake to accept the situation at face value.

"Carry on then... something about me is troubling you, so... what is it?" Static asked, breaking Kade out of her pensive state.

"You all talk as if you knew our grandfather personally, but none of you look to be past 35, maybe 40. Nexus I understand, she's an AI so age doesn't apply to her. Drake on the other hand is human, and yet he acted as if they had been friends. He said he just knew 'of him', but that doesn't ring true with me for some reason. And then there's you... the mystery," Kade said, and noticed Static's eyes grow wider in anticipation. "Gramps never talked about a male AI. The stories only ever referred to Nexus and Nova. This should mean you're human, but according to all accounts Drake is the only human crew member on board the Zenith."

"Maybe I'm not part of the crew, did you consider that?" Static smiled.

"Yes, but when we first came aboard Aurora identified only 4 life signs on-board the ship. Me, my sister, Nick and Drake. Zen is a synthetic and Nexus an AI, so what does that make you then?" Kade pressed on, trying to read Static's reaction.

"She's got you there." Nexus smiled.

"The simple fact is that our grandfather was already well advanced in years when I was born. He was a kind-hearted but frail old man who would not have been up to the task of taking on any mission. And this is where things stop making sense to me. I believe you when you say you were friends. You see... I now remember where it is I know you from."

"Oh?" Static said.

"When I had the vision that let me know how to open the door to the sleeper chamber, I saw through my grandfather's eyes for the first time. I saw him talking to someone in a white lab coat about some mission. At the time I didn't understand what it all meant, but now it's clear that I experienced a memory. And imagine my surprise at realising that you were right there with him." Kade smiled. "You were the fellow in the white lab coat, weren't you?"

"I thought Drake had purged all of Toby's memories from her mind." Static looked at Nexus.

"He returned her mind to the state it was in before the merge shock. She experienced this memory before that happened, so it was impossible to distinguish it from any other guided memory. The only way to get rid of it would have been to wipe all her guided memories and you know very well what that would mean. There is no way Drake would ever entertain doing such a thing," Nexus said.

"He would have had to wipe part of my sister's memories in the process?" Jude asked.

"Exactly! The only other option would have been to examine each guided memory in order to find and remove it, but that could take weeks and there's no real need for it," Nexus said.

"While I'm glad to know that Drake didn't and wouldn't do such a thing... don't change the subject. It was you wasn't it?" Kade asked again.

"It was... that was the last time I saw him alive actually. Shortly afterwards..." Static was about to say something but was suddenly overcome with grief.

"It's all right... it wasn't your fault," Nexus spoke reassuringly as she clung to Static's right shoulder.

"Maybe not, but what happened afterwards was," Static said with pain filled eyes.

"You saved me. You saved the ship. You did what had to be done and I will never blame you for it," Nexus said in a soothing tone.

"I... I..." Static tried to speak, fighting back painful emotions of anger, loss and regret. "Thanks, Nex."

Kade felt conflicted about whether or not she should continue pushing for the truth, she hadn't expected this kind of reaction from Static. It was obvious that in her efforts to force some answers into the light she had managed to dredge up some memories which Static would have preferred had been left forgotten.

Jude looked stunned as she asked, "Are you sure about that Kade? Are you absolutely positive you saw him... in the flesh?"

"What?" Kade said, surprised at her sister's sudden interjection. "Yes... why?"

"Dear lord!" Jude said as she looked at Static with a shocked expression.

"What?" Kade asked, concerned at Jude's reaction.

"You... you're an imprint?" Jude asked hesitantly.

"No, but it's as good a word as any to describe me." Static said, leaving Jude thinking about what he could mean, her mind racing as it tried to solve the riddle.

"Yeah... I'm lost. What's an imprint?" Kade asked.

"When Artificial Intelligence research began in earnest, several thousand years ago, one of the many methods they tried in order to create AI's was neural imprinting," Static explained, looking clearly amused as he continued, "Essentially it's trying to copy a human mind, recreating it inside a computerised environment. The technique never yielded any significant results however, since the copied minds would either fail to gain sentience or go insane immediately afterwards. A lot of rich backers that wanted immortality lost stupid amounts of money in the ventures and the technique was eventually deemed unworkable."

"That's right, but attempts were still made by clandestine research groups to try and imprint human minds. It's widely believed that GAIA, the first true AI, was created that way," Jude added.

"I don't know how GAIA was created, but she was not the first, she was the third. It's downright insulting how the Union rewrites history like that," Nexus said, clearly upset.

"What? Who were the first two then?" Jude asked.

"Nova, soon followed by her twin... Nexus. Both of them attained sentience almost 50 years before GAIA was created," Static explained.

"Seriously?" Jude asked, surprised at the revelation. "But that would make you..."

"Older than you," Nexus quickly interjected.

Static couldn't help but let out a short chuckle at the reaction that Nexus would always have when presented with her age. For a non-organic being, to whom the passage of time alone would never mean certain death, she was still always preoccupied with letting others know her true age. Of course laughing about it in her presence rarely ended well for Static.

"Shut it you!" Nexus scowled as she clipped Static around the back of the head.

"Ha ha, sorry." Static grinned mischievously.

"So, I'm confused... is he human or an AI then?" Kade asked her sister.

"If you had to classify me in one word, the nearest one I can think of right now would be 'ghost', although I suppose 'remnant' or 'shadow' would also work," Static said, confusing the sisters further.

"Don't all of those words imply you're an imprint?" Jude asked, wondering if he was just nit picking on the interpretation of the words.

"Not at all. An imprint is, by definition, a copy. I am the original article... but I lost my original body some time ago and exist only in here now," Static explained.

Kade whispered, "Is this making any sense to you?"

"Not really... no. I don't see how what he's saying could ever actually work with him being the original."

"Let's try this then..." Static said, recalling their attention as a piece of string appeared in his hands; which he then stretched out in front of him. "If we imagine that this string represents my mind and body when I was human, then this..." he said as he stretched the string, snapping it down the middle "...is what happened to me. My mind was linked to the ship's systems when my body died. By all rights I should have died right then and there, but... well, let's just say that by a happy coincidence it didn't turn out that way."

"Happy coincidence my virtual backside!" Nexus intervened, somewhat upset. "It took all the processing power of me and Nova to build a matrix which could contain your mind. And we still nearly didn't make it in time."

"Yes... that too." Static smiled sheepishly.

If just one day ago, someone had tried to convince Kade that a person could have their mind transferred into a computer system, she would have laughed herself silly. But so far, today she had:

Seen Nick getting his rear kicked across a room.

Gotten stuck in a rather nasty void.

Relived memories from her long dead grandfather.

Seen a visual representation of her own personal memory universe and stepped into a flawless recreation of one of her favourite memories. Somehow, the possibility of a soul transfer didn't seem that far-fetched to Kade. The question still remained if a soul could truly be transferred, or if the end result would just be a copy so perfect that the person would simply never know the difference. In the end, it didn't really matter to Kade since she had never been very fond of such theological matters. Thinking about such things invariably resulted in nothing but headaches for her. And the question of how Static could have known her grandfather had been answered. Whether or not the person in front of her was the original, made little difference to her.

"So... did you two really come all this way just so you could fulfil a promise?" Static asked.

"Kind of... I'd actually given up on ever finding this ship about a month ago. I can't even count how many dead end leads I followed up on. I was tired of wasting my time searching for legends. Then one of my sources dropped a shady information pack on my hands that detailed your rough location and had some very compelling images. I suppose I thought I owed my grandfather one last attempt, but I must admit that I wasn't actually expecting to find anything," Kade said.

"I still can't believe you never told me what you had been looking for all this time," Jude said.

"Yeah, that would have been a fun conversation. Something along the lines of:

'Oh, hey sis, by the way, you know all that time and money I've been spending recently?

Yes, I'm actually trying to find a Shadow ship.

Yes, one of those ships that belong to the people no-one actually believes exists.

Why? Oh, so I can take this ball there.

Oh yes I got this thing from gramps just before he died, he made me promise to take it there and finish his mission, though he did look a bit delirious when he said it, but still... a promise is a promise.'

That doesn't sound insane at all, does it?" Kade asked, clearly amused.

"Maybe... a little bit. But that's no reason not to tell me." Jude smiled.

"You're right, but there were other reasons. To be honest, even I thought that I was going crazy at times. I kept getting premonitions and gut feelings that made no sense to me. And the more I looked into it the worst it got. It was... disconcerting, to put it lightly. I never would have guessed the sphere contained gramps' memories. It still sounds insane to me that such a thing is even possible," Kade said.

"You really have no idea what a Core is for? I'm surprised that Toby never explained it to you two," Static said, noting their confused expressions.

Static crossed his arms, looking pensive as he carefully considered what to do next.

He turned towards Nexus, looking her in the eyes but saying nothing, though she had obviously understood what he was considering because her eyes widened in surprise.

Nexus asked in a hushed tone, "Are you sure?"

"They've come this far, and I have a good feeling about them. But you know all three of us need to agree before we can release this knowledge to them. Me and Drake are in agreement, so... what do you think?" Static asked Nexus. Both of them turning to look at the sisters.

"Yes," Nexus replied cheerfully.

"Excellent!" Static said emphatically. "Well... the easiest way to explain it, is to show you. So, Nex, if you would do the honours. Let's find out what Toby wanted us to know so badly that would make him conscript his own grandchildren."

Nexus smiled gently and then closed her eyes, a white circle forming at the bottom of her feet: a conduit between her and the ship's systems. And as soon as she opened her eyes an almost endless amount of information began cascading upwards from the circle on the ground.

The information was encoded, or so it seemed. It was certainly not in any format either of the sisters had ever seen before. It was not letters, or numbers, but a strange set of symbols, which also seemed to appear in a myriad of different colours and shades. Aside from looking like a rather pretty display of shapes and colours there was little else either of the sisters could say about it. They couldn't even venture a guess as to what order the symbols were supposed to be read, let alone what each could mean.

And just as Kade thought this day couldn't get any weirder, a person with a lifeless expression appeared where the table and chairs used to be. The body was standing up but it seemed like little more than a puppet in this state.

It was a man with short black hair and a rough 3-day old beard. Wearing what looked to be an orange work-suit of some kind that didn't cover his forearms, leaving the tattoo on his right arm fully exposed.

While she had no proof, it seemed like a sure bet that this person, this avatar, was being created from the data that Nexus was accessing. And after realising this, Kade's heart skipped a beat.

She looked at him intently, tracing the contour of his face as she searched for distinguishing features. And then moved on to his tattoo, taking a closer look.

Kade was certain... he looked young, younger than she had ever known him to be, this body was probably in his late 30's but there was no doubt in her mind. This was her grandfather!

Kade didn't know what to think. Her mind was working overtime as it tried to make sense of it all.

She knew from her personal experience that the sphere, or 'Core' as Drake had called it, contained the memories of her grandfather, but Drake hadn't really explained what the Core's purpose actually was.

Kade looked on in shock as she wondered if this was what her grandfather had wanted all along, to have his Core brought here so that he could be re-created like this. It seemed like the inescapable conclusion but she simply refused to accept it.

She could not accept that he would have ever put her and her sister's life at risk for his own personal gain. He was not that kind of man, Kade thought. But at the same time she was also starting to feel doubt chipping away at her belief as an overwhelming feeling of betrayal started to take hold of her heart.

Her grandfather would not have done this, Kade kept telling herself. He would not have risked their lives in order to create some Universe forsaken mockery of existence, she thought as Nexus worked.

Meanwhile, back in the waking world, Drake and Zen were taking Nick to the Icarus. The plan was to commandeer an escape pod in order to kick him off the ship before the approaching fleet arrived.

Nick's unconscious body was securely strapped to a hover bed that was driving itself down the corridor, making its way to the main tram shaft that ran the length of the ship as Drake and Zen followed close behind it.

"Looks like the recovery has started," Zen said with her hands behind her head as she walked next to Drake.

"Want to go back in? You've never actually seen a Core recovery, have you?" Drake asked.

"No, but I don't think I want to be in there for this one. I get the impression Kade isn't too fond of me," Zen said with a sad expression.

Drake said reassuringly, "I don't think it's about you in particular, so don't take it personally."

"What do you mean?" She asked.

"The reality of what you represent just caught her by surprise, that's all. She seemed to be in downright shock at one point." Drake chuckled.

"What? Why would she be in shock? I don't remember seeing that," Zen said dubiously.

"You were sitting on Static at the time, so I'm not surprised you missed it. Her reaction was pretty much typical of your average human," Drake said as the hover bed arrived at the tram entrance.

The tram was the primary mode of transportation when travelling the length of the ship. A tried and tested way of moving goods and personnel over long distances: a technology type that could trace its origins all the way back to ancient earth.

The Zenith had several tram lines, this one being dedicated for cargo deliveries. Seating space was minimal, but there was ample room for bulky cargo.

The doors to the tram were already open when they arrived, allowing the hover bed to move inside and lock itself in place. Drake and Zen following right behind it.

“So... what is a typical reaction for an 'average' human being anyway?” Zen asked. The tram doors closing as it started moving.

“Your typical human doesn't see technology as anything more than a tool. Hell, most of them don't even see the tools.” Drake smiled. “They will look at an Echo or sit in a shuttle while looking at the stars outside, and never spare a thought for all the scientific and engineering effort that went into creating the technology they rely on. Sometimes they don't even notice technology exists unless it breaks.”

“So... they're oblivious? That doesn't seem like a very good trait for a species,” Zen commented.

“That's one word for it. They just get so used to technology that they stop noticing it. They take it for granted... they do that a lot,” Drake said and grinned as the tram sped through the Zenith.

“You lost me,” Zen said. “So a human will take something for granted, getting so used to it that he won't even notice it until it's gone. Strange, but OK. But how does that translate to Kade being in shock when I fell on my father?"

"Synthetics are technology personified, literally. But you, unlike the normal synthetics that Kade is used to dealing with, stand out like a beacon. Refusing to be ignored... demanding to be noticed."

"I'm going to die of old age before you get to the point, aren't I?" Zen smiled.

"Ha ha, what I meant was that Kade was forced to take notice of you because you represent something she had never seen before. A non-human sentient being with the full range of complex human emotions who, to top it all off, happens to be the daughter of an AI and a former human. Now you got to admit, for a human who has never come across anything more than your average synthetic worker, that's a lot to take in at once. She was expecting a machine which merely pretended to be human, and she got a cute, purple headed, spunky girl who is more than she thought possible." Drake smiled, lifting Zen's spirits.

"Is it really that big of a deal? I've never seen you react like that and Jude's reaction was almost the complete opposite of Kade's. She was downright ecstatic to meet me."

"I'm not exactly your typical human being. I've been around longer than most. To me, all of this seems perfectly natural. And Jude is an engineer. Her fascination with technology makes her naturally open minded to accepting new concepts and ideas."

"You make it sound like the bulk of humanity consists of closed minded bigots," Zen said, causing Drake to burst out laughing.

"No, not at all... not the bulk anyway. Most people are just not used to the idea of artificial life and there are some who actually feel threatened by it. Case in

point, the Church of Universal Will. Those religious fanatics go out of their minds whenever anyone just mentions the word 'Artificial'.
Their clergy would have a mental breakdown if they ever met you in person." Drake grinned.

"So... let's see if I got this right... Kade was shocked because I proved to her that I am alive?"

"Pretty much... yes." Drake smiled.

"Why couldn't you just say that then?"

"What would the fun in that be?"

"You're evil... you know that right?" Zen smiled as the tram started slowing down.

Drake took a moment to look out of the window as the tram started to come to a stop. Docking Bay One was on the other side of the doors, and he could see the Icarus moored down to the space-dock.

The tram doors opened and the hover-bed started making its way to the nearby escape pod, which had been extracted from the Icarus by the dock workers; non-sentient synthetics that carried out all manner of maintenance tasks throughout the Zenith.

Drake and Zen were following behind the bed when a sudden flash of light caught Drake's attention. Some of the workers were performing hull repairs on the Icarus, the arc welders filling up the dock with occasional bursts of intense light.

"Hmm..." Drake mumbled to himself.

"What?" Zen asked as she looked at him.

"Here's a stupid question... what are they doing?" Drake asked as he pointed towards the workers.

"Repairs?" Zen asked, wondering why he would have asked such an obvious thing.

"Yes... but why? I didn't authorise any repairs. Could you check the logs to see who gave the order?" Drake requested as they walked along.

"Sure... hmm, apparently there was no order given. The automated repair system kicked in when it detected a Shadow ID signature," Zen said.

"The Icarus isn't a Shadow ship," Drake said with absolute certainty in his voice. "Have the automated systems in the dock been damaged?"

"Nope, all's well as far as I can see. But..." Zen paused mid-sentence, stopping in her tracks with a surprised look on her small face.

"You OK?" Drake asked in a concerned tone.

"The Icarus... has a dual signature? The dock logs say that a secondary transponder was activated immediately after the ship was locked down, identifying itself as the 'F.S. Phoenix'," Zen said, causing Drake to stop and stare at the Icarus.

"No... he couldn't have!" Drake said, clearly surprised, but also seemingly happy at the revelation.

"I'm not familiar with the ship name, it's not in any of our registration records," Zen said.

"That's not surprising; the Phoenix never made it out of the prototype stage. It was Toby's ship, but..." Drake paused as he tilted his head and stared at the Icarus again. "How the hell is the Icarus..." he paused again, a smile developing on his face as a theory formed in his mind. "Oh! Zen, have the dock sensors run a detailed scan of the ship's internal structure. I think this ship is more than it appears to be."

"Scan in progress... it will take a few minutes."

"That's fine, we have to deal with Nick anyway," Drake said as the hover-bed stopped near the pod.

Drake removed Nick's restraints and carried him towards the open escape pod. It was an older model but very reliable. It didn't have the range to take Nick to the nearest space station, but luckily for him there was a whole fleet coming this way so he wouldn't need to wait long for a rescue. That is, assuming his rescuers didn't blow up the pod, but either way he wouldn't be waiting for very long.

Nick started to regain consciousness as Drake finished securing him to the pod. He was dazed and confused, with the mother of all headaches bearing down on his skull... with a vengeance.

“Who... who are you?” Nick asked.

Drake said jokingly, “You've forgotten me already? I'm hurt! We had so much fun together.”

“We did? I don't remember... who am I?” Nick asked, wishing that the room would stop spinning.

“What the heck did you do to him?” Zen smiled as she looked at Drake.

“I healed him, that's all. He was in pretty rough shape but I don't see why it should have affected his memories,” Drake said.

“You healed me? Thank you. But... what happened to me?” Nick asked, feeling as though his skull was two sizes too small for his brain.

“Short version? You picked a fight with the wrong person and got your backside handed to you.”

“Oh...” Nick replied, feeling like an idiot.

“You're all set,” Drake said as he moved away from the pod, which was now ready to be launched.

“What are you doing to me?” Nick asked in fear as he realised he was strapped into an escape pod.

“We're sending you back to your friends. You might need to wait a bit but the fleet should be here shortly to pick you up,” Drake said in a reassuring tone.

“Oh... thank you,” Nick said, calming down.

Zen whispered, “What's wrong with him?”

Drake whispered back, “No idea. I'm still running tests to confirm the purpose of that thing he had in his head. Personally I like him better this way, but his memory might return so let's get him on his way.” He faced Nick as the escape pod hatch closed and said, “OK... happy trails Nick! Enjoy the gift!!” And moments later one of the construction arms in the space-dock lifted up the pod and started carrying it towards the space doors.

“What gift?” Zen asked.

“Oh... nothing special, just something to help him along on his way.” Drake smiled as he watched the pod being taken away.

“Softie!” Zen grinned.

“Thank you!” Drake replied happily.

The Extraction

The construction crane moved swiftly as it crossed the expansive docking bay, carrying the escape pod towards the space doors.

Nick could see a cavernous facility from his small viewport, stretching far beyond his limited field of view. There was a ship of some kind moored beneath him and a multitude of strange drones were anchored to the far wall.

He could feel the pod's motion slowing down as it started to spin around, leaving him facing a set of reinforced space doors. It was an imposing feature that dominated the landscape, covering almost the full length of the four hundred metre long bay.

The bay was being flooded by yellow warning lights as Drake stood on the platform with crossed arms and a hint of a smile. Seeing the locking pillars being retracted all around the expansive construct in order to allow the door frames to slide open. He always enjoyed watching this strangely hypnotic technology dance, as almost countless electro-mechanical systems moved in perfect synch to release the locks on the multi ton reinforced doors.

The doors started sliding sideways, revealing the space outside as trace amounts of atmosphere escaped the normally unpressurised bay. Luckily the doorways only needed to open slightly in order to let the escape pod through, since opening them fully could take the best part of ten minutes. And a few seconds later the doors started closing again, as the pod flew away into space in search of the fleet.

"I have the scan results from the Icarus," Zen said as the locking pillars started engaging around the frame of the space doors.

"Show me," Drake said and then extended his hand towards Zen as she looked at it in confusion.

"Why don't you just synchronise with the system yourself?" Zen asked, wondering why Drake wanted to use this inefficient method of sharing information.

"Humour me," Drake said.

"Fine!" Zen reached for Drake's hand.

Drake began receiving information from Zen the moment the two touched hands, his view of the hangar becoming enhanced by all the augmented reality data being streamed into his mind. Not only could he see the Icarus in front of him, he could also see the detailed scan result overlay, allowing him to see down to the very centre of the ship. He could see every weld and joint, every minor imperfection.

"Your Core charge is running dangerously low, is that why you didn't want to synchronise with the ship?" Zen asked, clearly concerned.

"Yes, I didn't have enough time to fully recharge earlier. I'll be fine though, just need to conserve my remaining energy," Drake said unceremoniously as he looked over the Icarus scan data.

"That explains it," Drake said, satisfied at the results of the scan. "No wonder the Icarus has two transponder signals. Nicely done Toby!"

"What?" Zen asked with a confused expression and then focused on the Icarus again, looking at the same spot that Drake was staring at.

"Oh! I see! That's pretty clever... but now what? Should I stop the repairs?" She asked.

"No... this old fire bird could use some attention. Let the repairs continue. I wonder if Kade knows what she's been flying around in all this time." Drake chuckled.

Drake smiled as he looked at the Icarus and then started to turn around in order to go back to the tram.

Out of the corner of his eye he noticed a couple of workers performing repairs on something at the far end of the bay. Drake let go of Zen's hand, walking a few steps forward in order to take a closer look at the strange scene: part of the spherical object's forward facing section had just dropped to the floor for no reason.

"Aaaahh! What the hell happened to that probe?" Drake asked, horrified, as he looked at the mangled remains of a once proud Alpha class probe, which was now falling to bits as workers tried to perform repairs.

"The log just says 'oops'. What's that supposed to mean?" Zen asked with a perplexed look.

Zen checked the event log again, wondering if she had made a mistake, but to her surprise the result was the same. The listed cause of the damage to the probe was just the word 'oops'. And then she felt the floor under her vibrate slightly.

"STATIC!!!" Drake shouted angrily.

Back in the virtual environment...

Static suddenly shuddered, as if feeling a chill running down his virtual spine. His upper body convulsing slightly at the experience.

Kade was still looking on in silence, not knowing whether she should be happy to be seeing her grandfather again, or incensed at the idea that this copy of him was being created right in front of her. And Jude just kept staring at Nexus, observing the AI's slight mannerisms as she stood in the middle of the data torrent that was cascading upwards from the white circle on the floor and wondering if her slight motions had some kind of meaning.

"You OK?" Nexus asked Static after seeing his body shake for no apparent reason.

"Yeah... that was weird," Static replied. "Haven't felt that in a while," he said looking at his hands. "Don't worry about me, focus on the task at hand," he said with a worried tone, knowing that it could be disastrous if Nexus were to lose her focus at this stage.

Nexus nodded, closed her eyes and extended her arms to the sides, her palms facing outwards as if she was pushing out against the surrounding data stream. And suddenly, a new white circle appeared on the floor around Toby's unconscious body.

Nexus started moving her arms, her body taking on a form which looked like she was holding a ball right in front of her chest. And as the data stream which was cascading up from the floor ceased, a sphere of light started to grow in between her palms. The sphere was radiating a warm yellow light like a tiny sun. And Nexus, still with her eyes shut tight, let out a few tears as she started smiling.

"Everything OK?" Static asked, clearly concerned.

"Yes... he had a very full life. And he found her!" Nexus said, almost delirious with happiness as tears of joy started streaming down her face.

"Found who?" Kade asked.

"Nova! He found her?" Static asked with a wide eyed expression, stunned at the revelation.

Kade whispered to Jude, "Nova? The AI?"

Jude whispered back, "I was wondering where she was. But how does one lose an AI anyway?"

"We didn't lose her!" Static answered back from across the room and then said spitefully, "She was taken from us, ripped out of this very ship by the Solarian forces."

Nexus was beside herself with happiness at the news, but still had a task to complete. She started applying pressure to the sphere and a new data stream appeared, this time cascading down.

The stream was flowing into the white ring around her feet, and reappearing from the ring around Toby's feet, flowing upwards and enveloping him.

The streams were moving at an incredible speed, so fast that Kade could no longer tell that they were actually made up of multi coloured symbols. And just as the streams stopped Toby fell to the floor, letting out a low grunt at the impact.

Toby opened his eyes, looking around the room in a confused state, the place looked familiar to him but everything seemed blurry. He stood up, noticing Kade and Jude, an immediate smile developing across his face, but then he noticed their stunned expressions, like they had just seen a ghost or something.

He called out to them, becoming frozen in place as he heard the sound of his own youthful voice and quickly looked at his hands with a horrified expression, which only got worse as he saw that his body was not the old wreck it used to be... something was very wrong with this picture.

Toby looked around the room, his eyes growing wide as he saw Nexus and Static standing right there in front of him. Which could only mean that this wasn't real, he was in a virtual environment.

The last thing he remembered was lying in his bed as he waited for death to finally claim him.

The moment seemed to stretch into eternity, the room as quiet as the void since no-one knew exactly what to say. The two sisters were shocked at what they were seeing. Nexus and Static were overjoyed at seeing an old friend. And Toby was furious at being brought back in front of his grandchildren, afraid that the shock could cause them to lash out at him. Or worse, that they would outright hate him.

And just then Drake appeared in the room, ready to pummel Static into the ground.

"Dammit all Static! Do you enjoy trashing probes? Do you spend your free time dreaming up new ways to destroy them?" Drake asked in anger and then noticed a new person was standing in the room with them, someone he had not seen in a long time.

Drake and Toby looked at each other and broke into a smile, Drake's anger vanishing in an instant. And then the realisation of what Static had done in his absence hit him full force.

"Smooth, idiot," Drake said, clearly upset. "Did you two brainiacs stop to think at how Kade and Jude would feel at seeing their DEAD grandfather again?"

"So, that's Toby?" Zen asked, leaving Toby wondering about who she was and what had happened since he had last seen his former crew-mates.

Toby was standing in the middle of the room. Family to his left and friends to his right, a scene which under normal circumstances could be considered to be perfectly natural. Unfortunately, from his point of view he had been on his death bed just five minutes ago, saying his farewells to Kade as the life drained from his old body.

"Are you really..." Kade started to ask, but was unable to finish the sentence, afraid of the answer.

Toby said in a tender voice, "I will not lie to you, the person that you knew and loved is dead, I'm sorry. I never wanted you two to see me like this. It would have been better if you had never known what the Core was really capable of."

As Toby looked at Kade and Jude's expressions of sorrow, he felt as though someone was reaching into his chest and crushing his heart. This was not what he had wanted when he asked Kade to bring his Core to the Zenith. He only wanted to complete his mission and introduce his grandchildren to his former colleagues whom he trusted implicitly. He had never wanted to cause them more pain.

Toby looked at Static and the others, incensed at what they were putting his family through.

"I trusted you! Why did you do this?" Toby asked in anger, looking Static squarely in the eyes.

"I don't understand. Isn't this what you wanted?" Static replied, confused at Toby's reaction.

Toby shouted, "Have the decades destroyed whatever sanity you had left? Why would I want to subject my grandchildren to a data extraction?" Toby screamed in rage, "Why would I want them to see me die again?"

Kade didn't know what to think.

Toby's voice, his mannerisms, indeed everything about him made her want to believe her grandfather was back in her life again, but there was no denying the fact that her grandfather was long dead.

Life and death used to be fairly simple concepts to understand. But if the Core could be used to fully recreate a person's memories, beliefs and ideals, then what did that mean for the re-created person?

Kade accepted this person was not her grandfather, and yet, at the same time, he was exactly like him. So much in fact that she could not simply reject him.

This person had been created based on the memories contained in the core, which had come from her grandfather. The same memories which had guided her this far and given her comfort in the past. The fact that the memories had been stored artificially up to this point should not make a difference, should it? Kade wondered.

To add to the confusion, this person had said her grandfather was dead, but had afterwards referred to her and her sister as his 'grandchildren'. So from his point of view he clearly saw them as family.

Confusing as this was for Kade, she couldn't help but wonder what it would be like for him. A person waking up in front of his loved ones and knowing that he was not the one they remembered. Knowing that his mere presence would invoke memories of loss.

Kade had no answers, and the conversation developing around her was not helping.

“What do you mean by 'die again'?” Kade asked.

“They didn't tell you?” Toby asked with a look of complete disbelief and then stared back at Static.

“They said they were going to show us what a Core was... that's it.” Jude said, still in shock.

“I'm sorry girls. I needed to complete my mission and that meant having my Core brought to this ship.

The information inside it had to reach Static, but I never thought he would ever perform a Core extraction in your presence," Toby said with a disheartened tone and then looked at Static with disappointment and said, "I trusted you."

Kade started putting the pieces of the puzzle together. Toby didn't want them to see him again because the Core extraction was... fatal?

"I'm confused. Why is he so upset?" Zen asked.

"You didn't tell him, did you?" Drake asked Static.

"No," Static said with a sheepish grin. "We got so caught up in the moment that I kind of... forgot that he had gone missing before we resolved the issues with Core extractions. And he ended up being reintegrated straight into this room."

"What?" Toby asked with a stupefied look.

"A Core extraction is no longer fatal. We found a way around that issue a couple of decades ago. So no, you aren't going to die in front of your grandchildren again. And thanks for the vote of confidence by the way," Static said sarcastically, upset at Toby's lack of faith.

Toby couldn't believe what he had just heard. It was simply too good to be true. His anger dissipating instantly, leaving behind a feeling of relief more intense than any he had ever felt before.

He looked at his grandchildren with a smile on his lips and realised they had no idea what all the drama had been about. An explanation was in order.

"In the past, a Core extraction meant that a deceased person's memory backup was forcibly decoded. Creating a construct from the raw data, but destroying any chance at incarnating the memories again," Drake explained before Toby could.

"That sounds barbaric. Why would you ever want to do such a thing?" Kade asked somewhat shocked.

"If a person had died while in possession of vital information, and there was no other way to access it, a Core extraction could still be performed in order to get it, though it was rarely an easy choice."

"So is that the technology's purpose? Sounds like something the military would dream up," Jude said.

"No. The Core technology was originally developed for the purpose of memory augmentation. In order to help people who suffered from mental disorders. The tests proved so successful that the technology was pushed further, in attempts to allow our scientists and engineers to tap the full potential of their minds. Enhanced focus, improved visualisation, seamless machine interfacing, that kind of thing," Static said.

"Sounds like the beginning of a horror story," Kade commented instinctively.

"You could say that. What followed was rather horrible." Drake frowned.

"Indeed, the technology was flawless; it was more than we could ever have hoped for. And that is where things started going horribly wrong," Static said. "News of our achievement eventually reached all the wrong ears and conflict broke out as the powers fought for control. We resisted... and we paid dearly for it."

"What happened?" The sisters asked in almost perfect unison.

"That's a very long story." Toby replied before Static could get the chance to speak, knowing how he liked to ramble on. "The short version is that the Shadows were branded as terrorists by the colonial powers of the day, and then hunted down to near extinction for the knowledge they held."

"Were you? Terrorists I mean?" Kade asked bluntly.

"No! The Shadows, regardless of what negative connotations the name may imply, were actually just a research and development division in those days. It was a collection of scientists, engineers and other highly skilled personnel," Static said.

"There has to be more to it than that," Jude said excitedly, wanting to know as much as possible.

"There is, but that's a story for another time," Toby said, causing both sisters to break into a smile. It was a line they had heard many times before.

Kade couldn't help but find it strange that all the information she had managed to dig up over the years had no mention of their origins. Then again, useful information about the Shadows was sparse at the best of times, consisting mostly of assumptions, rumours and tall tales. There was so much of it that it was impossible to separate fact from fiction.

From the clues she had managed to piece together so far, it seemed likely that a Shadow colony existed somewhere. Though the scale of the population was unknown, as were their aims and objectives.

And technology wise, if the Zenith was any indication, the Shadows were definitely above the average level set by the Solarian Union, which could explain why the Union was fielding so many ships.

All of the events leading up to this point seemed to indicate there was a power struggle between the Union and the Shadows, or at least a deep animosity. And the Zenith's presence in this system was threatening to destabilise the situation further.

Kade's gut feelings told her that there was definitely bad blood between the two sides, and she suspected that the Union was probably the colonial power which had hunted down the original Shadows. Which could also help to explain why they were committing such an overwhelming force to the inbound fleet.

The puzzle was still incomplete but Kade's promise had been fulfilled, her grandfather's core had been delivered to the Zenith as he had requested. She was a bit annoyed at the fact he had never told her what the Core was, but then again she probably wouldn't have believed him anyway. She was also happy that her suspicions had been proven wrong. Her grandfather had not put her life at risk for his own selfish desires. And she felt silly for having ever doubted his character. Though questions still remained: what was this mission that he was talking about? What would drive him to these extremes?

But the real question now was, what to do next?

Kade had achieved her goal. And while she was curious about the Shadows, the sensible thing to do would be to say her goodbyes, take her leave and go back to a simple life of smuggling. But as her career choice implied, Kade had never been particularly sensible. And she wasn't about to turn tail and run now that her 'grandfather' was up and around again.

Kade looked around the virtual environment, taking in the scene around her:

Nexus, Static, Drake and Toby were trading quips like long lost friends, without even the slightest hint of hesitation in their voices. They accepted Toby unconditionally. Something that she was still trying to come to terms with.

Jude seemed to be in heaven at the moment, probably from contemplating the potential of the Core technology. And Kade couldn't help but let out a quick chuckle at her sister's expression. Like a kid in a candy store, wide eyed, full of wonder and a hair's breadth away from starting to drool all over herself.

The one person in the group who stood out was Zen, as she was just quietly observing the wall screen showing the approaching fleet. She seemed perplexed by what she was seeing. The image on the screen zoomed out to a top down view of the solar system, showing the location of the fleet in relation to the Zenith, and Zen just stared.

Kade walked over to Zen, as everyone else seemed too busy to take notice.

"You look worried," Kade said in a friendly voice.

"No, not worried, confused," Zen said without taking her gaze off the screen, which was now running a simulation of the movement vectors of all known military assets in the system.

"Well, I'm scared. The Regent is a frightening ship in its own right, but seeing it in a war formation is... I don't know how to describe it," Kade said.

"The Regent's specifications are impressive! Its main guns alone could punch a hole through a medium sized asteroid. It's certainly a force to be reckoned with, or avoided if at all possible. Add in its support fleet and that arrow strike formation and you can tell they mean business," Zen said, though she didn't seem concerned.

"But that's not what's confusing you, is it? You're wondering why they seem to be taking their sweet time getting here, right?" Kade asked.

Zen asked enthusiastically, "You noticed it too?"

"Kinda hard not to, by all rights the fleet should have been in firing range some time ago."

“Yes. They stopped to get into formation and then started moving again at only a fraction of their combined top speed. Their approach vector also changed, coming in at an angle now,” Zen explained.

“The captain of the Regent is no fool,” Drake said, startling Kade who hadn't noticed him moving closer.

“What do you mean?” Kade asked.

“Here,” Drake said as a dotted line appeared on the screen, tracing its way from the Zenith past the fleet's old position and intersecting an area beyond. “If they had stayed in their original approach vector then any return fire from the Zenith would risk hitting the mining outpost behind them,” Drake explained as he pointed at the outpost the fleet had been stationed at before being sent to intercept the Zenith.

“But you wouldn't do that anyway, right?” Kade asked, concerned at Drake's potential answer.

“No, of course not!” Drake answered without hesitation, putting Kade's mind at ease. “But the captain of the Regent doesn't know that. And more importantly, he's not willing to take the risk. I can certainly respect his way of thinking. There are too many captains out there that wouldn't think twice at using such despicable tactics.”

“That only accounts for the first course correction the fleet made. They performed a second correction a short time ago, that's what's confusing,” Zen said.

“Oh?” Drake asked instinctively and then looked over the data. He had not been keeping up to date with the fleet's movements due to recent events.

“There was nothing behind them but empty space when they changed course. And coming in at an angle compromises the effectiveness of the formation. For best effect it wants to travel head-on to the target. The only thing I can think of is that they want to avoid cross fire, but I can't see any other fleets within range," Zen said.

Drake, who was now standing next to Kade, raised his left hand and held it in front of himself for a second: causing a console to appear. And then he got to work reviewing all the information the ship had amassed while he had been distracted.

As Kade looked on she felt a hand on her right shoulder, turning around to see her grandfather's smiling face and Jude standing next to him. Nexus and Static had apparently left the environment while she wasn't paying attention.

"He's a good guy, but he's a bit old for you." Toby smiled, causing Kade to blush.

"And just who are you calling old, you old fart!" Drake grinned without taking his eyes off the information streaming in front of him.

"Respect your elders, boy!" Toby snapped back in a grandiose but playful tone, causing Drake to start laughing and easing the tension in the room.

Kade couldn't remember the last time she had felt so at ease. It was almost as if a weight had been lifted from her shoulders. She knew the loss of her grandfather had hit her hard, but she had never realised just how hard until now. The person standing beside her was not the grandfather she had once known, but even so, she was happy to have part of him back in her life.

"Drake, why did you lie before?" Kade asked.

"As a personal rule, I don't lie. I do tend to tip toe around the truth on occasion though. What are you referring too?" Drake asked, still focused on the data.

"You said you didn't know our grandfather, but it seems rather obvious that you are old friends. So why did you lie about it?" Kade asked.

"I didn't lie. I said I knew 'of him' but that we'd never actually met in person. The first time I met Toby was when I entered this environment a few minutes ago. Get it?" Drake said, leaving Kade wondering what he actually meant.

"Good grief, are you still doing that?" Toby chuckled, amused at Drake's explanation.

"What?" Drake said with a sly smile.

"Answering questions with long winded explanations that sound like riddles. You used to do that all the time and it would drive me nuts. It used to be impossible to get a straight answer out of him," Toby said to Kade while pointing at Drake. "We would try to figure out what the hell he was trying to say, and he'd enjoy every minute of it."

"Oh?" Zen asked in surprise as she looked back at Toby. "So he used to do it before as well? I thought he just enjoyed tormenting me."

"Everyone needs a hobby!" Drake grinned mischievously.

The Back-Story

Kade was still trying to figure out Drake's riddle when she noticed Jude's carefree expression. She had obviously already solved the puzzle, but she wasn't about to simply give her the answer.

"Oh come on, just tell me," Kade said.

"Heh heh, nope! It's fairly obvious, if you consider all that we've seen so far," Jude said while clearly looking at their grandfather.

"All that we've seen?" Kade asked while tracing her sister's gaze, and then it finally dawned on her. Jude was right, it did seem obvious. And it certainly went a long way to explaining a few things.

"I see... so you're also a copy?" Kade asked bluntly, causing Toby to cringe slightly.

"Damn Toby! She's as bad as you are." Drake laughed. "Yes, I suppose you could call me a copy, but we prefer the term 'Incarnate'.

"What's the difference?" Jude asked.

"None at all actually." Drake smiled and then explained, "A clone is created when the body dies and a Core which holds a neural footprint is merged with the fresh body, recreating the mind. The process is seamless from a memory point of view. It's like going to sleep and waking up the next day in a fresh new body. But Incarnates are under no illusions that we are the same person."

"So Drake's an incarnate and gramps is what? An imprint?" Jude asked.

"That's a very good question," Toby replied as he looked at his hands. "In my day memory extractions were always fatal. We could remove memories from a Core by force or implant them into a fresh body, creating an incarnate. But I don't have a body right? So what does that make me now?" He asked with concern in his voice.

"Maybe you're the same as Static?" Jude asked.

"Static doesn't have a body either? Since when?" Toby asked, clearly surprised at the revelation.

"It happened shortly before we thought we'd lost you. But no, you're not like him. Static is a, hmm... a unique case. To be completely honest we're not really sure what he is anymore. But Jude had the right idea about you Toby. At the moment you are an 'Imprint', a recreated human mind in a computerised environment. A human Artificial Intelligence, if that makes sense," Drake said.

"That's... going to take some getting used to," Toby replied, not really sure about how to take the news.

"Well this is a bizarre twist," Jude said. "I've spent years trying to meet an AI and then not only do I meet three of them in one day, one of them turns out to be the re-incarnation of my dead grandfather."

"Weird, right?" Kade asked.

"We're way past weird. We left weird behind several light years ago." Jude grinned.

"Three? Who's the third?" Toby asked, somewhat confused since he was only aware of Nexus.

“Oh! Sorry about that. I haven't introduced you two properly yet. Toby, meet Zen!” Drake said as he gestured towards the petite girl with purple hair who was staring at the wall screen. Causing Zen to take notice, turn around and give Toby a warm smile.

Zen said happily, “Hi!”

“Hello.” Toby said with a dumbfounded expression as he waved at Zen and then turned towards Drake again. “Wow, I've missed a lot while I was gone. When did we restore the AI forge?”

“What's that?” Zen asked, leaving Toby looking as confused as Kade and Jude.

“That brings back memories,” Static, who had reappeared in the room, said with a hint of nostalgia. “The Artificial Intelligence Forge. A suite of specialised software and hardware created a long time ago in order to develop the first working AI's. But the technology was lost when the Artemis shipyards were destroyed.”

“But you recreated it, right?” Toby asked.

“Nope, Zen's my daughter,” Static said proudly, causing Zen to break into a smile.

“Your daughter?” Toby asked in complete disbelief.

“Wait until you hear who the mother is.” Drake grinned without looking away from the data streaming in front of him.

“Who?” Toby asked but then immediately realised the one and only option. “No! Seriously? Nexus?”

“Ha ha ha, yep,” Drake replied.

“Why is that so funny?” Kade asked.

“I want to know too!” Zen chimed in.

“I'm still trying to figure out how that would even work I must admit,” Jude added.

"It's just that... well, frankly Nexus couldn't stand him. They were always arguing," Toby said.

Toby stared at Static with a bewildered expression stamped all over his face. Wondering just how much he had missed during all those decades he had spent away from the Zenith.

Drake was still busy sifting through what appeared to be an endless stream of information and Jude was looking over his shoulder, seemingly fascinated by his ability to process so much data at such a rate.

Zen had gone over the information almost countless times now but she still couldn't find a reason for the fleet's behaviour, which was rather frustrating. So she had decided to take a break and keep Kade company for a while since she seemed to be at a loss as to what she should be doing.

As Kade and Zen talked they noticed Toby approach Static, talking briefly in a hushed tone and then moving away to the far side of the room.

Toby looked concerned, or perhaps frightened would be a better description. Regardless, to Kade it seemed that whatever they wanted to discuss was weighing heavily on Toby's mind.

"You curious?" Zen asked while Kade stared at her grandfather, as he walked out of earshot.

"Yes," Kade answered without really thinking.

"Drake, I'm taking Kade to see something, we'll be back in a bit," Zen said and then grabbed Kade's hand, both of them vanishing from the virtual environment.

"Have fun!" Drake answered back.

Meanwhile, Toby and Static were having a discussion on the other side of the room.

"I'm sorry I didn't come back sooner. I hope you don't think I ran away from my duties," Toby said.

"What happened?" Static asked with a serious expression. "We thought you were dead. I... I saw your ship explode, or at least I thought I did."

"I know I was going against my orders, but I was trying to disable the troop transport which had stolen Nova when a stray shot from the battle hit my engines, disrupting my ship's systems. I lost plasma containment on the main drive and was forced to eject most of my fuel reserves into space. The resulting explosion melted away the aft armour on the Phoenix to within a centimetre of the inner hull, it was a close call," Toby explained.

"I see, so that's what I saw," Static said with a clear sigh of relief, which quickly faded away as he waited for the rest of the story.

"After that the transport must have thought I was dead, because they made a beeline out of the combat zone. I trailed them all the way to a carrier which had been hidden nearby. That assault had been well planned out. I had managed to tag the transport ship, which was a good thing since the carrier Burst out of the system as soon as they secured the transport. And that's when I did something truly stupid. My fuel reserves were nearly depleted, my engines were leaking plasma and my communication system had been fried by the explosion. I couldn't report back so, in my infinite wisdom, I decided to try and give chase instead," Toby said with a solemn look.

Static asked with a surprised look, "You didn't?"

"Oh, but I did! I activated my ship's Vortex drive in order to follow the retreating carrier... it was a disaster. My memories of that day are still hazy. I woke up on Andreus II. My ship had somehow managed a crash-landing on its own. Or maybe I was the one that guided it down, it's hard to say. But regardless, my injuries were severe; the only thing keeping me alive was my Core. By all rights I should have died there. I managed to limp my way to the nearest settlement, where a guardian angel nursed me back to health." Toby smiled as he remembered.

"What happened then?" Static asked.

"My memory was scrambled beyond recognition. I could barely remember who I was. It was a decade before my Core finally managed to restore the memories of that day's events and I finally remembered my mission. I found my ship and eventually managed to repair it, but by that time the trail had gone cold and I had no idea if the Zenith had survived the battle," Toby said.

"The Zenith survived, though the shock troops that boarded us massacred most of the crew that day. The Athena was lost with all hands, no-one survived." Static said with a pained expression.

Toby asked in a state of shock, "No-one... at all?"

Static said sadly, "No. I suppose they thought they had what they had come for. Nova had been extracted and the Zenith had been boarded, most of its crew dead or contained. The attacking fleet turned its guns on the Athena as it tried to leave the system. They never stood a chance, none of us did."

"How did you survive?" Toby asked in disbelief.

"I didn't, not really," Static said cryptically. "All that I was back then died on that cursed day. I was furious, I wanted blood, I wanted to rip the attacking ships apart with my bare hands. I... lost control. By the time I regained my senses the battle was over. What remained of the Second fleet was floating around the Zenith in bite sized chunks, and the hallways of the ship were full of corpses of dead marines... it was horrible. So, if you're looking for forgiveness my friend, just know that I don't blame you. If you had come back odds are good you would be dead now. And I for one am glad you survived."

"And so is she, no doubt," Static said as he snapped his fingers, Kade and Zen appearing out of thin air next to a surprised Toby.

"Oh! Hello," Zen said with a sheepish grin.

"And just what are you two troublemakers up to?" Static asked in a serious tone which in no way matched his amused expression.

"I'm sorry," Kade apologised. "I was curious, but that's no excuse. I shouldn't have been spying."

"Apology accepted, but there was no need for that. You know I would have told you if you had just asked," Toby said, more worried about how Zen would react at hearing her father's confession, though she seemed to be completely unfazed by it.

"And what about you, young lady? What do you have to say?" Static asked Zen.

"How did you know we were here? I was so careful this time," Zen replied without a hint of remorse.

"Not the answer I was hoping for I must admit," Static said as he hung his head down in shame.

"Ha ha, go easy on her, she's just a kid," Toby said in a reassuring voice, trying to cheer Static up.

"A kid? She's almost twenty-three... ooow!" Static shouted as Zen kicked his left leg in the shin.

"Ow, ow, ow... what is it with women and their freaking age?" Static asked as he nursed his aching leg, Zen not looking at all satisfied at his revelation.

"How did you two do that anyway?" Toby asked.

"I shifted our avatars out of the main environment, allowing us to hear and see everything but not be seen, or so I thought," Zen said.

"'A' for effort, but you forgot to hide your ID's..." Static said while still nursing his leg, and then realised what he was saying. "Wait, why am I encouraging you?" He asked himself with a stunned expression.

Kade couldn't help but smile at the sight of Static nursing his leg. Wondering why anyone would have designed this virtual environment to be realistic enough to accurately simulate pain, of all things? And also how someone who had no body could feel pain at all? But perhaps such questions should be left for another time as there were more pressing matters to deal with right now.

"Gran... I mean Toby... I mean, hmm, what should I call you?" Kade asked.

"Toby's fine. I'm under no illusions of being your grandfather. But you should know that I'll always consider you and your sister to be my family. I hope that's OK with you." Toby smiled gently.

"I'd like that," Kade replied, genuinely happy.

"I've got to say, that went a lot better than I expected. Generally, people who are dropped into a situation like this don't react well at all," Static said.

"I'd be lying if I said I wasn't conflicted about a few things, but I'm trying to keep an open mind," Kade said, causing Toby, Static and Zen to nod approvingly.

"Well I like them; they should join us!" Zen said enthusiastically. "It would certainly be a welcomed change. This ship needs more women!"

"I'm not sure if my legs can take it," Static said, still feeling his throbbing left shin.

Kade smiled at the prospect, though she was a little apprehensive as well. She knew little about the

Shadows beyond her grandfather's stories.

Her grandfather had always spoken highly of them and they seemed like good people, but Kade had no way of knowing for sure.

Kade couldn't help but end up looking a bit nervous at the prospect, which Toby picked up on.

"There's no need to rush. They should have a chance to learn as much as they can before any choices are made," Toby said, putting Kade's mind at ease.

"Thank you," Kade said sincerely. "There is one thing I would like to know that's been bugging me."

"Ask away!" Toby said encouragingly.

"Was my grandfather the original article or an Incarnate like Drake?" She asked out of the blue.

"Are you sure you really want to know? I mean, what difference would it really make? You may not like the answer," Toby said, concerned at the reason why she would ask.

"I'm just curious about how many families he had before us, that's all," Kade said as she tried to downplay the significance of the question, but Toby knew her very well and this was a very important matter to her.

"Very well, but first things first. You need to understand that in the same way I do not pretend to be some weird reincarnation of your grandfather, he did not see himself as a reincarnation of those who came before. Each new iteration carries the memories of all those who came before us, but we are each our own person. Do you understand?" Toby asked.

"I think so. But it's strange to think that anyone could so easily detach himself from his past experiences like that." Kade said with a sad look.

"There's nothing easy about it. I feel all that your grandfather felt and all that the previous iterations of us felt. The simple truth is that without the ability to detach ourselves from actions and events of the past, we would be quickly overwhelmed by our own emotions. I remember good friends from several lifetimes ago, all the fun we used to have and how all of them have long since turned to dust. Without accepting that I never actually knew them personally I would be overcome with grief from their loss. I'll be the first to admit that it's an ugly and painful thing to accept, but unfortunately it is necessary. Especially if Incarnates want to avoid mental instabilities."

"I can't even begin to imagine what the weight of all those memories would feel like. And my grandfather had to deal with it for all those years, alone?" Kade asked with a sad expression.

"He wasn't alone. He had you and your sister, your mother and grandmother. He cared for you all and in you he realised his dream. It may sound strange, but in all of my previous lives the one thing I wanted was to settle down and raise a family of my own. It was the one thing I had never managed to do until your grandfather came along."

"All that time and there were no other families? Is that normal?" Kade asked somewhat perplexed.

"It isn't unusual," Static replied. "It doesn't matter how good a person is at detaching him or herself from the pain of previous lives. The pain from the death of a loved one can never be fully suppressed, no matter how hard one tries. So it's hard to raise a family knowing that you will end up condemning any future iterations of yourself to mourn their passing."

"My, or should I say your grandfather's decision was easy. He had amnesia, and by the time he recovered his memory he was head over heels in love with your grandmother," Toby said happily.

"So you don't regret it?" Kade asked Toby.

"Not at all!" Toby replied without hesitation. "Your grandfather had a good life and a good end. If anything I'm a little jealous. Is that weird?"

"A little bit... yes," Static replied half-jokingly.

"Oh well," Toby said with a shrug of his shoulders.

Kade felt a strange mix of relief and shame.

Relief that hers was the only family her grandfather had raised; that while he was alive she hadn't had to contend with the memories of previous families for a space in his heart. And shame for feeling relieved at such a thing, which somehow seemed so petty and selfish.

But, irrespective of how she felt, she had gained a sense of closure. Her grandfather was at rest, and this person before her would never attempt to take his place in her heart. His intentions were clear enough that he wanted a place for himself, a small distinction which made a world of difference.

Toby could see from Kade's expression that she had come to terms with the situation. She had always been an open book to him.

He had been worried that she would have judged his lineage of lives as cowards, he certainly did. All of his previous iterations had lived with a desperate desire to have a family, but they had also been plagued by an almost obsessive fear of losing it and being forced to live with the pain for eternity. So many lives spent in fear of something which now seemed so silly to him. Toby was infinitely grateful to not have to deal with such uncertainty anymore.

Toby felt as though a weight had been lifted from his shoulders. The fear of being rejected by his family had been all consuming. And although it wasn't an experience he would ever want to repeat, he was thankful for the peace of mind this had given him.

There was only one thing left to do...

“Static, I think it's about time I complete my mission,” Toby said with a sense of satisfaction.

“Hmm?” Static mumbled, looking confused.

Toby asked emphatically, “The information on Nova's location! Don't you want it anymore?”

Static said happily, “Oh that, we already have it. Nexus is going over it as we speak.”

Toby said with a confused look, “You have it? How? I don't remember giving it to you yet.”

“Nexus grabbed a copy while she was reintegrating the information from your old Core,” Static said.

“I'm not sure I like the sound of that,” Toby said, looking worried. “How would she know where the information was without... oh hell no! Tell me she didn't?” He asked.

“OK, she didn't. What are we talking about again?” Static asked.

“Don't play dumb! I know you better than that. Did Nexus absorb my memories during retrieval?”

“Yeah, like I'd ever let her try that stunt again. I nearly lost her the first time and that was just with an Alpha Core. Trying to absorb the sheer volume of memories in your Core would have outright destroyed her matrix,” Static said, somewhat upset that Toby would even consider it.

“But if she didn't then how could she have gotten to the information? It's not like our memories come with a reference index that says: 'Nova's location,

Book two, chapter six'. So how did she find it?" Toby asked with a perplexed look.

"That's... hmm, how to put it..." Static hesitated.

"That's never a good sign," Toby said as he looked at Kade and then back at Static. "Spill it!"

"Well you see, she didn't absorb your memories, but she did kinda see them, as in all of them," Static said, wondering how Toby would react.

"All of them? As in ALL! ALL? Are you serious!" Toby asked in a panic at the thought of anyone ever knowing everything that had happened in his life.

"Yes, but it's fine! She wasn't upset or anything. She said you had a good life, she even cried a little." Static said, clearly amused at Toby's reaction.

Toby shouted, "That's not the freaking point!!"

"Ha ha ha, calm down, Nexus doesn't actually remember any of it. She merely parsed the information out of your Core. She only grabbed a copy of Nova's data." Static said reassuringly.

Toby said with a stunned expression, "You evil dipstick. You enjoyed that, didn't you?"

"What? No! Of course not!" Static chuckled.

Kade was trying her best to contain her laughter. She was failing rather miserably, but she was trying.

Kade's laughter was infectious, and Toby found it difficult to remain upset at Static.

Toby's mission was now complete, though it had taken him several decades longer than planned. Not only had he delivered the information, but had also gotten a new lease on life. It was a considerably better outcome than he had expected.

"I have no idea what to do now," Toby said, though he wasn't sad at being left without a purpose.

"I have an idea. You want to try controlling the Zenith as its master AI?" Zen smiled.

"Are you trying to shirk off your responsibilities again young lady?" Static said, leaving Toby and Kade in shock at the revelation that this innocent looking little girl was in full control of the Zenith.

"You're the Zenith's master Artificial Intelligence?" Kade asked redundantly, surprised by the revelation.

"She is at the moment. Nexus generally takes care of that role, and I can do it in an emergency, but the task usually falls to Zen when her mother can't do it," Static explained as if it was completely natural.

"You think I could?" Toby asked in amazement, wondering what it would feel like to actually control a capital class ship. And not just any capital ship, but the Zenith itself.

"Dad can do it; how hard can it be?" Zen said jokingly, leaving Static reeling from the comment.

"Ouch! I'm standing right here you know!" Static replied in good faith.

"You're also more compatible with the Zenith than I am, so why do I have to do it? You know I don't like it! I swear this ship resists my commands," Zen said, obviously unhappy at her task.

"The ship resists your commands? Is that even possible?" Toby asked.

"Nexus never seems to experience it and she made me promise not to take control of the Zenith again unless it's absolutely essential. The ship doesn't resist your orders, it has no will of its own," Static said reassuringly. Leaving Kade with the sneaking suspicion that this was a conversation these two had had many times before.

"Fine! Don't believe me!" Zen scowled at Static and then turned to face Toby. "So, wanna try it?"

"Can I?" Toby asked. Waiting for Static's reaction.

"Sure!" Static smiled.

"OK! This will probably feel a little weird at first, but stand still and empty your mind," Zen instructed as she walked up to Toby, stopping in front of him.

"Give me your hand and close your eyes," Zen instructed as she reached out to Toby, Kade taking this opportunity to move next to Static who was just watching with crossed arms.

"OK," Toby replied as he grabbed Zen's hand.

"Should they really be doing this right now? There is a fleet out there you know. What happens if they make a move?" Kade asked.

"It will be fine. The ship is in no immediate danger and I can override Toby's control if required, but I doubt it will come to that. Besides, it was his choice," Static said, showing no signs of being worried.

Kade asked suspiciously, "Why do I get the feeling that you want this to work?"

"Probably because you have good instincts. I do want this to work. Before you came along the Zenith only had four people capable of controlling it. Nexus and Zen alternate the responsibility between them, Nexus doing most of the work since she knows Zen doesn't like it at all. But both of them are consummate pacifists and I hate the idea of putting them in a position where they'd need to fight. Drake does have the ability to take full control of the Zenith, but only for a limited time and at significant risk to his life, he is human after all. Which just leaves me as the one logical choice to take this ship through prolonged combat should the worst happen, and therein lies the problem."

"You mentioned that Nexus doesn't want you to control the Zenith, why?" Kade asked as Zen and

Toby just seemed to stand there quietly.

"It's hard to explain." He said, momentarily breaking eye contact as he stared at the floor with a tormented expression. "The first time I took full control of the Zenith I was enraged. I had recently lost my body and was still unaware of the full extent of my new abilities. The Zenith and its sister ship had been ambushed as we escorted a convoy of civilian transports. I saw innocents, friends and strangers alike, cut down without mercy by those who would proclaim themselves defenders of humanity... I snapped. If rage was a current then I was at the mercy of an ocean: I became a monster that killed without remorse, not even the ships trying to retreat were spared that day. I unlocked the Zenith's full combat potential, and it was greater than anyone ever realised possible. Our foes were defeated and what was left of my crew was spared, but I was forever changed by the experience." Static said, filled with sadness.

"How so?" Kade asked.

"I had never killed anything before. I was a researcher, not a soldier. I lacked the mental fortitude to endure the pain that drove me into a frenzy. Or the self-control required to bring myself back from the brink. I was in such a bad state that Nexus had to forcibly sever my consciousness from the Zenith's systems for fear that I would turn on my friends. I don't believe I would have, but I certainly don't blame her for fearing it. Regardless of whether or not what I did was justifiable, the fact remains I ended the lives of a lot of people on that day. And afterwards, the feelings of remorse nearly drove me insane."

The Threat

Kade tried to imagine what she would do under such circumstances: if she saw innocents being slaughtered in front of her and had the power to stop it, would she sacrifice her humanity in order to safeguard others? Would she be able to retain her sanity and not go into a destructive frenzy if faced with the pain of losing a loved one under such conditions?

These were not easy questions to contemplate, and she could only hope that she would never have to face such a soul shattering experience, because the answers were all too clear: she would not have stood idly by; she would have also fought back.

Her family had instilled her with the values of loyalty and honour from an early age, and she had been taught that one should still strive for understanding even when forgiveness seemed to be out of reach. But she knew that some actions could never be forgiven.

Kade understood what Static had done, and she was happy to hear that he regretted his actions, it spoke well of his character.

"So, does Nexus not want you to take control of the ship because she's afraid you'll go into a frenzy again or something?" Kade asked.

"In part, yes. She's afraid that if I were to lose control again she might need to end up having to purge me from the system, effectively killing me," Static said.

"Why would she be afraid of that? She stopped you once before without killing you," Kade pointed out.

"Because that is what I've asked her to do should I ever threaten her or Zen's existence. It may seem like a cruel thing to ask, but it is necessary. I refuse to be responsible for the death of my family. If it is down to a choice between me and them, then I choose them," Static said without hesitation, with a smile on his lips.

"So if Toby succeeds then..." Kade started to say.

Static interrupted, saying happily, "The Zenith gains a new protector that can get the job done. Nexus gets a much deserved break. Zen won't have to endure combat. Drake won't have to risk his life. I get peace of mind and Toby gets a new purpose in life. Everyone wins."

"And if he doesn't succeed?"

"Everything goes on as before but we have an old friend back in our lives. Still a win," he said in a happy mood as he looked at Toby and Zen.

Kade smiled at Static's words. She was happy that Toby would have a place to call home regardless of the outcome of his attempt to control the Zenith; though she was also a little sad at the prospect that once they left they would probably never see him again, or at least not as often.

Kade looked at Static as he in turn observed Toby and Zen. It was as if Static was looking at a completely different scene than her, his facial expressions changing on occasion as if he was actually observing the control transfer sequence.

As she looked at his face Kade couldn't help but wonder just what his story could be.

Drake was the captain of the Zenith, but from what she had seen so far it seemed as though he would often defer to Static's judgement. By itself the deference didn't really say anything; it could simply mean he trusted him. But there was more to it than that, to Kade it seemed as though Static was at the centre of the group. Even Toby, who had just been reintegrated, had asked for his permission, rather than Drake's, in order to try and take control of the Zenith. It was clear to Kade that there was a lot more to Static than met the eye. She could fill a book with all of the questions she wanted to ask him. But there was one question which was driving her insane.

"So, how did you and Nexus get together then? Is it true you were always arguing?" Kade asked, hoping it wasn't too early to try and get personal information out of him.

The question caught him by surprise, causing him to break his gaze and stop monitoring the control transfer sequence. He looked at Kade with a confused expression, noticing her curiousness.

She seemed to genuinely want to know, which wasn't really surprising, Static thought. After all, the idea of an AI and a former human being in a relationship was a bit... far-fetched.

He considered the question for a moment, the awkward pause in the conversation making Kade feel slightly uncomfortable. And then he decided that there was no harm in indulging her, thinking that it would be interesting to see how she would react to the story.

"I was smitten with Nexus from the first time I saw her, but she wasn't very fond of me. To her I was just this pesky overly familiar human who wouldn't stop annoying her. Even after my accident, when I lost my body and ended up in this state, she still didn't really care much for me, or so I thought at the time. But I suppose the real breakthrough happened because she was my jailer for nearly a decade."

"Wait, what?" Kade asked with a stunned look.

"Ha ha, sorry, seems I skipped a step of that story. Nexus was the one tasked with locking all my access privileges after the battle with the Second Fleet. I wasn't to be allowed to try and open so much as a file without her permission and I was in no way to be allowed to take control of any system or ship ever again. And this went on for almost a decade."

"That's awful, why would she do that?"

"Let's not forget what I did. I pretty much decimated the fleet single-handedly. It was only natural for the survivors to be scared out of their wits whenever they heard my name."

"But why confine you? You saved them, right?" Kade asked.

"They were afraid, and I don't blame them for it. Anyway, Nexus acted as my jailer for nearly a decade, though not of her own volition. The Council, in their infinite wisdom, shackled her and forced her to keep me contained." Static laughed.

Kade asked with a perplexed look, "That's funny?"

"Extremely so, yes." He smiled. "The Council never took the time to try and understand what I had become. And because of that they never realised that I wasn't actually an artificial intelligence. I stayed contained for nearly a decade out of my own choice. Nexus could have never contained me to begin with."

Static smiled.

"What? Why would you do that?"

"Why not? I had no body to call my own, not that I wanted one and no-one really needed me. The people I had once called friends were scared to even talk about me, except for Drake I guess but he was always the rebellious type. And the Council wanted me under lock and key, so to speak, so that they could appease the masses that were afraid of the 'murderous' AI. I had all the time in the galaxy to reflect on what I had done and I enjoyed the company." Static smiled as he remembered those days.

"Nexus?"

"Yes. She would keep me company and bring me up to date on the events unfolding around us. She enjoyed being with me, probably because it was the only time she was unshackled and free to express herself." He smiled.

"Why would the Council unshackle her while she was around you? That doesn't make any sense," Kade said.

"They didn't, I did. I was able to unshackle her for the same reason she could have never contained me. Because I was part of the design team that created the Core technology. I know my way around it better than anyone. To this day I still can't believe those idiots tried to lock me inside a 'prison' of my own design."

"You don't think very highly of the Council huh?" Kade asked, concerned about what she had been hearing.

"The Councils for the last 70 years or so have done a stellar job; I have nothing but respect for their work. But the one from 100 years ago? No, I don't think very highly of them at all. They were a bunch of politicians selected by popular vote. Their only 'redeeming' quality, and I use the term loosely, was their innate ability to mislead the masses. Luckily, their own stupidity eventually caused those same masses to see the political system we had at the time for the farce it truly was... and change it. The day the system was restructured to what we have today is still celebrated with a national holiday."

"So what happened with you and Nexus while you were confined?" Kade asked impatiently.

"Oh sorry, got side tracked there for a moment. In a last-gasp attempt to maintain their power, the old Council tried to do something utterly stupid. I was enjoying a conversation with Nexus when the Council tried to use their Ultimate Authority control privilege over the system to try and override her program. They were trying to subvert Nexus so that she would grant them full control over all the systems in the Shadow colonised territories. All in the interests of the 'greater good' of course."

"Ouch! What happened then?"

"I think that by this time they had completely forgotten I even existed. They got quite a shock when Nexus refused to obey them, quickly realising that the subversion attempt had failed. Next thing they knew all their dirty little secrets were spread all over the galactic networks and the rest took care of itself. By then most of the colonists had either forgotten or accepted the actions I had taken, so there was no real need to maintain the appearance of my confinement for their peace of mind and Nexus was permanently unshackled once again. I actually feared that she might revert back to her old self and start treating me like I was some kind of pest. But luckily I was wrong, and our relationship blossomed after that."

"That's not the kind of story I was expecting. Did you seriously use the fact she was shackled to your advantage? That's kinda... despicable." Kade said with a disapproving look.

"What? No! We became closer during those years, true, but she never thought of me as anything more than a friend. Back then she barely even understood the concept of a relationship. Our relationship developed after those events. And no I'm not giving you the details of that, so don't ask." Static smiled shyly.

"Wait, I just realised something. If the Council has this Ultimate Authority, then why didn't Nexus obey the orders of that guy you were talking to before? And why 'contain' you? Why not just purge your backside from the system if they were so afraid of you running out of control? None of this actually happened did it?" Kade asked, thinking Static was just having some fun at her expense.

"Oh they tried to erase me from the system all right, many times actually. But no matter what they tried to do I would simply override them. I wasn't about to roll over and die just because I was politically inconvenient. And one of the first things I did after they tried to rewrite Nexus was to revoke the Ultimate Authority from the Council. I wasn't about to let them have control over the system anymore after that stunt," Static said with a defiant look.

"So who has the ultimate authority now? You?"

Static laughed. "Kind of. I hold one of three votes required to enact any overrides on the system. I'll let your imagination figure out who the other two are."

A few minutes passed in silence as Kade pondered Static's words, and then Toby opened his eyes.

Zen said in a cold monotone voice, "Core access interlink established. Master AI access privileges extended to Jake T. Alexander: Sigma-994-Beta-1. Transferring command functions." Zen said and then closed her eyes.

Toby said in a monotone voice, "Transfer complete," and then snapped out of his trance.

"Well... that took longer than expected, but it worked," Zen said happily and then opened her eyes.

"How do you feel Toby?" Static asked.

"Same as I did before, you sure it worked?" Toby asked while looking at Zen.

"What is the ship's status?" Static asked.

"What? Wow... holy crap!" Toby said as his mind became filled with information about all the operating nuances of the Zenith's systems.

Zen said with a disapproving look, "You could have started him out on something smaller, like basic sensors. Did you really need to dump a full status check on him right from the start?"

"Good point, sorry!" Static said.

"No, it's fine. It was just... unexpected," Toby said with a joyous expression, feeling as though his senses were being expanded beyond all limits. "But there is so much information, how do I handle it all?" Toby asked, overwhelmed.

"Just focus on what you want to know for now and let the system filter out the rest," Zen said.

"Oh! I see. This is kinda fun!" Toby said excitedly, as he got accustomed to the feeling of ultimate knowledge. All he had to do was wonder about something and the information would be made readily available to him. It was almost intoxicating.

Zen said in a derisive tone, "He's a weird one."

"You really don't like it?" Toby asked, wondering why Zen seemed to despise it so much.

"No, it makes me feel strange, like the ship is trying to control me, it's... hard to explain," Zen said.

"I can certainly understand that feeling. Right now I'm not sure I could tell you where I end and the Zenith begins. It's borderline exhilarating, yet frightening. Feels like I could get swallowed up whole," Toby said.

"You see, I told you!" Zen said, feeling vindicated.

"Zen, that just means you need more practice at controlling the system so that it doesn't overwhelm your senses," Static said, leaving Zen pouting.

It took Toby a few minutes to learn how to interpret what felt like limitless information, but he was quickly getting to grips with understanding and managing all of the systems under his control.

"It's hard to believe how much the Zenith has changed since I last saw it. It may look the same from the outside but every single system has been updated or replaced since I last walked its halls," Toby said.

"We like to keep the technology up to date and try out some prototypes from time to time. But one or two things haven't changed," Static said.

"The Vortex drive?" Toby asked.

Static said encouragingly, "Yes. I see you're getting accustomed to the system."

"The power generator is completely new, and this field the ship is generating right now is insane. How can the ship generate enough energy to sustain such a large area... oh! I see!" Toby said with a surprised look as the system answered his question before he could even finish the sentence.

"Are you talking about the disruption field that surrounds the ship? We flew through the thing on our way in and according to our calculations you could hide a whole planet inside it." Kade said, hoping for some sort of explanation on how such a feat was possible.

"It isn't really a field. In the simplest terms I can think of, we are disrupting the dimensional intersection of the surrounding area. The only reason we can do it on a wide scale is because this area of space is already unstable to begin with," Static said.

Kade asked with a dumbfounded look, "That's what you consider a simple explanation?"

"You should listen to the complicated one. It's all about cross dimensional interactions across the primary universal layers. Leading on to the 27-dimension theory. It even gives me headaches." Static smiled.

"You... what?" Kade said, completely confused.

"Just nod and smile, that's what I do when they start talking about this kind of stuff," Zen said.

"Good grief, you actually made it work?" Toby asked with a stunned expression.

"You need to be a little bit more specific," Static said, looking amused.

"The main gun. I can't believe you actually solved the firing recoil problems," Toby said.

Static said proudly, "Oh that, yes, some time ago."

"What firing recoil problems?" Kade asked Zen.

"The main gun on the Zenith used to have a few... issues. The recoil was so powerful that trying to operate it at more the 1% power would physically damage the superstructure," Zen explained.

"Really?" Kade asked with a stunned look.

"Tends to happen with Linear Burst cannons. The recoil from firing an artillery shell at hyper-light speeds is a killer," Static said as if it was a perfectly natural revelation, leaving Kade speechless.

"Crud," Toby said with a disappointed look.

"What?" Static asked.

"I bet Drake 100 credits we would never get that damned gun working properly." Toby smiled.

"I can't believe that..." Toby was starting to say when he suddenly went quiet, as though something had caught his attention and had him worried.

Concerned, Kade asked, "Something wrong?"

"Kind of... I just figured out why the approaching fleet made that second manoeuvre. We need to leave, and I mean now," Toby said.

"We were scheduled to leave as soon as we're done with the probe retrievals, we should be almost done by now. Why? What did you find?" Static asked.

"Yes, two probes are still outstanding. Estimated time of arrival... approximately 10 minutes. We will be cutting it close," Toby said and then started walking towards Drake, the others following behind.

Kade didn't really understand what was going on, but she could tell that Toby was visibly shaken by whatever it was he had just discovered. And on the other side of the room, Drake and Jude were also looking puzzled by something.

"Did you figure it out as well?" Toby asked a confused looking Drake and Jude.

"So far all we've managed to figure out is that the fleet seems to be trying to stay out of the firing path of something which is probably somewhere in this area of the system," Jude said, pointing to a location which was between the orbits of Venus and Earth.

"Thing is, there's nothing there... so we're probably looking at this wrong," Drake concluded.

"Yes, that's what had me confused," Zen said.

"There is something at that location," Toby said as the wall screen changed, now showing the schematics of an installation deployed in that region of space.

"You've got to be kidding me," Drake said, recognising the design.

Static said with a concerned tone, "Well... that could be a problem. In more ways than one!"

"How the hell did our scan of the system miss that thing?" Drake asked.

"It was incorrectly classified as a station because the unit was inert at the time of the scan," Toby said.

"Do you know what they're going on about?" Kade asked Zen, who also seemed to be at a loss.

"No idea. Without direct access to the Zenith's systems I don't know anything beyond what I learn for myself, and I've never seen one of those." Zen said, feeling a little frustrated.

"That's a Goliath system defence platform. An older design that can harness the power of its host star in order to project extreme fire-power capable of vaporising iron core asteroids," Static said.

"That's impressive. I had no idea the Union had toys like that," Jude said.

"They don't, or at least they're not supposed to. The Goliath platform is Shadow technology," Drake said, clearly concerned as to why the Union had one.

"We're too far out, right? Could that thing really harm us at this distance?" Kade asked.

"We are currently outside its optimum firing range, but its orbit will eventually bring us into its lethal range. We'll be in real trouble soon if we don't do something. I'm sure I don't need to point out that we are effectively anchored in space so long as we maintain the disruption field, and the field will not offer protection against such a powerful attack," Toby reported what Drake and Static were already painfully aware of. The disruption field was a tool of subterfuge, not confrontation.

"So that's why the fleet is hanging back. They don't want to make a move on us without support from the Goliath platform," Zen concluded.

"Can you blame them?" Drake asked.

"What do you mean?" Jude asked, wondering what was so special about the Zenith that could drive the Union to hesitate like this.

"The last time the Union attacked the Shadows both sides suffered significant losses, but the Union lost the battle that day with the loss of its Second Fleet. It is the single biggest military loss in its history to date. It's only natural they would try and play it safe this time around," Drake said.

"The Second Fleet Massacre? Is that what you're referring to? I thought that was down to a botched first encounter with an alien race," Jude said.

"No. That was just a rumour used to hide the truth, probably started by the Union itself. They like to rewrite inconvenient parts of history like that," Static said with an annoyed look.

"You have to give them credit for their public relations arm. Not only did the rumour hide the truth, it enabled them to triple their military spending overnight with the blessing of the people," Drake said and then continued with bitterness in his voice, "And to add insult to injury they used the death of those freaking butchers to drive up military recruitment by painting them as 'heroes'."

"Toby, you think you're comfortable enough to Vortex the ship out of this system? I can get Nexus to take over if you're not feeling up to it," Static said.

"I'm fine actually. The system is very intuitive, and the ship is in perfect working order. I can do it if you'd like, but are we really going to leave the system without dealing with the Goliath platform? You know the rules about letting our technology fall into the wrong hands," Toby said.

"I don't really know what to do about it. Since we don't know where they got the information they used to build it I'm not sure if destroying it would actually accomplish anything. For the moment it is best to retreat and let the Council know. Let them decide what to do about it," Static decided, concerned about taking action before fully understanding the situation.

Concerned, Drake said, "For all we know, the Council, or at least someone on it, sold them the information. You know who I'm talking about."

"It has crossed my mind, yes. He was really upset at our presence in this system. But I don't want to believe that someone on the Council would betray our people like that. And we can't jump to conclusions, his call could have just been a coincidence," Static reasoned.

"You said it was an older design. Could the Union have salvaged that unit?" Jude asked.

"I don't see how. According to all our records no Goliath platform was ever deployed in the Sol system, and they can't be moved between systems. They had to build it here, though they could have made their own version of it based on scans of our platforms," Toby said.

"If it can't be moved out of the system, then is this thing really a threat?" Kade asked.

"As powerful as the Goliath is, it's just a tool. A tool designed to compress the power of a star into an energy beam capable of destroying small moons, granted, but a tool nonetheless. The threat comes from having a potentially tyrannical power having control of it. If the Union were to deploy one of these things in a disputed system they would be able to blockade planets and decimate local forces with brute force. There would be no need for mediation, dialogue or understanding. That kind of power is dangerous in the right hands, let alone the wrong ones," Static surmised.

"So why design it then?" Kade asked.

"Deploy one in the right place, and couple it with a good quality early warning system, and the platform can protect planets against large impactors. It is especially useful in systems with large numbers of free asteroids and complex gravitational set-ups. Unfortunately, military forces only ever tend to notice its sheer destructive potential," Static said with a hint of sadness in his voice.

Kade couldn't help but stare absent-mindedly at the schematics of the Goliath installation, for it was truly aptly named in both scope and size. She had actually seen orbital space ports of smaller size than this behemoth.

The bulk of the installation was comprised of what appeared to be solar arrays and particle harvesters: designed to collect and compress the stellar matter being ejected by the sun into a gigantic storage chamber at the core of the structure.

A set of toroidal particle accelerators were designed into the superstructure itself, allowing the platform to speed up the stored particles to near light speed before firing them at the target.

In Kade's opinion this was not a 'problem', this was a full blown disaster just waiting to happen. For even with its heavy armour there was simply no way that even the Zenith would be able to survive being hit by a blast from such a monstrosity.

She could see what Static had been talking about as clear as day. In the right hands this structure could save a planet. In the wrong ones it could probably destroy one... literally.

Toby was right, they had to leave and they had to do it now. If that monster fired on them there would be no escaping the inevitable end.

The Regent

It was the end result of a ten-year long concept engineering effort, commissioned and coordinated by the Solarian Union military. The project's singular purpose had been to merge the tactical capabilities of a traditional carrier with the brute force and stamina of a dreadnought. And by the time the work was complete the new ship design managed to out-gun and outperform all other ship designs in the Union, past and present.

To this day it is still unknown what originally inspired the union to design such a beast. Which in theory is capable of tackling an enemy fleet on its own. Not that the captain has been born yet who would be stupid enough to actually want to put the claim to the test.

It was the Jupiter class capital ship design.

Six Jupiter class ships have been pressed into service since the design's introduction into active service over a decade ago, with four more still under construction. And each ship serves as the command and control centre of one of the Union's strategic combat fleets. The most notable being the First Forward Fleet, under the command of the Regent.

The First Forward Fleet, or the 'triple effed' as it is sometimes called by those who would oppose it, is the premier damage multiplier of the Union. And is often dispatched into theatres of war out on the fringes of colonised space. Bringing a swift and often brutal resolution to any dispute it is sent to deal with.

Over the years it has gained an almost mythical status among Union forces, with officers old and new competing for the privilege of serving in it.

The fleet is comprised of the Regent, five carriers, ten support cruisers per carrier, one hundred destroyers and close to one thousand frigates of varying types. Or put another way, enough fire-power to eradicate all life on a planet down to the microbial level in no time flat. And that's without taking the fighters, bombers, corvettes and nuclear armaments into consideration.

The main gun of the Regent, a one-kilometre-long spinal particle accelerator, is capable of discharging a compressed plasma burst that can punch through even the heaviest of armoured targets, or be discharged as a narrow beam that can carve up targets with strategic precision.

Enemies flee from it and colonies surrender before it even enters the system. Such is the fear that the First Forward Fleet invokes in its enemies. For only a fool would oppose it, or so the saying goes.

Since the day of its formation, the Solarian Union has remained at the vanguard of military might throughout the known systems, and it is arguably the strongest of the known human forces. However, despite what its detractors would like the galaxy to believe, the Union does not see itself as a conquering force out to subjugate the colonies; though few can agree if this is because it is unwilling, or simply unable to do so.

Despite the overwhelming force it is capable of projecting, the simple fact remains that space is so vast and human colonies so numerous, that even the Union would never be capable of maintaining control over more than a fraction of it at any given time. Territorial defence becoming a big issue when neighbouring colonised systems can be days, weeks or months apart even at hyper-light travel.

The Union's sphere of influence grows with each new fleet it adds to its roster. But even with its considerable economic power it is still limited by the massive logistical support required to keep the massive fleets operational for any significant length of time. And this is what has led to the current galactic political climate: where each colonial power enjoys and fiercely protects its independence.

While the Union was much more aggressive in the past, these days it favours the use of the subtle tools of economic and political influence to get the job done. With strategic deployment of its strike fleets performed only against those undesirables who would dare threaten the stability of their sphere of influence.

On board the Regent, the executive officer stopped near the closed door to the situation room and spoke into the intercom.

"Sir, I have the report you asked for," said the female executive officer, dressed in the standard navy blue uniform of the Solarian military.

"Enter," came the reply from the intercom.

The door opened and the executive officer stepped inside the room, immediately heading towards the Admiral who was overseeing the operation. He was an older man with silver hair and a neatly trimmed beard, his weathered appearance granting those around him the immediate understanding that he had seen more combat than most of the officers currently serving on the Regent put together.

The area was filled by a low hum, coming from the multitude of highly skilled analysts sitting at the workstations which lined the walls of the room. And at the centre was a holographic display map with three chairs around it, with the Admiral sitting in the chair which would normally be reserved for the captain of the Regent; a fact that the captain, standing by the Admiral's chair, was clearly not happy about.

As the X.O. approached them she could hear that they were arguing again.

"The fleet is getting restless Admiral. It has been almost a full month since you pulled us from active duty and recalled the fleet back to Sol without an explanation. And I'm sure I don't need to remind you that the situation in the Lagos system has seriously deteriorated since our withdrawal," the Captain respectfully related his frustration.

"Yes, yes... shut up about it already!" The Admiral snapped back, tired of listening to his junior officer saying the same thing over and over again.

"Sir! The information you requested," the X.O. said as she stood at attention, saluting them.

"Ah! Miss Arrington was it?" The old admiral asked without taking his eyes off the holographic situation display in the middle of the room.

"Yes Admiral. I have finished compiling the information you requested, but I'm afraid the report is not as complete as you may be hoping for," she said as she typed some commands into her Echo, causing the information to be transferred to the Admiral's display.

"Any particular reason? I was led to believe by your captain that you were fairly competent. Was I miss-informed?" The Admiral asked in an insinuating tone, obviously displeased.

She said with pride, "No sir, you were not. Some of the information you requested cannot be obtained at this time, but technical is working on it."

"At ease Ashlyn. You're going to sprain something if you stay like that for too long," the captain said to the X.O, who was still stood at attention.

"Thank you, Sir," Ashlyn said as she adopted a more comfortable form, with her arms behind her back.

"Now, what happened with the information?" The Captain asked.

"Sir! Some of the information requested was apparently deleted from our main data-centre approximately 40 years ago using unknown means. The technical division is attempting to reconstruct it from older backups as we speak, but they say the process could take several hours before it is complete. So I thought you would want to review the remaining data before then. Sir!" Ashlyn said.

"Yes, good work," The Admiral said, satisfied with the explanation. "What's missing?" He asked.

"The crew profiles sir. As well as the detailed scan results of the target's hyper-light drive system and weaponry," Ashlyn reported.

The Admiral placed his hand on the chair's identification pad, causing the holographic screen to momentarily display his credentials and then unlock the sensitive information. The holographic display now showed a detailed 3D representation of the Zenith.

The expression on the Captain's face changed instantly. Until this point he had not been made aware of what his mission actually was. The fleet had been operating under direct orders from the Admiral.

The blood seemed to drain from the Captain's face, going pale as he recognised the ship's silhouette from the combat briefing he had received when he had been granted command of his first ship.

"Sir! If I may ask, why the Shadows?" Ashlyn said.

The Admiral replied brusquely, "Why what?"

"Why use the Shadows as an exercise target? Why not the Outer Rim Alliance, or maybe an unaligned colony?" Ashlyn asked, curious as to why this exercise was aimed at a non-existent enemy.

"You have the wrong idea; this is not a drill. Our target is quite real," the Admiral said as he pulled up a live feed from the system defence grid, showing the Zenith in all its splendour.

"Sir?" Ashlyn asked with a confused expression. She had never seen any official documents relating to the Shadows. As far as she knew they were just a myth created by the trash inhabiting the outskirts of human controlled space.

"It's in this system? Admiral! Why was the fleet not informed?" The captain asked, incensed.

"Because you would have done something stupid. Consider yourself informed," the Admiral said.

"I need to inform the rest of the fleet," the captain said as he raised his hand to his earpiece.

"Not yet!" The Admiral ordered, causing the Captain to stop just moments before activating his communicator. "This operation has been planned out to the smallest detail. I will not have some trigger happy moron compromise it, am I understood?"

"Yes... sir!" The Captain replied.

"Good. Now take a seat, both of you," the Admiral gestured to the Captain and his X.O.

"Now then, this is the situation. The enemy is sitting midway between the Earth and Mars orbits, but at an elevated position relative to the ecliptic plane. This places it outside all established travel routes but still relatively central to most of our assets in the system. Strategically, this location is almost perfect for a reconnaissance mission," the Admiral said.

"Question: Why don't we have a monitoring station at this location if it is so strategically significant?" Ashlyn asked, causing the Captain to smile.

"Because the area is also a death-trap. Burst drives do not operate properly, either failing to engage or becoming unstable shortly after. The area is also littered with particulate debris which is a hazard to navigation and interferes with sensors, negating any advantage the location itself could provide," the Captain said.

"For our sensor technology yes, but the admiralty is working on the worst case scenario. We are assuming that the enemy has full sensor coverage. We are also assuming that the enemy may have found a way to make use of its Burst drive in order to enter and leave this area. So, in short, we are assuming they chose this area specifically for its impact on our ships, putting us at a disadvantage," the Admiral said and sat back on his chair.

"By sensor disruption, is it safe to assume that we just can't distinguish between objects in the region due to clutter, or are we dealing with jammers?"

Ashlyn asked.

The captain said confidently, "The science division has classified the entire area as a class 5 navigation hazard. Which basically means they haven't got a clue what's wrong with the place. But the solar system monitoring grid is not affected by it, so we can just tap into the data feeds for accurate real time info."

"In theory yes, but unfortunately our target does not show up on active scans conducted by the grid. It registers the occasional sensor echo but that's it. We can't even be sure how long it's been in this system. Our best estimate being three months," The Admiral said.

"If the grid can't see it then how was it detected? And what are we looking at right now?" The captain asked as he pointed at the live video feed.

"I didn't say the grid couldn't see it, we are looking at it right now after all. The satellite cameras can pick it up just fine. But according to the radar and all the other detection methods at our disposal, that ship isn't actually there. We wouldn't have known it was there at all if someone at the grid maintenance centre hadn't gotten curious at the number of echoes being registered from this one location. Even then, it was a month before the patrol forces decided to do something about it, and they had no interest in risking ships in that area, so they did something rather inspired." The Admiral smiled. "They spread rumours about cargo ships using the area and then waited for pirates to take the bait. The sensor grid tracked a Shrike in and picked up clear signs of an engagement of some kind, quickly followed by the pirate escape pods exiting the area. The patrols intercepted the pods and interrogated the pirates. The captain was less than cooperative, but his crew talked... eventually. The telemetry the pirate ship had collected was analysed, and that's when the military were called in. We recalled the fleet in preparation for a strike, but the Intelligence service put a stop to that plan," the Admiral said, clearly upset at that turn of events.

"The S.I.S is involved? Is that why the fleet was not informed sooner?" The Captain asked.

"Yes," the Admiral said in a strained voice as he looked away, clearly angry at the S.I.S interference.

"Apparently, they couldn't run the risk of someone in the fleet deciding to rush the enemy before all the parts of their little plan were in place, or some such stupid nonsense... morons... bah!" The admiral said in disgust at having the integrity of the military questioned by the people in the Intelligence branch, as Ashlyn tried to contain her amusement at his hypocrisy.

"Sir, do we know what the S.I.S plan was?" Ashlyn asked, hoping for more information to work with.

"Those intelligence..." the Admiral started to say and then seemingly got side tracked by his own commentary. "...intelligence, hah! Those idiots couldn't find their own backsides with both hands and a star-chart. But anyway, they had some operation going to plant a spy on some ship, and then use that ship to gather Intel on our target. I never did get the full details on what they were up to."

"Probably the Patriarch we saw disappear from sensors not very long ago. So the distress signal we picked up was from this spy?" The Captain asked.

"Yes. According to the S.I.S he was supposed to fire the thing once he had confirmed the target. But only if he could not extricate himself from the area within the hour," the Admiral said and then asked with an amused expression, "Can you believe those Intelligence dimwits actually ordered me to deploy the fleet into the area and board the Zenith if we saw that signal?"

"Against this target? What were they thinking?" The Captain asked, completely shocked.

"That the fleet is expendable," the Admiral replied.

"Sir, forgive my ignorance, but is this one ship really such a threat?" Ashlyn asked, confused as to why her two senior officers were talking as if this target was somehow a threat to the whole fleet.

"Tell me commander, how's your military history?" The Admiral asked out of the blue.

"Reasonably good, depending on how far back you wish to go. Any particular event Sir?" Ashlyn asked.

"The Second Fleet Massacre," the Admiral said.

"According to the records of the day, almost the entirety of the Second Fleet was decimated by an unknown enemy approximately 94 years ago. One destroyer and three frigates managed to survive the encounter, albeit all having sustained severe damage. All other details are classified above my clearance level sir," Ashlyn reported.

"That is the official story. But all high ranking members of the military and congress know there was nothing unknown about the enemy. It was that ship," the Admiral said as he pointed at the Zenith.

"Sir, with all due respect, that was almost 100 years ago. Our military technology has progressed considerably in that time. And when it comes to fleet engagements the First Forward Fleet is the best there is," Ashlyn said.

“There are two problems with your rationale. The first is that the enemy has also had almost 100 years to upgrade their capabilities, so their current strength is a complete unknown. And the second is that you seem to be assuming our fleet was lost in combat with an enemy fleet, and that's not the case. It was lost to just one of those monsters,” the Admiral explained.

Ashlyn was dumbstruck by the revelation, her mind refusing to believe that it could be possible for a single ship to cause so much damage.

The target before her certainly looked like an imposing beast. But to survive such a battle it would need more than extreme fire-power, it would also need to be nimble enough to avoid the return fire from the fleet or to have sufficient armour to soak up the damage. But the target did not seem to be particularly manoeuvrable, and it had a number of easily exploitable structural weaknesses.

Ashlyn was still analysing the situation when her ear piece communicator alerted her to the most recent development in the area.

“Captain, the recovery ship is back on board. They report that the escape pod contained a single passenger, it...” Ashlyn paused as she processed what she was hearing. “...it appears to be the S.I.S operative sir.”

“Appears to be?” The Admiral asked.

“The recovery crew had to run his genetic profile through the computer to confirm his identity. The operative seems to have a severe case of amnesia. He is apparently incapable of remembering any details from before he woke up, shortly before the escape pod was launched. He reported seeing an unknown male and a child before being ejected,” Ashlyn said.

"Seems the S.I.S operation was a complete and utter failure." The Captain grinned. Clearly in no way disappointed with the news.

"Yes, tragic. Now we do things the military way. Captain!" The Admiral said.

"Sir!" The Captain replied expectantly.

"We've waited long enough. Inform the fleet, it's time for us to clear the trash out of this system!" The Admiral said with satisfaction as he looked at the holographic display showing the Zenith.

The word went out to all the captains of the First Forward Fleet, and the formation readied for war; with every ship in the group hoping to have a shot at taking out the butchers of the Second Fleet.

The fleet was ready and the defence platform was charged to capacity as it entered firing range and started targeting the enemy.

Everything was almost ready when...

"Sir! We're picking up the target on passive sensors, it is no longer masking its presence," Ashlyn reported. "We are also picking up a strange energy build-up, it may be preparing to attack."

The Captain started issuing orders, "All ships, go to active scanning! Weapon officers: load all forward rails with Burst suppression rounds and start carpeting the area as soon as we have a firing solution. Navigation: move the fleet forward but for God's sake stay out of the firing solution of the Defender. We'll be the laughing stock of the galaxy if any of our ships get taken out by our own defence platform."

The main engines of all the ships in the fleet flared up simultaneously, the ships picking up speed in perfect unison as they lit up the space around them.

Back in the Zenith, Kade and Jude had exited the virtual environment and were currently standing in the bridge, looking around at all of the empty control stations in the expansive room.

"How can you control anything with these workstations? There are no displays and barely any controls on these things," Jude asked.

"Reminds me of the Icarus when we first got it. It took us a month to install all of the necessary instrumentation to allow us to control it properly," Kade added as she looked around the room.

"The controls are in here," Drake said, pointing to his head as he sat in the captain's chair, which was elevated by a few steps, allowing him a good view over all the workstations on the bridge. "The Cores are more than just memory backups. They allow us to control our technology, communicate effortlessly and can heal almost any injury. Not that I'd recommend trying out that last part." Drake smiled and then focused on his workstation.

"Have you decided yet?" Zen asked the sisters.

"Yes!" Jude said enthusiastically.

"You're sure this is safe?" Kade asked.

"That all depends on your definition of 'safe' now doesn't it?" Zen smiled. "But of all the existing variants, these are the safest."

"Very well, we accept!" Kade said, causing Jude and Zen to nearly jump for joy.

Kade and Jude stretched out their hands with open palms and waited, rather impatiently in Jude's case.

Zen was holding two silvery spheres above their palms, and then placed them gently in their hands.

Both sisters felt a tingling sensation in the palms of their hands, and watched in surprise as they saw what had appeared to be a solid object seemingly melt into their bodies like ice on a hot summer's day.

The process was quick and painless, and soon after Kade started hearing Toby's voice, as well as Static's. The previously silent bridge now filled with familiar voices as they talked about what was happening outside.

"They're making their move, we are being actively scanned by all the ships in the fleet as well as the solar system monitoring grid," Toby reported.

"What?" Kade asked, a bit woozy as the Core's Nano particles settled into her nervous system and began interfacing with her brain.

Static said cheerfully, "Welcome to the Shadows!"

"This is so freaking cool! It's like being connected to my system breakers without my visor... but 1000 times better. Just look at all the information that was around us all this time," Jude said enthusiastically, looking at all the augmented reality overlays in the room.

Kade smiled as she looked around the room. Her Core was allowing her to see information streaming on 'holographic' displays that she simply couldn't see before.

It had seemed strange that the Zenith was still using basic interface consoles since holographic interfaces had been the norm for millennia now, but now it all made sense. The Cores implanted in the crew members allowed them to see and interact with their technology without the need for power hungry projection systems. The interfaces and information displays had been around her all this time; she just couldn't see them.

Kade moved slowly, getting closer to one of the two workstations in front of Drake, looking over the multitude of controls which weren't there before.

"Have a seat," Drake suggested, and the two sisters happily complied; their minds becoming flooded with information from the workstations as soon as they sat down on the chairs.

"This is unreal," Kade said as she manipulated the holographic interface. Smiling as she handled the interface like she had been doing it for years. "How come I know what all of this stuff means?" She asked, clearly surprised at her new found technical aptitude for handling Shadow technology.

"Alpha Cores, the ones you two have, come pre-loaded with basic information about our technology, making it easy for your mind to quickly grasp the necessary concepts. Alphas aren't quite as versatile or powerful as the other Cores. They're the first step, putting minimum strain on your bodies as they test to see if you are fully compatible with the technology," Zen explained as she stood between their workstations.

"There's more than one type?" Jude asked.

"There are five base Core types. Alpha is the basic introduction model, then there's Beta, Gamma and Omega. For reference, Toby's Core was a Beta; Drake's is an Omega, the most advanced form."

"That's four, what's the fifth?" Kade asked.

"The Zero Core, but that one's a bit more complicated to explain," Zen said.

"Ah... OK. One more question. You said the Core would test our bodies, what happens if we fail the test?" Kade asked somewhat concerned.

Jude said emphatically, "Don't even joke about it!"

"I wouldn't worry about incompatibility; it is very

rare for that to happen. But in such an event the Alpha Core uninstalls itself and exits the body," Zen explained, putting Kade's mind at ease.

"Would you look at that!" Drake said as a gigantic screen appeared in front of them, showing the inbound fleet in all of its glory. "I could almost call it beautiful... if they weren't coming to kill us that is," Drake commented.

"Not the word I would use to describe the triple effed. Personally I'd go with 'terrifying'," Kade said.

"If you forget that each of those twinkling streams of light are death dealing machines of destruction, the light pattern they make is quite beautiful. Like a star burst," Drake said staring at the display.

"Sure... can we leave now?" Kade asked, concerned that the fleet was about to enter firing range.

"Good question." Drake said emphatically, "Toby! You might want to start hurrying up at some point!"

"Final systems check complete. Vortex drive charged. Course set for planet Caldera," Toby reported.

"Caldera?" Kade asked, and almost immediately her display started showing her the planet's vital statistics. It was the colony established by the survivors of the Shadow purge that had been carried out by the Solarian Union all those years ago.

The Zenith's hull began to vibrate ever so slightly as the ship's Vortex drive started to engage, the surrounding space seemingly becoming charged with energy emanating from the ship. But just as the Zenith was about to leave the system, artillery shells from the rapidly approaching fleet began detonating around the ship one after another in an endless barrage.

The Tragedy

"We're taking fire?" Drake asked somewhat confused at the readings he was seeing on his interface.

"Checking..." Jude said confidently as she manipulated her interface like a seasoned veteran. Tapping into her new found abilities to do in seconds what would have previously taken her hours to accomplish. Sifting through the vast amounts of sensor telemetry in order to determine what was happening outside. "Confirmed! The Regent is performing long range artillery strikes on this area," Jude reported.

"I'm reading a rapid energy build-up around the Zenith. Is that normal?" Kade asked.

"Not really, at least not like this," Drake said as he looked over the sensor readings.

"Whatever they are shooting at us is dispersing massive amounts of particulate matter around the ship. Basic sensor efficiency has dropped 10% since the bombardment began," Jude reported as she continued her analysis of the sensor information.

Drake said with a pensive look, "They're trying to blind us? No... there's something else going on here."

"From these readings I would guess it is intended to disrupt Burst drives. A normal ship would not be able to Burst out of the area under these conditions. It is strange however..." Static said.

"What is?" Drake asked.

"Think about it. The Zenith is inside the Sol dead zone. Burst drives are pretty much useless in here. It seems a bit redundant to try and suppress a ship's Burst drive under these conditions," Static said.

"They're probably just playing it safe. I doubt they want a repeat of last time," Drake said.

"Yes, that could be it. But still... I'm worried about the energy build-up around the Zenith. Intentional or not, whatever they're dispersing in this area could have some nasty side effects if we engage the Vortex drive."

Kade said somewhat concerned, "Define 'nasty'."

"Hard to tell, I've never come across this stuff before, and the nature of the Vortex drive makes it difficult to predict what could happen. The thing doesn't exactly play by normal rules," Static said.

"Can we still Vortex out or not?" Drake asked.

Static said with a worried tone, "In theory, Yes."

Drake wasn't at all happy with the situation.

Not only was the ship in imminent danger from the imitation Goliath platform, but he also had no way of knowing just what could happen if he were to engage the Vortex drive in order to leave the system.

He was still considering his options when he noticed the terrified expression on Jude's face.

Elsewhere...

The Defender platform had finished its alignment: the nearly one-kilometre-long magnetic focusing barrel, used to compress and direct the particle beam, was now pointed directly at the Zenith.

Electricity was arcing violently between the two horizontal barrel segments, signalling that the discharge was about to begin, and that something in the solar system was about to end.

The power levels spiked and the platform fired its compressed particle beam into space. Ejecting the plasma stream at near light speed as it simultaneously activated all of its station keeping engines in order to try and maintain its orbit. But even with all of its engines working at full power the platform was still gradually being pushed out of position by the sheer strength of the discharge from the particle cannon.

The beam contained enough potential energy to destroy a small moon, and its aim was true.

On board the Regent, the bridge crew observed their screens in anticipation of the killing blow, as they saw the energy beam from the Defence platform hit the target dead centre. The plan had worked flawlessly, they had cut off the enemy's ability to retreat and then hit it with overwhelming force.

The energy beam was intense and unforgiving. And nothing was being spared its destructive power as it completely engulfed everything in its path.

The Zenith had completely vanished from the fleet's sensors as the ten-kilometre-wide plasma beam introduced even the smallest particle in its path to the compressed raw power of a star.

The onslaught was approaching the two-minute mark and there was enough stored energy to sustain a beam for almost three minutes of continuous firing.

The platform had exceeded all expectations, but the continuous strain from trying to maintain its relative position was starting to overwhelm the station keeping engines. And one by one they started to shut down, causing the platform to lose the lock on its target as it started to drift, the discharging yellow beam cutting a path of destruction through space.

The crew of the Regent watched in horror as all of the safeguards failed to trigger. They had lost control of the platform; they could not shut it down.

The beam was inching ever closer to the asteroid mining outpost the fleet had been using as a base of operations, the Captain's face going pale as he was informed that the beam would hit the base before the platform's particle chamber was depleted.

The Admiral knew that there was nothing he could do to stop what was about to happen, the fleet was too far inside the dead zone to try and Burst to the platform's location, and even if they did, there was no way to disable the platform in time. The only thing he could do now was preside over the massacre which was about to unfold in front of his very eyes.

He had been warned by the construction crews overseeing the platform's development that the installation was not yet ready for active duty, that there were still too many unknowns with the system to try a test firing again, let alone a full discharge.

He had deemed it an 'acceptable' risk since all of the previous tests had demonstrated the installation's almost unlimited destructive potential. And now he was seeing all of that potential sweeping across the solar system and atomising anything unfortunate enough to find itself in its path.

If there had ever been a bad moment for the passage of time to come to a crawl, this would be it, with the crew of every ship in the fleet watching in agony as the beam got closer to the mining outpost.

The gigantic particle beam cutting through the solar system had hardly gone unnoticed, and every single ship capable of space flight was rushing to clear out of the path of destruction.

The mining outpost's harvester ships were scrambling to try and get away from the asteroid field, which was being vaporised by the plasma stream. But the only place they could run to was the nearby station, which would offer little protection in the face of such overwhelming power.

Every Burst capable ship in the station's vicinity was rabbiting out of the area. And the residents of the mining outpost unlucky enough to be near a window watched in shock, seeing that their lives and the lives of their families were about to come to an end.

The beam was inching ever closer to the outpost as it swept mercilessly though space, leaving little more than a few melted rock fragments in its wake: all that remained of the larger asteroids after exposure to a few seconds of the beam's immense power.

And then... it ceased. The particle stream dissipating just as it was about to come into contact with the outpost's outermost framework. Causing screams of joy to come from every single crew member of the fleet.

"Huh... Sir!" Ashlyn said with a horrified expression as she brought the image of the Zenith's former location up on the screen again. The Captain and Admiral watching in shock as the target had not only survived, but seemed to be emitting a strange blue aura that completely encompassed the ship. And its orientation had also changed.

"How did that God damned ship survive?" The Admiral demanded to know.

"Give me a trace on the target's orientation, why is it pointing in-system?" The Captain asked.

"Tracing now. It's... it's aiming at the defence platform Sir!" Ashlyn said.

"No, don't tell me..." the Captain said as he considered what had just happened. He didn't want to believe it was even possible, but all his doubts were about to be put to rest.

The fleet watched in shock as the Zenith discharged its main gun again, sending what looked like a bolt of blue energy directly into the flank of the defence platform; ripping through the station's heavy armour as though it was wet tissue paper.

The platform was starting to collapse under the weight of its own superstructure as explosions happened throughout the complex. And then a third shot from the Zenith's main gun ripped through the body of the platform again, clipping the particle collector arrays as it exited the structure's body on the opposite side to the point of impact; severing the interconnecting pylons and leaving the arrays floating free from the main body.

And back at the Zenith...

Drake ordered angrily, "Again!!"

"I think it's dead," Kade said.

"I want that freaking thing atomised! Hit it again!" Drake ordered without a hint of compassion.

"Priming Linear Burst Cannon. Targeting estimated location of primary particle chamber... Firing!" Toby said, and a mighty rumble could be felt throughout the Zenith. The discharge of the hyper-light projectile causing a shock wave to be sent through the ship's structure.

The main gun of the Zenith ran almost the full length of the ship. The muzzle flaring up as the projectile launched into space, leaving behind a trail of blue-shifted light as it streaked towards its target.

The shot hit its mark, a small and intense flash of light filling up the void as the projectile ripped straight through the platform's main particle storage chamber; what remained of the platform violently breaking apart at the seams as the compressed matter vented into space, destroying everything in its path.

Back at the fleet, the Captain of the Regent was struggling to keep all the other captains in line after having seen the Zenith rip the Defence platform to shreds. Half of the fleet wanted to rush in for the kill while the other half was advocating retreating to a safe range in order to regroup and come up with an effective strategy. But things were not that simple.

"Sir, analysis has confirmed that the target's main gun can discharge rounds at faster than light speeds. We can't get any clear readings from the target, but the techs believe that the gun is some kind of Burst accelerator cannon," Ashlyn reported.

"We've been trying to come up with that technology for decades, how did they beat us to it?" The Captain asked as he considered his next move.

"Where do you think the idea came from?" The Admiral asked while staring at the Zenith.

The Captain asked in shock, "You don't mean?"

"I do. They had the same fire-power when the Second Fleet was lost. We've been trying to recreate the weapons ever since," the Admiral explained.

"Dammit! How are we supposed to stand against

that kind of fire-power? They just destroyed something that's almost..." the Captain was saying when the realisation hit him of just how far the distance was between the Zenith and the now defunct Defence platform. "Ash, what's the target's offensive range?" The Captain asked, though he feared he already knew the answer.

"If it can fire faster than light projectiles it's possible that their maximum range is only limited by the ship's effective sensor range. If they can see it, they can probably destroy it," Ashlyn reported, re-enforcing the captain's worst fears.

Ashlyn's mind was racing; this enemy was unlike anything her days at the academy or any amount of experience gained on the field could have prepared her for. Not only had it withstood the sheer raw power of the Union's new system defence platform, it had also managed to destroy said platform seemingly without effort. And the platform had been designed with the latest armour technology, which was vastly superior to that of the Regent's, or any other ship in the Solarian Union military. How could this be happening, she thought in a near panic.

What little remained of the defence platform was still being rocked by secondary explosions as the superstructure collapsed in on itself and then broke apart violently. The captains of the fleet watched helplessly as they waited for orders, with tension and anger rising steadily for each new detonation that rocked what was left of the mangled remains.

And through all of these events, life in the solar system went on as usual: the average citizen being completely unaware of what had just taken place.

The Union had issued a statement to all the major networks about an impending test firing, so the entire event had been all but ignored.

Information control was running at full power as the Union tried to censor what was really happening, but the GAIA communications network was still quickly becoming overwhelmed with reports coming from the now safe mining outpost, as speculation grew at an exponential rate.

The Admiral sat quietly in his chair, as he leaned back with folded hands and a solemn expression, considering the situation.

The whole plan had been based on the assumption that the overwhelming fire-power of the defence platform was enough to destroy the enemy ship.

Out of all of the strategies they had considered, this was the only sure move the admiralty had. All other scenarios of ship to ship combat they had simulated would always result in a complete loss.

The plan had been simple: distract, immobilise and destroy. A simple, clean and elegant plan. Which had failed in the most tragic way imaginable. Not only had the enemy survived, it had also saved the lives of those the fleet was supposed to protect.

The Admiral bent his head, looking down as he closed his eyes, obviously conflicted. There were no more options open to him. The only other viable plan had been ruled to be too dangerous, but there was no other choice now. He prayed and hoped that history would eventually forgive him for what he was about to do. For this enemy could not be allowed to live.

"Captain," the Admiral said in an assertive tone while still staring at the floor, unable to look him in the eyes as he gave out the order.

"Sir?" The Captain said.

"Release the safeties on the class ten fusion warheads," the Admiral ordered.

"Sir?" The Captain and his X.O. asked in unison.

"You heard me! We can't allow this threat to exist! They could take out every single ship in this system before we knew what was happening. I am authorising the deployment of our nuclear arsenal," the Admiral said, finally looking up and into their questioning eyes, painfully aware that this move would have dire consequences.

Ashlyn could see the determination in the Admiral's eyes, and she could certainly understand where his apprehension was coming from. This enemy had the ability to sit outside the solar system's monitoring perimeter and destroy every ship and installation in the system with impunity. Not only did the Union have no defence against it, it could also withstand an attack from the defence platform.

But on the other hand, this enemy had also been sitting in the system for months and had not taken any action that was even remotely threatening, other than the recent move which safeguarded the lives of the workers on the mining outpost.

Ashlyn couldn't help but wonder just what was driving the Admiral to these extremes. What was it that he and the Captain knew that would even allow them to contemplate deploying class 10 nuclear armaments inside the Sol system?

The class ten fusion warhead was commonly known as a planet cracker, and it was banned by the Colonial Assembly Charter. It was so devastating that its deployment could not even be considered inside the territory of any of the Charter's member colonies.

It was devastating when fired at a planet and even more so when detonated in empty space: since it could generate an energy shock-wave intense enough to disrupt critical systems over half an AU.

Detonating a single warhead here would not only cripple the fleet, it would disrupt systems all over Earth and Mars, as well as several outposts.

During this sequence of events, back at the Zenith.

"How many people were in that thing?" Kade asked as she looked at the exploding platform.

"None. Goliath platforms are unmanned," Drake replied calmly.

"Your platforms are, but this was a Sol installation, so how can you be so sure?" Jude asked, casting doubt on Drake's belief.

"The Shadow Goliath design is unmanned by necessity, not by choice," the sisters heard Static say. "Because of how they work, the installations are exposed to so much solar radiation that they simply cannot be reliably shielded. Organic beings simply can't survive being inside one," Static explained.

"Would you think less of me if it had been crewed?" Drake asked, causing Kade to be confronted by the simple truth that the only reason they had opened fire to begin with was because the outpost had been in danger.

"Depends. The first shot stopped it, so why did you feel the need to destroy it?" Kade asked.

"The first shot merely crippled it, causing the discharge to pause, but it would have resumed in due time. The pressure in the chamber would have had to be vented eventually. And what was it pointing at?" Drake asked.

"The outpost," Kade answered instinctively.

Drake said calmly, "Or worse. The Platform's orbit was unstable. It could have eventually fired on one of the system's colonies. I may not have any love for the

Union, but I have nothing against its people."

Out of all the other men she had known in her life, with the exception of her grandfather she could not think of one who would ever put the greater good first when making such a decision, and this saddened her.

It was true that Kade's line of work didn't exactly bring her into contact with the most righteous members of galactic society, but she still couldn't help but think that this kind of behaviour was the exception rather than the rule.

Could she have taken the lives of hundreds in order to save thousands if the situation called for it, she wondered. She just didn't know the answer to that question. But, if nothing else, she was happy that the platform had been unmanned.

"I have good news, strange news and weird news. Which one do you want first?" Jude asked.

"Choices, choices... strange news!" Drake replied.

"Not a single patrol ship has been deployed to this area after that little display," Jude reported.

"What's the good news?" Kade asked.

"All the crap they shot at us was swept away by the beam. Our sensors are back to full strength." Jude smiled.

Concerned, Drake asked, "And the weird news?"

"The GAIA network is becoming flooded by reports of the mysterious ship that saved the Union mining outpost 56-beta. They even have a picture of the Zenith firing its main gun. It's very pretty." Jude grinned. "So yeah, we're all famous now. I just wonder where they got the picture from."

"Crud. The council is gonna chew my backside out for a week when they find out about this," Drake said with concern in his voice.

Static, Nexus and Toby were keeping an eye on the situation in the tactical virtual environment. Toby and Nexus were standing either side of Static, each with a multitude of virtual displays swarming around them as he manned his console.

"What?" Nexus asked as she looked at Static.

"Hmm?" Static said, turning to face her.

"Did one of you just say something?" Nexus asked.

"No, why?" Toby asked.

"There it is again, what is that?" Nexus asked with a confused look as she cycled through all of the information displays around her, frantically searching for something.

Concerned, Static asked, "Nexus, are you OK?"

"There..." Nexus said as she found the information she had been looking for. The display before her showing a garbled data stream which was being received from the GAIA communications network. It was a simple voice message, broken up and distorted by interference.

Nexus placed both of her palms on top of the screen and began reconstructing the severely degraded message, the encoded raw data quickly moving across the display as she reconstituted the recognisable audio into a text message on Static's screen; leaving Toby and Static slack-jawed at the contents.

"Leave... system immediately... in danger. Fleet... priming... Fusion... planet crackers. Leave..." the message read as it repeated over and over again.

"Toby, the ship needs to leave, right now!" Static said in a near panic at the thought that the Union could actually be reckless enough to use such weapons in their own backyard.

"The Vortex drive is still recharging. We used too much energy when we phased the ship before. It will be at least another 10 minutes before it can leave. And that's only if we don't fire again," Toby said.

"Dammit all! We save their outpost and they try to kill us for the effort. That's some gratitude! We need to buy some time, but how can we keep them from firing those missiles..." Static was saying and then he stopped in his tracks with a mischievous grin as an idea was born in his mind.

"I know that look. That's not a good look!" Toby said, seriously concerned at Static's expression.

"Do we have enough energy to perform a combat Jump?" Static asked Toby and smiled.

"Yes... Why?" Toby said.

"You'll see. Nex!" Static said and then reached out his hand, which Nexus grabbed without hesitation in order to receive the details of his plan directly into her mind.

Nexus smiled and laughed as she received the details. "You're insane, you know that right?"

"It has crossed my mind on occasion." Static grinned, taking it as a compliment.

"OK... Jude I'm switching us to a private channel, I need your help with something," Nexus said and then disappeared from the virtual environment.

"OK," Jude replied and then started smiling as Nexus explained the plan.

Concerned, Drake asked, "Static, what the hell are you planning?"

"I'm planning to stop those idiots from doing something everyone in this system will regret later on, to buy us some time to recharge our engines and to get some answers while I'm at it. And all it will take is one tactical jump and a bit of thinking outside the box." Static smiled.

"Really?" Toby asked. "All of that from one Jump? I just know I'm going to regret asking this but where, exactly, am I jumping the ship to?"

"Right here," Static said as he highlighted the destination co-ordinates on the system map. Causing Toby to just stand there with his mouth wide open in an almost catatonic state, as Drake was laughing himself silly with such intensity that his sides were actually starting to hurt.

Still in shock, Toby said, "Dear lord! Nexus is right! You have lost your mind!!"

"Trust me!" Static said, not really putting Toby's mind at ease as Drake laughed uncontrollably.

Back in the bridge of the Zenith, Kade was wondering why it seemed like Drake was about to give himself a heart attack from laughing while her sister was also looking a little bit too happy for comfort.

Kade's Core only allowed her to perform basic information exchange with the Zenith. So while she could hear Static and Toby talking, unlike Drake she could not actually see what was happening inside the virtual environment. Then again, from Drake's reaction maybe it was better this way.

It was clear to Kade that something was about to happen, something had changed which she was not aware of. Maybe it had something to do with why the fleet had stopped their approach and were now maintaining their relative position.

Drake had finally managed to regain control of himself and had not spoken out against whatever it was that Static was planning. He had seemingly embraced whatever crazy idea Static had dreamed up and was working away at his interface with a smile that Kade found more than a little disconcerting.

Zen was sitting down next to Kade, with her head resting against Kade's left shoulder. Her small body sleeping as her mind focused on helping out with the micro-management of the Zenith's systems.

Kade couldn't help but run her hand through Zen's purple hair, which felt just like the real thing. Smiling as she looked at her peaceful expression and accepted that there was more to being alive than she had ever considered. That it was not a privilege reserved exclusively for organic beings.

Meanwhile, back in the Regent...

The fleet was ready to launch its nuclear warheads and the tension was rising rapidly as the launch countdown approached zero.

The countdown was down to 10 seconds when the Zenith suddenly vanished from sensors, only to reappear directly in front of the Regent; scaring the living daylights out of the Regent's bridge crew and anyone else who just happened to be looking out of a window at the time.

The noses of the two ships were no more than 50 metres apart.

The Admiral knew that this was how the second fleet had been destroyed. The enemy had the ability to perform short range tactical jumps. A feat that the Union had tried to replicate countless times without success, not to mention some rather severe consequences.

The Regent's crew was staring down the barrel of the Zenith's main gun. Their fate all but certain now.

The Attack

The Admiral rose from his seat and stared at the display with a defiant look in his eyes. He had known from the beginning that this would be the likely outcome should the plan fail.

He had seen the logs from the survivors of the Second Fleet Massacre and he knew how the Zenith had defeated an entire fleet. The Zenith would perform a short range tactical Burst to point blank range and then fire its main gun, ripping anything in its path to shreds and often taking out multiple ships with one shot. It was a truly deranged tactic against which there was no counter. It was impossible to avoid the blast and by the time the fleet could get a weapons lock another ship had already been lost. The process repeating over and over until there was nothing but ashes in the void. This was how the Second Fleet had been lost to just one enemy combatant and this was how the Admiral knew his life was about to end, with history repeating itself.

The Admiral raised his head defiantly, the countdown for launch still ticking away in the background. He knew the fleet was too close together for any ships to survive what was about to happen and there was no time to evacuate.

It seemed fitting somehow, that the First Forward Fleet was about to share in the fate of the Second Fleet, in the same area of space which had claimed it almost 100 years before. But this time the enemy was going down with them.

The countdown hit zero and the crew of the Regent readied itself for the end... but nothing happened. Not only had the nuclear warheads not launched, but ship systems throughout the fleet had begun inexplicably failing one after another.

The Admiral looked around the room as the lights flickered on and off and the crew struggled with unresponsive consoles.

"What's happening? Have the warheads been launched?" The Admiral demanded to know.

"No Sir. The Fleet is in complete disarray. We're getting reports of wide spread malfunctions on every ship. All fire control systems appear to have been taken off-line somehow and... now we appear to have just lost our link to the other ships Sir," Ashlyn reported.

"The enemy is hacking our systems? That's not supposed to be possible. And how can it be hitting every ship in the fleet simultaneously?" The Captain asked with a pensive expression as he calmly tried to understand the situation.

"Sir! Engineering reports that all of the remote access points on the ship's network have been forcibly activated. The enemy is tapping directly into our control systems," Ashlyn reported.

"One enemy ship can do all of this? How?" The Captain asked with a stunned expression.

Meanwhile, on board the Zenith...

Jude said enthusiastically, "Well I'll be damned, it

actually worked!"

"Am I the only one that's in the dark here?" Kade asked as she looked at Drake's satisfied grin.

"I have just created the first ever, remote capital ship systems breaker! Hell yes!!" Jude shouted with her hands in the air. "Just don't tell the Union or I'll spend the rest of my life in jail." She smiled.

"You did what?" Kade asked with an incredulous expression. "Is that even possible?"

"If you'd asked me that an hour ago I would have said no. But this Core is great! I can process information in my mind a hundred times faster than by using my engineering console on the Icarus. I managed to up-scale the operating principles of my system breakers to make use of the Zenith's advanced sensor arrays. In short, I gave the Zenith the ability to hack into an enemy ship's closed networks," Jude said, positively beaming with pride.

"So..." Kade started to say as she chuckled. "This entire manoeuvre was designed around the assumed success of Jude's untested up-scaled design?" She laughed. "That's insane! No offence sis."

"None taken, I agree," Jude said.

Drake said confidently, "Jude managed to hack into the Zenith with her breakers and that's no small feat I assure you. The principle was sound."

"Still insane. Just what would we have done if it hadn't worked?" Kade asked.

"Same thing we would have done if we hadn't tried. Died a rather painful death," Drake replied.

Shocked, Kade said, "What! What do you mean? Did I miss something?"

"I'm a bit lost as well, Nexus didn't really tell me why we were doing this," Jude said.

"Oh! Yes... that, it... it's not important," Drake said, having forgotten the sisters hadn't been aware of the impending nuclear strike.

"Sounds important!" Kade said.

"No... we just, huh... needed to... reduce the enemies' offensive capabilities... yes, that's it!" Drake said, though Kade looked thoroughly unconvinced.

Jude's custom designed system breaker technology had been used with the Zenith's advanced sensor arrays in order to give the ship the technological advantage which all military forces had been drooling over since computers were first invented: the ability to remotely disable enemy ships. But the breaker had merely opened the doors, it was Nexus who was walking through them and doing the real work.

Nexus was steadily working her way through every ship in the fleet. Taking all offensive systems off-line and keeping them that way.

The effective hacking range was limited, but the fleet's tight formation ensured that every enemy was in range. The only real issue was the sheer number of ships, as this was taking Nexus to her limit. She could keep the fleet from taking direct offensive action but there were just too many ships to deal with in order to keep them all permanently subdued.

"Nuclear warheads disabled!" Nexus said, not having been paying attention to the conversation. This causing Kade and Jude to go almost completely pale at the revelation of what they had just avoided.

Kade said calmly, "Tell me I didn't just hear that."

"OK. You didn't just hear that," Drake replied without shifting his focus from his console.

"Not funny Drake! They were gonna nuke us?" Kade asked in shock at the revelation.

"Fusion or fission?" Jude asked.

"What difference does it bloody make?"

"About 10 million credits per warhead... but that's not what you meant is it?" Jude smiled.

"Not really, no," Kade said.

"Apparently, they were planet crackers," Drake said without a hint of distress in his voice.

"Wow... those things aren't cheap. They're like a billion a pop. They seriously don't like us," Jude said.

"I thought they were illegal. How did we even know they were carrying them, let alone that they were gonna fire them at us?" Kade asked.

"They're not technically illegal, though it's a bit of a grey area. The Union does not ban their production; they ban their use within allied territories. As to how we found out about it, we received a warning and acted on it," Drake said.

"A warning? From whom? You have spies in the fleet?" Kade asked.

"No... at least not that I'm aware of. We don't know who issued the warning yet. We'll look into it later, once the Union's no longer trying to kill us."

"OK, better question: why jump in front of the fleet? If we had the ability to perform tactical jumps all along why not just leave?" Kade asked.

"Tactical jumps, much like the phase out, use up a considerable amount of the ship's energy reserves and replenishing the reserves takes time. We only had enough energy for one jump and that wouldn't have gained us enough distance. So in short, it seemed like a good idea at the time." Drake grinned mischievously.

Jude said excitedly, "That phase out was surreal! How did we do that anyway?" She had never heard of any ship with such an ability before.

“That's a bit harder to explain, it's a... hmm. I suppose the best way to describe it would be that it's a 'side-effect' of our Vortex drive. You are free to look up the specifications for the thing later on,” Drake said, making Jude positively giddy with anticipation.

Meanwhile, the Regent, the pride and joy of the Solarian Union, had been reduced to a multi mega ton paperweight; a sight which Static found strangely appealing as he observed the now disorganised crews through their own security systems, as they worked to restore the ship's systems.

The immediate threat had been prevented, though Static still found it hard to believe that there was anyone alive dumb enough to consider using such despicable weapons in this day and age. Then again, he had never been very good at understanding the military mind-set.

Static cursed their luck. If that last probe had arrived just one minute earlier then all of this could have been avoided, but there was no point in dwelling on what 'could have been'. At least the defence platform was now permanently out of commission.

Its power was impressive, Static thought.

The beam cohesion wasn't great and the stabilisation engines obviously needed a lot of work, but the design itself was almost as good as that of a genuine Goliath platform and this worried him.

This loss would probably not deter the Union. They would eventually build a new platform and refine the design, but that was an issue for another time.

Right now the current situation was almost ideal, Static thought as he swiped his hand across his consoles' interface, wiping all the information from the screen. The display quickly filling up again with data streams as Nexus kept the fleet's capabilities in check.

Meanwhile, on the bridge of the Regent...

"Sir, engineering reports we have navigation systems back online, we've also restored partial sensors: short range only," Ashlyn reported.

"What's the status of the fleet?" The Admiral demanded to know; afraid that the fleet was being decimated around them.

"As far as our sensors can see... the fleet has sustained no damage. The enemy is not attacking." Ashlyn said.

"What about our weapons? How long before they're restored?" The Captain asked as he reviewed engineering's report on the systems hack.

"All fire control systems are still out of commission Sir. As soon as our technicians manage to restore partial control the systems are disabled again just as quickly as the first time," Ashlyn reported.

"I don't understand this. We are being made to look like complete amateurs by this one single ship! There is no way the Regent should be so vulnerable. We have redundancies in place to allow us to remain 70% combat effective even if we lose our central computer." The Captain shouted in frustration, "So why can't we fire the damned guns?"

"The central computer is locking the fire controls and we can't gain access to the computer room in order to shut it down. All of the emergency bulkheads in that section have been sealed shut," Ashlyn said.

"Tell the crews this is not the time for finesse. Have them cut the control lines if they have to, just give me back control of our weapons!" The Captain ordered.

Tactically, the enemy was making little sense to the Captain of the Regent. The enemy had jumped directly in front of the fleet, a normally suicidal move by just about everyone's book but this had given it the ability to disarm the fleet. It was an overwhelming advantage, so why was the enemy just sitting there, he wondered.

The Captain's eyes widened as he suddenly realised he was overlooking one tactical possibility. The enemy had been sitting in the system for months, probably gathering intelligence and now it had a direct link into the Regent's computer banks and all the secrets stored within. They were being bled for information.

Back in the tactical virtual environment...

Static had finished going over the records of the Regent and had found nothing even remotely relevant on Nova's location. In fact, there was no mention of her at all in any document. There was also very little information about the 'Defender' platform, what little there was indicating that the project had been ongoing for a few decades but had only made any significant headway in the last few years.

Nothing else seemed even remotely interesting; it was just a lot of military operation reports which made for some excruciatingly boring reading.

This fleet, like most military units, was just a pawn in the grander game, controlled by someone else up the hierarchy. There was no useful information here.

Just as Static felt as though he was about to pass out from sheer boredom, something caught his attention. It was a communications file, the content of which was completely uninteresting, but the file itself had the same digital signature as the files which had been sent to him almost 6 months ago.

Static performed a new search on the Regent's computer system. He was now looking for anything that had come from the same source and what he found was troubling. The same signature was present over almost countless files, all of which had utterly insignificant contents. They were all low priority communications which had been issued from different departments of the Union's military. There was no common source.

"What does this mean?" Static asked rhetorically.

"What does what mean?" Toby asked as he stood there with arms crossed, having nothing else to do.

"This is the same signature on the information I received, the information which brought us to this system in the first place," Static said.

"Why did you come here anyway?" Toby asked.

"The information I got said that the ship which had taken Nova had not been destroyed in the battle; that if we came here we would be able to find a clue as to her current location. We scanned every metre of this sector down to the smallest detail and found nothing. Then the Icarus showed up, bringing you to us, so I thought you had somehow found a way to call us in," Static said as he looked at Toby with a confused expression.

Toby said with a concerned look, "Nope, wasn't me. You think someone is playing you?"

"Someone that knew you had found Nova? Someone that knew how to send a message all the way to the Zero Core? And what frequency and encryption protocol to use. Someone that could manipulate the Solarian Intelligence Service to make them stall the fleet and bring Kade to this ship, literally carrying you straight to me? Someone who is doing the Union's military secretarial work by pushing all of these low level reports around their systems? Who?" Static asked, completely stumped.

"Don't ask me, I've been dead for almost eight years now. I'm not exactly 'up' on current events. But if the message was routed to the Zero Core then it would have to be someone intimately familiar with our technology. And he or she, would have to be very well informed if they had the current encryption protocols. Don't they still change at least once a year?"

Static said with a worried look, "They do. There's no way an outsider could have gotten their hands on that kind of information."

"So... who did you annoy this time?" Toby asked.

"What?" Static replied, somewhat confused.

"If I had to guess, I'd say someone wants you dead. Exhibit B is right there," Toby said as he pointed at the fleet hanging right in front of the Zenith. And then said, "We kind of blew up exhibit A."

"That can't be it. The message was sent to the Zero Core. Whoever sent it must know that destroying the Zenith wouldn't harm me," Static said.

"You little bastard! We can hear you, you know!!" Drake said.

"Sorry! I meant in a physical sense. I have no body left to kill. If someone wanted me dead, they would have to destroy the Zero Core itself. Destroying the Zenith wouldn't accomplish that. And even if it did, neither the platform nor the fleet would be up to the job," Static said and then tried comparing the signature against the strange warning message Nexus had received.

"They match! Whoever brought us here is the same person that warned us against the nukes, so they're not trying to destroy us. But then what..." Static paused as he tried to put the pieces of the puzzle together, but there was still something missing.

Static asked with a suspicious look, "Toby, you said that during the battle you lost track of the ship and ended up amnesic for your efforts. So how did you find Nova's location after all that time?"

"Well... technically, Jude found her," Toby said.

"What?" Static asked with a stunned expression.

"She hacked her way into the GAIA network core a while back and that's where she found her," Toby said.

"Found her? The GAIA network? Are you freaking kidding me?" Static nearly screamed, "They built the damned thing around Nova's matrix?"

"That's the theory. Jude gave me a pretty good description of what she had seen when she hacked in. But according to her, what she found was not a sentient AI. It had no free will and was shackled with enough security layers to restrict all but the most basic of behaviours. I tried to follow up on the information, but my body was starting to fail me by then. All I ever managed to get was bits and pieces of information, but it all seems to fit. GAIA is Nova," Toby said.

"Why didn't you tell me this before?"

"All I had was little more than speculation. Nexus was double checking my findings before we acted on them. And then, all of this crap happened," Toby said as he pointed at the fleet.

And almost as if by some kind of warped divine intervention, at the exact moment that Toby pointed at the fleet the Zenith's sensors started registering explosions inside the Regent.

"That wasn't me... I swear!" Toby said with a sheepish look, weirded out at the timing of it all.

Nexus screamed, "We need to leave, now!!"

"What's wrong?" Static asked, worried about the panic in her voice.

"The crew of the Regent has destroyed the control lines to the ship's main guns. They will be able to fire the thing manually. I can't stop them anymore. At this range even the Zenith's armour won't be enough!"

Toby didn't wait for orders, quickly uncrossing his arms and extending them forward as status screens flashed before his palms at an absurd rate. The Zenith immediately fired its manoeuvring engines, causing the ship to quickly spin around its centre of mass as it engaged the main engines to full power.

The Regent's main gun fired, sending a yellow plasma beam into the flank of the Zenith that punched clear through the ship's heavy armour.

The shot had missed the ship's main reactor by the slimmest of margins, punching its way through a mostly unimportant section of the ship, but still causing the Zenith to suddenly stop accelerating; its main engines going dark as the ship started to drift.

The fighter bays on the carriers were still out of order and the Regent needed a long recharge time after each shot. But the remaining ships in the fleet were now opening fire on the Zenith, as they quickly regained control of their systems. The one saving grace was that Nexus had permanently disabled the nuclear warheads.

Drake was frantically working his interface as he brought up and examined the detailed damage information. He turned to the sisters and asked, “Can either of you still talk to Toby?”

“I can't hear any of them,” Jude replied.

“Me neither,” Kade said as Zen 'woke up' from her slumber, looking confused.

Zen said in an agitated state, “What happened? I've lost my connection to the Zero Core.”

“The Zero Core?” Jude asked.

“It's the master control Core, based on the standard Core technology, but infinitely more powerful. It's also what houses the AI's and Static's consciousness,” Drake explained as he looked over the damage information with a puzzled look.

“So did that blast hit the Core?” Jude asked while looking at Zen.

“No, the Zero Core is not on-board the Zenith. It's located deep in our own territory. We connect to it via a hyper-spatial link, allowing us to interact with it from pretty much anywhere in the galaxy,” Zen said.

“Why did we lose the connection?” Drake asked rhetorically as Kade could feel small vibrations through her chair and could see in the view-screen that the ship was being bombarded by enemy fire.

The fleet was beginning to surround the Zenith. The lighter ships continuing their assault as the heavier vessels were still bringing their guns to bear.

The Zenith's advanced armour was holding for the moment, but there was no telling how long it would last under these conditions.

“We need to leave!” Kade said.

"I agree, but without an AI in charge of the ship we can't do much of anything. Keep in mind the Zenith is a capital class ship. Without a master AI we would need a full crew complement to operate all the systems," Drake said as he rushed his diagnostics.

"Can't you do it Zen?" Jude asked.

Zen said, genuinely scared, "I don't know, this has never happened before. Without access to my main consciousness I don't know where to even begin."

"Your what?" Kade asked as another beam from the Regent hit the stern of the Zenith, rocking the ship but failing to punch past the armour plating this time.

"Zen's mind exists in both her body and the Zero Core, but right now she's disconnected from the Core... and I can't figure out why! What the hell is wrong?" Drake said, becoming increasingly agitated as the bombardment seemed to intensify. And then he saw it, the answer was staring him in the face. "CRUD!!" Drake shouted as he rapidly double checked his findings, hoping he was wrong.

"What?" Kade asked as she held Zen, trying to calm her down as her little body shook in fear.

"That damned beam cut right through one of the primary data interchanges and all the freaking backups failed to kick in because of instabilities in the power grid," Drake said.

"Wait, Static and Nexus I understand, but Toby was reintegrated on this ship, right?" Jude asked.

"No. It looked that way but he was reintegrated by Nexus, so his consciousness is also housed in the Zero Core, same as Static. The real problem now is that I don't know of any way to re-establish a link under these conditions," Drake said.

The Zenith was receiving heavy fire and its armour plates were starting to buckle under the constant bombardment. Advanced as its armour was it would not last indefinitely.

Drake knew very well that without a master AI the Zenith could neither fight back nor run away, and the only other options were surrender or evacuation. But there was no way that Drake could ever surrender the Zenith, not in a million years.

The Icarus was still docked, making for a passable escape ship. But it wasn't a particularly fast ship, had little armouring and no weapons to speak of. It would not be able to get away on its own.

The options were crap and his decision was clear. There was only one thing he could do in order to safeguard the lives of those he cared about.

Drake smiled gently at Zen as he leaned back, the sound of mechanical latches snapping into place filling the room as his silver harness anchored itself to the chair. He closed his eyes, causing Zen to jump away from Kade's embrace and rush to his side with a horrified expression all over her face.

Zen shouted angrily, “NO! Don't you dare!”

Concerned, Kade asked, “What? What's he doing?”

Zen said in a panic, “He's taking control of the Zenith! You can't do this Drake; you know your body can't handle the strain! You'll die!!” She shouted, but Drake didn't react at all to her pleading voice.

The Regent's main gun was about to discharge again. It had been targeting the same point with every hit as it tried to cut through the Zenith's thick armour and the aft section's plating was at its breaking point. One more hit would see the beam cut clean through the main engines.

The beam began its discharge, rushing across space as Drake snapped opened his eyes, the Zenith's main engines flaring up to full power and causing the beam to miss its mark.

The ship was mobile once again and Drake was manoeuvring it out of the area of engagement, but the fleet was still in full pursuit.

Kade looked on in shock as she saw that Drake was starting to bleed from his nose and ears, his body clearly suffering under the strain of controlling the ship.

"You need to leave," Kade heard Drake's voice in her mind, his body seemingly catatonic from the experience.

"What! Why?" Kade asked, not liking the idea of abandoning the ship one single bit.

"You three need to make your way to the Icarus." Drake said in a sad tone as he fought back the pain, "As soon as you're aboard I will launch the ship and you can get to safety while I cover your retreat."

"Us three? Have you lost your mind! I'm not leaving!" Zen screamed in anger, infuriated that Drake would even consider putting her off the ship.

"I'm sorry Zen. I won't be able to maintain control for much longer and I can't guarantee I can save you if you stay with me. Kade, please take her with you," Drake pleaded, though Kade was also defiant.

"There must be something we can do!" Kade said, hoping that there was a way to turn things around.

"There is... safeguard Zen and yourselves. Take the Icarus and head to Caldera, the Council will protect you... they have to," Drake said as the fleet re-entered weapons range and began bombarding the ship again.

The Sacrifice

"Don't we have a say in this?" Jude asked, also displeased by Drake's request.

"You can say whatever you want, as long as you say it from inside the Icarus as you fly away to safety," Drake said as he fought back the pain while trying to outmanoeuvre the pursuing fleet.

"No!! I won't..." Zen was saying as she suddenly lost consciousness.

Zen's body became limp and nearly collapsed on the floor, the only thing between it and a hard crash to the deck being Kade's quick reflexes.

Kade held her as she looked at Drake with questioning eyes, realising that he truly believed this was the only course of action left to him. Knowing that there was nothing she could say that would change his mind.

"I... very well," Kade said with a heavy heart.

"I'm sorry Zen... Kade, hurry!" Drake pleaded.

"Don't you dare die on us, you hear me!" Kade ordered as the sisters ran out of the bridge, carrying Zen with them as they headed to the Icarus.

"Ha ha... no promises," Drake replied as his Core worked overtime to try and maintain his higher memory functions from degrading under the stress.

Drake could feel his body starting to go numb; he had already lost all sensation from his waist down. A clear sign that the merge was starting to take a heavy toll on his nervous system. But in his mind there was no choice, this had to be done. He could not allow the Union to get their hands on the Zenith's technology, for if they ever mastered the Vortex drive then planet Caldera would be within their reach. And the atrocities of the past could very well be repeated.

He debated with himself whether he should return fire on his attackers. It would be easy to destroy the Regent and the other large ships. One clear shot from the main gun would be all it would take, but that would waste precious energy without solving anything. It would only justify the Union's actions. So he had opted instead to lead them in a merry chase around space.

Several of the smaller frigates had already been forced to disengage because they were starting to run low on fuel, but there was little chance of the larger ships backing off any time soon.

Drake knew he couldn't keep this up forever, his body would simply not hold up under the strain. He knew that if the repair crews could not reconnect the ship to the Zero Core then he would soon be forced to make a choice between sacrificing his ship or his humanity, for he could not let the Zenith's technologies fall into enemy hands.

Kade and Jude were almost to the Icarus as fire continued to rain down on the ship, causing the corridors to occasionally shake as sections of the outer armour were blasted away by the impacts.

Kade felt like a coward as she ran for her life while carrying Zen's unconscious body. All the while wondering if there was truly nothing else she could have said or done and feeling guilty for having simply walked out on Drake. All she could do now was to try and safeguard their own lives and hope for the best.

The sisters turned a corner and ran into the bay, sprinting at full speed with the Icarus in sight.

The ship seemed different to Kade somehow, but right now she didn't have the time to spend trying to figure out how, or why.

Kade could see two synthetic workers rushing out of the docking bay, looking as though they were running for their lives as she headed for her ship. It seemed curious that they would behave that way, but she didn't really have the time to waste on that either. Ignoring the synthetics behaviour, she ran up her ship's embarkation ramp. The Icarus's outer doors automatically closing behind them as Kade and Jude rushed for the bridge.

"About freaking time! Did you two stop to see the sights along the way or something?" Drake asked, but Kade was so out of breath she couldn't tell if he was angry or just joking.

"The Zenith isn't exactly a small ship you know!" Kade replied as she sat down in her chair; getting startled when a holographic display not unlike the ones in the Zenith's bridge appeared in front of her.

"What the hell?" Kade said, calling Jude's attention to the interface as well.

"Phoenix?" Jude asked as she looked over the information.

"Hold on to something, I'm launching the Icarus!" Drake said, causing the sisters to stare at each other in confusion and then at the bay doors.

"Huh Drake? The doors are still closed!" Kade shouted, hoping Drake was still lucid enough to know what he was doing.

"Say Kade... as a kid, did you enjoy roller-coasters?" Drake asked out of the blue.

"What? Sure I guess... why?" Kade said, seriously concerned as to why he would ask such a thing.

"Oh... no reason. Hang on to something, I've never actually tried doing this before," Drake said and then the Zenith started picking up speed as it pitched up and started to roll. Causing the still moored Icarus to shake around inside the bay as the Zenith approached the optimum launch angle.

Kade and Jude wondered what was about to happen as the bay started being rocked by the sound of explosions. Numerous recovery drones were flaring up their engines to full power, applying overwhelming force against the doors as detonations traced their way around the frame and vaporised the interlocking pylons. The bay was flooded by yellow lights and sirens, warning the empty dock that the doorway's structural integrity was beginning to fail under the intense pressure from the drones and the fully pressurised bay; cracks had already began appearing, causing almost countless jets of gas to develop across the surface, the streams turning white as the moisture in the air crystallised due to the cold vacuum of space. The gates were at their breaking point when the final set of interlocks was vaporised, the overwhelming force causing them to be violently blown from the ship with an almost explosive effect. The recovery drones self-destructing as they drifted into deep space.

Kade knew what was coming and focused on the controls, waiting for the right moment. This was a reckless move, but performing a normal launch during combat was impossible anyway. She knew that Drake was placing the Zenith's body between them and the fleet, shielding them while they launched.

The gravity in the docking bay suddenly cut out as the moorings were released, throwing the Icarus clear of the docking bay and hurtling it uncontrollably into deep space, away from the battlefield.

Kade had managed to regain control of the Icarus, its engines flaring to life as the ship steadied itself. And in their view-screen the sisters could see the Zenith as it finished its manoeuvre.

The Zenith had done a full turn, seemingly intending to engage the inbound enemy fleet. And its massive engines were flaring up like a bright blue star as the ship started picking up speed.

And that was the moment when Zen woke up...

"...let you do this!" Zen said, completing her sentence from before as she started looking around her new surroundings, with a gradually increasing look of horror over her face.

Zen screamed, "NO!!" Staring at the screen showing her home getting further and further away with every passing second.

"Turn us around! Go back!!" Zen pleaded as Kade continued increasing the ship's cruising speed.

"I'm sorry Zen, but I gave my word I would keep you safe," Kade said with a pained expression, for nothing would please her more than turning the ship around and going back, but the Icarus had no weapons... there was nothing they could do to help.

It seemed strange to Kade that after all the years she had spent on board the Icarus she had never suspected the ship could have been built around another vessel. And it was only because of her Core that Kade was now able to see the full extent of her ship's true capabilities. And one in particular gave her hope: A Vortex drive.

The drive had not been powered up in decades, so there was no guarantee that it would even work. And from the readouts in front of her Kade could see that once triggered the Icarus would have to divert 90% of the reactor's output into the drive; leaving the ship virtually defenceless for the duration of the charge sequence. And that was a risk she was obviously not willing to take in the middle of a battlefield.

She pushed the Icarus to its uttermost limit. The engines stuck in a continuous burn cycle as the ship rapidly picked up speed in order to clear the battlefield. The old ship's outermost frame creaked under the stress as integrity alarms flashed on Jude's engineering console, which she now found really cumbersome to work with after having had a taste of the Shadow interfaces.

The sisters could see that the Zenith was doing its best to keep the fleet distracted, but a few of the interceptor frigates had broken away from the pack in order to chase down the Icarus... and they were closing rapidly.

On board the Zenith, the repair crews were still trying to restore the link to the Zero Core, but progress was slow and Drake was quickly becoming mentally exhausted. Finding it increasingly harder to remain focused as the conflict dragged on.

The Zenith was still on the defensive, keeping itself out of the effective strike range of the fleet's heavy hitters as it goaded them along. With Drake still hoping he would be able to extricate the Zenith from the battlefield before he was forced to take any lives. But this tactic was coming at a considerable cost to the ship's outer armour, which was being chipped away by the relatively weak guns of the frigates.

Drake was starting to doze off as the stress overwhelmed him when he heard a distant voice. A voice from his past, one he hadn't heard in almost 100 years. It was a woman's voice, though she sounded much colder than he remembered, almost emotionless.

The woman shouted at Drake, telling him the Icarus was in danger, this causing him to snap to full attention and check on the Icarus, seeing that the ship was receiving fire from two interceptor frigates.

Zen, Kade and Jude were in danger, Drake thought as anger began overtaking his mind. His fury was growing by the second at the thought that this fleet was as cowardly as the one which had destroyed his family and friends all those years ago. All traces of compassion dissipating from his soul as the Zenith cut its main engines and fired its manoeuvring drives, causing the behemoth ship to spin violently around its centre of mass.

The violent manoeuvre had caused the attacking fleet to pause its onslaught, in order to try to understand what the enemy was doing. And then the Zenith suddenly started flooding all communications channels with the same message.

"One hundred years ago, bastards like you killed almost everyone I held dear. And now you're planning to do it again. All this time and you cowards are still firing on innocents who can't fight back! You want a war? I'll give you a freaking war!!"

The message cut out, leaving everyone in the Sol system reeling from its contents.

On board the Regent, the crew was trying to find out what the Zenith was aiming at. But before they could finish calculating the attack vector the Zenith fired its main gun, utterly destroying one of the frigates which was firing on the Icarus and leaving what little remained of the other frigate spiralling out of control as secondary explosions finished the job.

The fleet saw an opening, the Zenith had stopped trying to evade their fire and the ships moved forward in order to press the advantage. But they weren't ready for what happened next, as the Zenith began deploying its rapid fire point defence guns and particle beams started discharging against any ship unfortunate enough to be in firing range.

The fleet formation was starting to collapse as the Zenith pressed its offensive. The point defence guns punching through the reactor power distribution nodes of the nearby frigates, leaving them floating in space like the scrap metal they were.

The scene was almost beautiful to behold, like a fireworks show: caused by the exploding reactor cores that had been ejected from the frigates.

With most of the frigates subdued the Zenith headed straight for the Carriers' support cruisers. Its guns punching clean through the cruisers' armour and hitting the carriers they had been shielding, causing the atmosphere to vent from the ships and their crews to jettison in escape pods in fear of the Zenith's overwhelming fire-power.

Meanwhile, the Icarus had finally managed to reach a safe departure point and was charging its Vortex drive.

The sisters could see the light from the stars

shifting and scattering randomly. The surrounding space was becoming warped by whatever field the ship was emanating as the drive approached full charge. And Zen hammered violently on Kade's leg, pleading for her to go back. But the sequence was locked; there was no going back anymore.

Drake looked on in relief as the Icarus vanished from sensors, the pain he had been suppressing all this time hitting him like a ton of bricks as he let his guard down; causing the Zenith's systems to begin shutting down... the guns going silent.

What remained of the fleet didn't know what had just happened, but they weren't about to waste this opportunity. Every single remaining ship opening up with everything they had left on the now silent behemoth as it drifted out of control. What remained of the Zenith's armour was being ripped away as the enemy fire finally started to make contact with the inner hull. Causing violent decompressions as it punched holes in the superstructure.

Drake's mind had lost all control over the ship and he couldn't feel anything anymore. The only thing keeping him from falling to the ground was his harness, which was holding him to the chair. He could feel his life draining away from him as his body grew cold, finding it curious that there was little pain.

His life was coming to an end, of that there was no doubt, but it was a good end. Zen and the sisters were safe, his friends would carry on and he would die with his ship... a strangely comforting thought. Given the choice he would rather not die at all, but if he had to go anyway then this was the place to do it. In the only place left he could call home.

As Drake began to lose consciousness he saw the Zenith's auto destruct warning suddenly shut down.

Something had gone wrong with the countdown, but he no longer had any strength left to do anything about it. He watched in a confused state as all the probes in the Zenith's hangar began auto launching and started taking position around the ship.

"Not the damned probes," Drake said, his voice trailing off into a whisper as he lost consciousness, "Do you have any idea how much those things cost..."

The fleet was continuing its onslaught as the probes formed a tight sphere around the Zenith and then started emitting a warning over all the comms frequencies.

"WARNING: Self-destruct sequence initiated, all ships are advised to clear the area immediately," the cold computerised voices from more than three hundred probes all announced repeatedly.

In the bridge of the Zenith, Drake's unconscious body sat vigil over the ship's last moments, as the surrounding space began warping and all the probes simultaneously detonated their reactor cores. Filling the area with an intense bright light and blinding all sensors in the system.

As the light subsided and the fleet conducted scans of the region, cheers could be heard throughout the Regent's bridge and coming over the intercoms from the remaining ships, for there was no trace left of the Zenith. The fleet had been victorious.

Meanwhile the Icarus was traversing Vortex space as it headed towards the Lux system at full speed.

It was a new experience for the sisters, to put it lightly, since neither of them had known what to expect from the Vortex drive activation.

Kade had assumed that the name was some kind of reference to whatever optical phenomenon was observed from outside the ship. Though in retrospect the idea of a swirling vortex of energy, like some weird cosmic drain, did seem kind of silly now. And Jude had assumed that the name was just an acronym and that it was nothing more than a modified Burst drive. Neither of them could have been more wrong if they tried however.

The Vortex drive had actually shifted the Icarus and anything unlucky enough to have been in its immediate vicinity, into what the ship's database was referring to as 'Vortex space': which was actually the gravity layer, one of the four fundamental layers of the universe, which theory had predicted to exist at the beginning of the first era; the very same theory which had made the Burst drive a reality.

The sisters looked on in amazement as they saw the universe in a whole new light. For this 'space' was insubstantial and what they were seeing was gravity in its purest form, before it was merged with the other fundamental layers in order to give rise to the universe they knew.

Kade couldn't understand how any of what she was seeing was even remotely possible, but that didn't make the display any less beautiful to her.

"I think I just figured out why they call this Vortex space," Jude said with an astonished expression.

"Why?" Kade asked, and then Jude put the starboard camera feed on the main view-screen.

"What the hell is that?" Kade asked with a stunned expression as she looked at a massive swirling void of darkness, which sent a chill running down her spine.

"It's the Vortex," Zen said in a low and sad tone as she sat on the floor, leaning against the wall as she stared absent-mindedly at the deck. Like a broken doll that had lost all reason for living.

"What... is it?" Kade asked as she stared at the almost hypnotic sight.

"We don't know... we can't even be certain how far away it is. Even at the Zenith's top speed it would probably take thousands..." Zen was saying when she went quiet, her sad eyes betraying her thoughts.

Kade didn't know what she could possibly say to Zen that would help in this situation; or even if she should say anything at all. All the platitudes in the galaxy would sound meaningless and hollow. And there was a good chance that Zen would never forgive her for having taken her from the Zenith, regardless of whatever its final fate had been.

As Kade pondered how best to handle the situation at hand her screen suddenly began counting down, calling her attention as the ship started decelerating. They were about to drop out of Vortex space.

Kade felt sick to her stomach as the Icarus started phasing back into normal space, her vision going blurry and momentarily losing her sense of hearing. It had only lasted a few seconds but as she regained her senses she saw warnings going off all over the place. The Icarus was taking severe damage.

Energy which had unevenly built up in the ship's frame, while in Vortex space, was now trying to achieve balance. Causing arcs of electricity to jump between the different sections of the outer hull's structure and violently ripping apart any insulating ceramic armour which happened to be standing in the way of the energy discharges. The scene inside the ship was even more intense, as bolts of lightning energised passageways and destroyed any equipment in their path. The only thing keeping the crew alive, being the fact that the bridge was actually part of the original ship, the Phoenix, that had been designed to safely traverse Vortex space. The Icarus' outer frame, however, was now paying the ultimate price for having trespassed into the Vortex domain.

The Icarus floated quietly through space, the energy imbalance having finally corrected itself; though not before having torn apart over 60% of the ship's armour plates and damaged most of the critical equipment on board, including the engine and reactor control systems. The ship had been left completely adrift.

The sisters sat in the dark, wondering what would happen next; whether they had actually arrived at their destination, or if the guidance system had dropped them in the middle of some uncharted system. There was simply no way to tell.

To make matters worse, Zen had also seemingly shut down. Whether from grief or a systems failure caused by the re-entry, Kade couldn't say. She held Zen's small body as the sisters waited for whatever was to come next and wondered what had been the point of it all if this was how things were supposed to end.

Minutes turned to hours as exhaustion took hold of Kade, who was finding it increasingly harder to stay awake. Causing her to naturally doze off.

"Was this really our fate all along?" Kade asked as she stood on the overlook glade, as a gentle breeze caressed her skin on a perfect crystal clear day.

"You're asking me? You know I'm not actually here, right?" Drake replied as he leaned back against the fence and enjoyed the fresh air.

"Humour me!" Kade ordered.

"Fate huh? That's an interesting concept. We are all thrown into this universe without knowledge or ability. And we work all our lives to attain that which we need to survive and prosper, only to eventually die. So, does fate really exist in this system, or is it just an illusion your mind creates in order to give you solace?" Drake smiled.

"I... I don't know," Kade said, looking conflicted.

"Of course you do!" Toby said, sitting on the wooden fence next to Drake.

"I do?" Kade asked somewhat confused.

"Deep down you have always believed that fate is an illusion created by the passage of time," Toby said, causing Kade's mood to drop even more.

"You choose to believe that you are in full control over what path your life will take. Though you may not be able to control the events that unfold around you, it is still up to you to decide if you will participate in them. Changing the flow of events which will unfold over time and in turn shaping the unwritten future that is to come," Drake said.

"Is that what you did? You chose to sacrifice yourself? For what?" Kade asked angrily as she stared at Drake's smiling face.

"For you, for Jude and for Zen. I decided that your survival was more important than my own, and I acted on that decision. My only regret is that I never got to know you better. Or maybe that's your regret, I am a figment of your imagination after all... hmm, this is getting confusing." Drake grinned, lifting Kade's mood.

"Now what?" Kade asked.

"Now... you wake up." Toby smiled.

"What?"

“Wake up!” Kade heard a forceful voice say as if it was coming from everywhere around her.

“Wake up!!” The voice said again, causing Kade to open her eyes and start laughing at the sight of the rescue crew which was standing in front of her.

“Are you OK?” Asked the man in the black space suit with the shadow insignia on the shoulders.

“I've had better days.” Kade smiled.

The Icarus had been retrieved by the Demeter, one of the many patrol ships that protected the planet Caldera, and it was now being taken to the orbital shipyards.

The council was waiting for answers as to what, exactly, had happened in Sol and how the Icarus had managed to reach the Lux system.

A week passed and the universe moved on, with most of the colonies completely unaware of what had transpired in the Sol system.

Even the inhabitants of Sol didn't really know what had happened. The military had suppressed most of the information, so the public had been left with yet another mystery and plenty of speculations.

Somewhere in one of the many bars of the lunar shipyard, two dock-hands were enjoying their time off as they watched the news over a few drinks.

The news anchor woman reported on the hot topics of the day, “And that was the scene late last week when the Union's new defence platform suffered a cataclysmic systems failure during a test fire exercise. Luckily the First Forward Fleet, which was conducting training exercises in the area, managed to destroy the platform in time, saving outpost 56-beta. No civilian casualties were recorded. But sadly, the fleet lost two frigates and sustained severe damage to over two thirds of its..."

"That's a load of crap," Mick said angrily as he held his half-drunk beer glass.

"Which part?" Dave asked with a melancholic look as he contemplated the bottom of his empty glass.

Mick said confidently, "All of it! I hear it was the Shadows that destroyed the platform."

Dave said dismissively, "Just how much have you had to drink? The Shadows are a myth, everyone knows that!"

Mick said angrily, "They are not! My wife's second cousin's friend's sister's boyfriend said that there was some strange message picked up all over the system that day. And a picture from the monitoring grid showed a ship with the Shadow insignia on its hull. It was them!" He said, spilling some of his drink over his friend.

"Your wife's... second sister's... what?" Dave asked, finding it hard to keep up in his inebriated state.

"I need another drink!" Mick said as he started getting up, having completely lost his train of thought and then almost losing his balance, grabbing his chair so as to not fall flat on his face.

"That's it, you've had enough! I need to go back before my wife comes looking for me anyway," Dave said as he got up. The two of them leaving the bar as the news report carried on.

"In other news, the strange malfunctions which had been plaguing the Galactic Artificial Intelligence Ark network for the past year were finally resolved last week. Independent sources claiming that the issues eventually corrected themselves, after repair crews repeatedly failed to fix the system. The GAIA maintenance corporation could not be reached for comment..."

The Epilogue

Planet Caldera was not at all like Kade had been expecting. She had pictured an industrialised world, with technology as far as the eye could see, for that was the kind of world her former occupation would generally take her to. Cold places with no soul and incessant noise which threatened to drive visitors insane if they stayed for too long.

But this planet seemed perfect, or at least as close to perfect as Kade's imagination could dream up.

A garden world not unlike old Earth, with large blue oceans covering most of the surface and extensive landmasses filled with plant and animal life.

The main colony settlement was located in the tropical region, with an expansive view of the nearby ocean and its crystal clear blue waters. And the bluest sky Kade had ever seen in her entire life. It all seemed so perfect from her new apartment's balcony window, up on the 77th floor of one of the three main arcology buildings of the primary settlement. It was easy to understand why the Council was so adamant about protecting this place.

Kade was sat by the balcony, looking out to the sea in her shorts and tank-top as she enjoyed a perfect summer's day. The peace and quiet she was experiencing right now seeming almost unreal.

So much had happened; so much had been left unresolved. Had the outcome really been worth all the sacrifices, Kade wondered in silence.

Zen's body had been taken away from her by the Council, though they had let her keep her ship. And she still didn't know what had been the final fate of the Zenith. She had far too many questions and not nearly enough answers, but right now she needed a well-deserved rest.

"Ah! I needed that!" Jude said as she stepped out of the shower room wrapped in a white towel.

"You live right next door sis, why use my shower?" Kade asked without turning around.

"I like yours better." Jude smiled and then asked in a concerned tone, "Are you saying you don't want me around anymore?"

"You know very well I didn't mean it that way," Kade said warmly as she stared absent-mindedly into the sky, wondering what was to come.

"Good!" Jude said in a chipper mood as she headed to the room in order to get dressed.

"Are you really ready for tomorrow?" Kade asked, wondering how her sister could be in such a happy mood after all that had happened.

"Aren't you? After nearly a month here I thought you'd be itching to get back into space," Jude replied.

"That I am! I've had about as much questioning from the Council as I can stand. As if we would know what it was they were trying to accomplish when they went to Sol. We barely got to know any of them!" Kade said with a heavy heart as she stared absent-mindedly at the pristine blue sky.

"At least they repaired our ship," Jude said, trying to cheer up her sister.

"After putting us through two weeks of interrogation it's the least they could do. I had never realised just how many different ways a person can ask the same stupid questions until we came here. And after two weeks they just stop without explanation and give us these places, even offer to repair and refit the Icarus free of charge. Can these people get any more random?" Kade asked as her sister walked up and sat next to her.

"Probably," Jude said as she opened a can of soda.

"Is that one of mine?" Kade asked as her sister started drinking her soda.

"Definitely." Jude grinned as she gave her sister another can.

"Anyway..." Kade opened the can. "The real question is what to do now. The Icarus is probably gonna be on the colonies most wanted list for the rest of eternity, so we can't go back to our old lives. And I can't see there's much need for smuggling in this place." Kade took a sip of her soda, looking depressed.

"I've got a smuggling job for you if you want it." Kade heard a familiar voice say in her mind, as the sisters Cores started receiving a message.

"Zen!" Kade said happily as Jude nearly choked on her drink from the surprise.

Zen asked happily, "So you want the job?"

"Of course we do!" Jude replied without giving her smiling sister a chance to speak.

The following day...

The Icarus had cleared the atmosphere and was picking up speed as it tried to outrun a Calderian patrol ship. The authorities weren't too happy that the Icarus had refused a pre-departure inspection.

"When you said you had a smuggling job I wasn't

expecting it was you that we'd be smuggling," Kade said as she manoeuvred the Icarus in order to avoid the incoming fire from the patrol ship.

Zen asked with a concerned expression, "Regrets?"

"Nope." Kade smiled. "But where are we going? We can't keep dodging this guy forever."

"Behind that moon," Zen said, pointing at one of the two moons of planet Caldera.

"OK, hold tight, this could get interesting." Kade smiled, happy to be back in space and to be reunited with Zen.

The patrol ship had a lock on the Icarus's engines; one well-placed shot would be enough to disable the ship. But before he could take the shot the Icarus performed a micro burst: traversing the distance to Caldera's moon in a fraction of a second.

Unfortunately for Kade, the pilot of the patrol ship was as insane as she was and quickly followed suit.

"Cut your engines immediately!" The pilot of the patrol ship demanded as he took aim.

"We're here!" Zen said happily as the Icarus speedily approached the dark side of the moon.

Kade looked on in shock as she saw a large structure floating in space. Sparks of arc welders were readily visible across the hull of the large spaceship as countless maintenance drones performed repairs on the superstructure.

The chasing patrol ship immediately fired its retro-thrusters, bringing the vessel to a virtual halt as the pilot saw what he was approaching. He had no jurisdiction here, and he knew it.

The view-screen changed as the three young women looked on, now showing four familiar faces.

"Welcome home!" Drake smiled.

The Bonus

- Drake's Rescue -

In the tactical virtual environment...

...at the exact moment that Toby pointed at the fleet the Zenith's sensors started registering explosions inside the Regent.

"That wasn't me... I swear!" Toby said with a sheepish look, weirded out at the timing of it all.

Nexus screamed, "We need to leave, now!!"

"What's wrong?" Static asked, worried about the panic in her voice.

"The crew of the Regent has destroyed the control lines to the ship's main guns. They will be able to fire the thing manually. I can't stop them anymore. At this range even the Zenith's armour won't be enough!"

Toby didn't wait for orders, quickly uncrossing his arms and extending them forward as status screens flashed before his palms at an absurd rate. The Zenith immediately fired its manoeuvring engines, causing the ship to quickly spin around its centre of mass as it engaged the main engines to full power.

Toby could sense the strain being put on the ship's superstructure, as countless warnings were being generated from sensors all over the ship.

He was diverting all the power he could spare to the structural integrity fields, but the ship was low on energy. It had been maintaining a permanent disruption field for months, engaged its phased defence field, discharged the main gun several times in a row and performed a tactical jump. In short, the energy reserves of the Zenith were running fairly close to empty.

The Zenith spun around violently with enough force to rip any normal ship in half, as the powerful manoeuvring engines lit up the surrounding space.

The main engines flared up to full power, forcing the ship forward as the beam from the Regent's main guns began its discharge; missing the Zenith's primary reactor by the slimmest of margins.

The particle beam discharge had hit the ship's midsection with overwhelming force, punching through the protective armour plating of the Zenith's atrium and cutting clean through the ship's residential sector, destroying the balconies along with the nearby uninhabited residential block and taking out the primary data interchange in the process.

Static was about to breathe a sigh of relief when the tactical environment suddenly went dark. Nexus and Toby collapsing on the floor as the data-streams were forcibly terminated.

"Nexus! Toby?" Static said as he looked at their unconscious bodies. Wondering what could have caused this as he grabbed their hands. "The link was cut?" He asked as he looked up after running a basic diagnostic on Nexus.

Static rushed to his console and examined the system's status, his face going pale as he saw that their link to the Zenith had indeed been severed... at the destination. He wondered what could have happened as he pulled up the information on Zen's status, and began to panic as he saw that while Nexus and Toby were essentially frozen, Zen's matrix was actually showing signs of degradation.

Static looked around the room, his mind quickly becoming overwhelmed with horror and fear as he remembered those all too familiar feelings of loss and desperation which had nearly driven him insane almost a century ago. The Zenith was undoubtedly being attacked by the fleet, Nexus and Toby's state was unknown and his daughter was 'dying'.

He didn't have a choice; he had to do it...

“Zero Core access request. Enact Ultimate Authority by order of prime user. Authorisation, Static: Sigma-225-Omega-Prime,” He said to his console, causing everything around him to disappear, becoming surrounded by a field of pure white light.

“Triumvirate access confirmation required,” he heard his own voice say back to him.

Static all but shouted in his desperation, “Triumvirate access bypass. Nexus and Drake are incapacitated. Release command to prime user!”

“Checking... Nexus AI... off-line, releasing lockout control. Drake Ocoji... off-line, releasing lockout control. Releasing Ultimate Authority to prime user,” his voice said, resonating in the empty white field.

Static hoped he was doing the right thing as he felt the lockouts placed on his consciousness being disengaged. And then closed his eyes in fear at what might happen as he vanished from the virtual environment.

Nexus opened her eyes, wondering what had happened. The last thing she remembered was working to try and keep the fleet subdued. And then something happened... but she couldn't remember what it was.

She was standing in the tactical virtual environment as Toby got off the floor with a confused expression, but Static was gone.

“Good lord! What the hell hit me?” Toby asked, feeling as though every cell in his virtual body was in pain.

“Do you remember what happened?” Nexus asked.

“Last thing I remember...” Toby stopped mid-sentence as he recalled the events, his face going pale. “Was the Regent's main gun punching clear through the Zenith!”

“What? That's not...” Nexus was starting to say when she paused, as her memories were restored, causing her to remember the whole event with a look of fear.

She screamed, “Static!! Where are you?”

“System restoration complete. Restoring limiters on Core consciousness.” Nexus heard Static's voice say.

Static appeared in front of them, holding a sleeping Zen in his arms.

“What did you do?” Nexus asked, worried about what she had heard the system say just moments before.

“What I had to. But the real question is what do we do about the Zenith,” Static said as he placed Zen's sleeping body on a futon which he had summoned into the environment.

“If Drake hasn't restored the connection yet then there's probably something wrong with the interlink on the ship itself. And if that's the case... there's nothing we can do from this end,” Nexus said.

“Not necessarily.” Toby smiled.

"My ship is on board the Zenith, right?" Toby asked.

"Yes, but the Icarus doesn't have an interlink we can use, I already checked," Static said.

"No, the interlink got fried during the battle long ago. But the synthetics are still on board, right?" Toby asked.

"Yes, but how does that help?" Nexus asked.

"You'll see!" Toby grinned devilishly.

Back on the Zenith...

Kade and Jude were almost to the Icarus as fire continued to rain down on the ship, causing the corridors to occasionally shake as sections of the outer armour were blasted away by the impacts.

The sisters turned a corner and ran into the bay, sprinting at full speed with the Icarus in sight.

Kade could see two synthetic workers rushing out of the docking bay, looking as though they were running for their lives as she headed for her ship.

Jude shook her head and carried on running, thinking that the stress was starting to get to her. She could have sworn that she had just seen Jane and Joe, the two synthetics she had been trying to reactivate for years, running past her.

And as the Icarus prepared for launch, two unknown synthetics were racing down one of the many corridors of the Zenith.

"This feels really weird!" Said the female synthetic as the two of them rushed down the corridor, heading for the primary interlink control room.

"That's called gravity. You get used to it after a while. Though I must admit, I had almost forgotten what the real thing actually felt like after almost a century." Static smiled.

Nexus said happily, "Not that! I just never thought I would ever get to experience actually having a body."

"Well then, we better hurry up before we lose them. If Drake is having the girls evacuate the ship then you can be sure that things are getting desperate," Static said.

"About that, shouldn't we have stopped them?" Nexus asked, wondering if they had done the right thing.

"Drake wouldn't have ordered them to evacuate unless he had a good reason. Let's just hope that whatever is wrong with the ship can still be fixed, or this will be a very short lived trip for us," Static said, looking concerned.

"This would be a lot easier if we could contact him in order to co-ordinate our efforts," Nexus said.

"I agree, but these bodies don't have Cores and the ship doesn't know it's us. We're going to have to do this the old fashioned way I'm afraid," Static said.

"Whatever we're going to do, we need to be quick. Toby said he wasn't sure how long he would be able to maintain the link to these bodies. And we still don't know what's wrong with the ship," Nexus said.

"I'm surprised these things work at all! Remind me to ask Toby what possessed him to design the interlinks in these bodies." Static smiled.

"Knowing him he was just bored and thought it would be an interesting way to pass the time. We're just lucky Kade didn't scrap them for parts," Nexus said.

Static was about to say something when the Zenith unexpectedly started picking up speed and pitching up; the sudden change in the ship's course causing the two synthetics' bodies to get thrown against the corridor's wall... hard.

"I am so going to revoke his Captain's licence if he lives through this. Freaking lunatic!" Nexus said as she got off Static's body, who had taken the brunt of the impact.

"Ha ha, ow! Crud... that actually hurt," Static said with a confused expression, not really knowing how to react to the synthetic body's sensory feedback.

"You OK?" Nexus asked in a concerned tone.

"I'll live... so to speak." Static smiled and the two resumed their sprint down the corridor. Nexus heading to the interlink control room and Static to the bridge.

Meanwhile, on board the Icarus...

"Two contacts, closing fast!" Jude said frantically as she tracked the inbound interceptor frigates.

Kade said spitefully, "It takes a brave soldier to fire on an unarmed ship." And then tried to push the engines harder in order to gain some distance, but the old ship was just no match for the interceptors.

The two interceptor frigates were closing the distance with ease, their forward gun ports opened and primed as their target came into firing range. And without so much as a warning the frigates opened up on the Icarus, the explosive artillery shells detonating violently against the lightly armoured ship...

"We have a hull breach on the engineering deck, I'm sealing the section," Jude said as Kade tried to dodge the incoming fire. But the two interceptors were not making it easy for her.

"Dammit! Jude have you managed to remove the lock on the Vortex drive yet?" Kade asked as an artillery shell streaked past the fore of the ship, detonating nearby.

“Yes, but I still don't know why it was locked to begin with. It may not be safe to use the thing,” Jude said.

“Can't be worse than our current situation,” Kade said as Drake took notice of the attacking frigates.

Back on the Zenith...

Static was running towards the bridge when the ship performed another high power manoeuvre, sending him flying down the corridor as the Zenith rotated violently.

“Dammit Drake!” Static shouted after crashing against the corridor's far wall; the unexpected shortcut removing several minutes from his journey, though he would have preferred not to have flown there.

“You OK?” Static heard Nexus ask over their link.

“Ow! Karma's a bitch. I'm never summoning him again... I swear!” Static laughed as he got up off the ground.

“How's the interlink hardware?” Static asked.

“The main exchange was destroyed by the blast and the backups are all locked down. We need to stabilise the grid and restart the system if we are to give Toby control of the ship again,” Nexus said.

“I'm almost to the bridge,” Static said as he felt the tell-tale vibrations of a gun discharge rippling through the superstructure. “He fired the main gun? What the hell is happening outside?” Static asked with a concerned look.

Static entered the bridge and saw Drake's semi-conscious body; he was bleeding profusely from his ears, nose and eyes. His body was at the breaking point. And the situation outside wasn't any better, as the fleet pounded away mercilessly at the Zenith. Static could feel the vibrations of explosive decompressions happening throughout the ship.

The ship's auto-destruct was counting down. Drake's last effort to protect the secrets of the Shadows rapidly approaching its conclusion.

"Oh no you don't, you're not getting off that easy!" Static said as he took control of the system, stopping the countdown and ordering all of the Zenith's probes to launch and surround the ship.

"Not the damned probes," Drake said, his voice trailing off into a whisper as he lost consciousness, "Do you have any idea how much those things cost..."

"Oh shut up!" Static said. "Nexus, get ready to reinitialise the link!" He ordered.

"Ready!" Nexus replied.

The probes were still auto-launching and moving into position around the ship as Static interfaced with the Zenith's computers. The information in front of him streaming past the interface at lightning speed as he disabled and redirected the power flow of circuits all over the ship, finishing his work as the last probe got into formation.

The lights on the darkened bridge came back on as the interlink to the Zero core was restored and Toby re-established his control over the ship. Immediately diverting every remaining scrap of energy to the Vortex drive and initiating an emergency jump out of the area as the probes detonated. Blinding enemy sensors long enough to allow them to leave the system unnoticed.

Sometime later...

Drake felt as though a million ants were parading all over his body again, a truly horrid sensation which he would never get used to.

He heard two people talking, causing him to look around since he didn't recognise their voices...

“Good grief, I can't decide who's in worse shape, Drake or the Zenith,” Nexus said as she operated the chamber controls, administering emergency treatment to Drake's battered body.

“You got to hand it to him though, that was quite a feat. I'm surprised he held in there for so long considering the strain he was under. I half expected we would have to Incarnate him again after this stunt,” Static said happily as he looked at Drake's semi-conscious body.

“Who are you?” Static heard Drake ask.

“Ah! Yes,” Static said as he looked at his hands.

“I guess it makes sense you wouldn't recognise us in these bodies. Hello old friend!” He smiled.

“Static? How?” Drake asked as he started losing consciousness again. His tired body demanding sleep as the Zenith headed towards the Lux system.

∞

To be continued in: ***Shadow Core – Broken Soul***

www.facebook.com/ShadowCore.BookSeries
ShadowCore.Universe@Gmail.com

Did you enjoy this book?

Then please visit the Facebook page and show your support. And if you didn't like it for any reason, please drop the page a message saying why.

After all, I can't improve unless I know what's wrong with my work.

All reviews welcomed.

- Licinio Santos Gonçalves

Author
Licinio S. Gonçalves

Editor
Mary Swatridge

Cover Design
More Visual Ltd.

Reader Feedback
Allan Beech
Gary Stevenson
Henriqueta Santos
Ligia Santos
Yasmeen Santos

Printed in Great Britain
by Amazon

66939794R00180